P.S. I HATE YOU

WINTER RENSHAW

COPYRIGHT 2018 WINTER RENSHAW
ALL RIGHTS RESERVED

COVER DESIGN: Louisa Maggio

EDITING: The Passionate Proofreader

COVER MODEL: Renato Menezes

PHOTOGRAPHER: Sandy Lang

All rights reserved. No part of this book may be reproduced or transmitted in any form, including electronic or mechanical, without written permission from the publisher, except in the case of brief quotations embodied in critical articles or reviews.

This is a work of fiction. Names, characters, places, and incidents either are the product of the author's imagination or, if an actual place, are used fictitiously and any resemblance to actual persons, living or dead, business establishments, events, or locales is entirely coincidental. The publisher does not have any control and does not assume any responsibility for author or third-party websites or their content.

E-Books are not transferrable. They cannot be sold, given away, or shared. The unauthorized reproduction or distribution of this copyrighted work is a crime punishable by law. No part of this book may be scanned, uploaded to or downloaded from file sharing sites, or distributed in any other way via the Internet or any other means, electronic or print, without the publisher's permission. Criminal copyright infringement, including infringement without monetary gain, is investigated by the FBI and is punishable by up to 5 years in federal prison and a fine of $250,000 (http://www.fbi.gov/ipr/).

This ebook is licensed for your personal enjoyment only. Thank you for respecting the author's work.

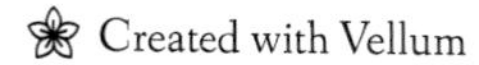

IMPORTANT

If you did not obtain this book via Amazon or Kindle Unlimited, it has been stolen. Downloading this book without paying for it is *against the law*, and often times those files have been *corrupted with viruses and malware* that can damage your eReader or computer or steal your passwords and banking information. Always obtain my books via Amazon and Amazon only. Thank you for your support and for helping to combat piracy.

DESCRIPTION

Dear Isaiah,

Eight months ago, you were just a soldier about to be deployed and I was just a waitress, sneaking you a free pancake and hoping you wouldn't notice that my gaze was lingering a little too long.

But you did notice.

We spent one life-changing week together before you left, and we said goodbye on day eight, exchanging addresses at the last minute.

I saved every letter you wrote me, your words quickly becoming my religion.

But you went radio silent on me months ago, and then you had the audacity to walk into my diner yesterday and act like you'd never seen me in your life.

To think ... I almost loved you and your beautifully complicated soul.

Almost.

Whatever your reason is—I hope it's a good one.

Maritza the Waitress

PS – I hate you, and this time ... I mean it.

For Sandy Lang.

The thought of what could have been is as painful as a broken heart. – Bridgett Devoue

1

MARITZA

"WELCOME to Brentwood Pancake and Coffee. I'm Maritza and I'll be your server," I greet my millionth customer of the morning with the same old spiel. This one, a raven-haired, honey-eyed Adonis, waited over seventy minutes for a table by a window, though I suppose in LA time that's the blink of an eye.

He doesn't so much as acknowledge me.

"Just you today?" I ask, eyeing the empty chair across from him. The breakfast rush is about to end, and lucky for him, I only have one other table right now.

He doesn't answer, but maybe he doesn't hear me?

"Coffee?" I ask another obvious question. I mean, the diner is called Brentwood Pancake and Coffee for crying out loud. Everyone comes here for the coffee and plate-sized pancakes, and it's considered a Class-D felony to order anything else.

Placing his mug right side up on his saucer, he pushes it

toward me and I begin to pour. Waving his hand, he stops me when the cup is three-quarters of the way full. A second later, he adds two creams and one half of a sugar packet, but the way he moves is methodical, rigid. With intention.

"Ma'am, this really can't be that interesting," he says under his breath, his spoon clinking against the sides of the porcelain mug after he stirs.

"Excuse me?"

"You're standing here watching me," he says. Giving the spoon two final taps against the rim of the mug, he then rests it on the saucer before settling his intense amber gaze in my direction. "Isn't there another table that needs you?"

His eyes are warm like honey but his stare is cold, piercing. Unrelenting.

"You're right. There is." I clear my throat and snap out of it. If I was lingering, it wasn't my intention, but this I'm-sexy-and-I-know-it asshole didn't need to call me out on it. Sue me for being a little distracted. "I'll be back to check on you in a minute, okay?"

With that, I leave him alone with his menu and his coffee and his foul mood and his brooding gaze ... and his broad shoulders ... and his full lips ... and I get back to work, stopping at table four to see if Mr. and Mrs. Carnavale need refills on their house blend decafs.

By the time I top them off, I draw in a cleansing breath and head back to Mr. Tall, Dark, and Douche-y, forcing a smile on my face.

"We ready to order?" I ask, pulling my pen from behind my ear and my notepad from my Kelly-green apron.

He folds his menu, offering it to me despite the fact that my hands are full, but I manage to slip it under my arm without dropping anything.

"Two pancakes," he says. "Eggs. Scrambled. Rye toast. Butter. *Not* margarine."

"I'm so sorry." I point to a sign above the cash register that clearly reads ONE PANCAKE PER PATRON - NO EXCEPTIONS.

He squints, his expression calcifying when he reads it.

"So that's *one* pancake, scrambled eggs, and buttered rye toast then," I recite his order.

"What kind of bullshit rule is that?" He checks his watch, like he has somewhere to be.

Or like he doesn't have the time for a rule that I entirely agree is pure bullshit.

"These pancakes are *huge*. I promise one will be more than enough." I try to deescalate the situation before it gets out of hand because it's never pretty when management has to get involved. The owners of the diner are strict as hell on this policy and their day shift manager is even more so. She'll happily inform any and all disgruntled customers there's a reason the "pancake" in Brentwood Pancake and Coffee is singular and not plural.

I've seen many a diner walk out of here and never return over this stupid policy and our Yelp review average is in the dumps, but somehow it never seems to be bad for business. The line is perpetually out the door and down the block every weekend morning without fail, and sometimes even on weekdays. These pancakes are admittedly as delicious and more than own up to their reputation, but that stupid rule is nothing more than clever marketing designed to inflate demand.

"And what if I'm still hungry?" he asks. "Can I order a second?"

Wincing, I shake my head.

"You've got to be fucking kidding me." He sits up a

little, jaw clenching. "It's a goddamned pancake for fuck's sake."

"Not just *any* pancake," I say with a practiced smile. "It's a *Brentwood* pancake."

"Are you trying to be cute with me, ma'am?" he asks, directing his attention at me, though he isn't flirting. His nostrils flare a little and I can't help but let my mind wander the tiniest bit about how sexy he looks when he's angry—despite the fact that I would never so much as entertain the idea of getting down and dirty with an asshole like this.

He's hot AF but I don't do jerks. Plain and simple.

I'd have to be drunk. Like, really drunk. And I'd have to be desperate. And even then ... I don't know. He's got some kind of chip on his shoulder, and no amount of sexiness would be able to distract me from that.

"Let me put your order in, okay?" I ask with a smile so forced my cheeks hurt. They say good moods are contagious, but I'm starting to think this guy might be immune.

"As long as it's the *full* order, ma'am," he says, lips pressing flat as he exhales. I don't know why he keeps calling me "ma'am" when I'm clearly younger than he is. Hell, I couldn't legally drink until three years ago.

I am not a "ma'am."

"The cook won't make two," I say with an apologetic tone before biting my bottom lip. If I play it coy and helpless maybe he'll back down a little? It works. Sometimes.

"Then it's for my guest," he points to the empty seat across from him. His opposite hand is balled into a fist, and I can't help but notice his watch is programmed in military time, "who happens to be showing up later."

"We don't serve guests until they're *physically* here," I say. Yet another one of the restaurant's strict policies. Too many patrons have tried to use that loophole over the years, so they had to close it. But they didn't just close it—they battened the hatches with hurricane-proof glass by way of a giant security monitor in the kitchen. They even make the cooks check the screen before preparing orders, just to make sure no one's breaking the rules.

The man drags his hand through his dark hair, which I'm realizing now is a "regulation cut."

Military.

I bet he's military.

Has to be. The hair. The watch. The constant swearing juxtaposed with the overuse of the word "ma'am." He reminds me of my cousin Eli who spent ten years in the U.S. army, and if he's anything else like Eli, he's not going to let up about this.

Exhaling, I place my palm gently on his shoulder despite the fact that we're not supposed to put hands on the guests for any reason, but this guy is tense and his muscled shoulders are just begging for a gentle touch.

"Just ... bear with me, okay?" I ask. "I'll see what I can do."

The man serves our country. He fights for our freedom. Despite the fact that he's unquestionably a giant asshole, he at least deserves a second pancake.

I'm going to have to get creative.

Heading back to the kitchen, I put his order in and check on the Carnavales one more time. On my way to the galley to refill my coffee pot, I pass a table full of screaming children, one of which has just shoved his giant pancake on the floor, much to his gasping mother's dismay.

Bending, I retrieve the sticky circle from the floor and place it back on his plate.

"Would you like the kitchen to fix another?" I ask.

They're lucky. This is the only time they'll make an exception, and I'll have to present the dirty pancake as proof.

The child screams and I can barely hear what the mother is trying to say. Glancing around the table, I spot five little minions under the age of eight, all of them dressed in Burberry, Gucci, and Dior. The inflated-lipped mother sports a shimmering, oversized rock on her left ring finger and the father has his nose buried in his phone.

But I'm not one to judge.

LA is lacking child-friendly restaurants of the quality variety, and it's not like Mr. Chow or The Ivy would welcome their noisy litter with open arms. I don't even think they have high chairs there.

"I don't want a pancake!" The oldest of the tanned, flaxen-haired gremlins screams in his mother's face, turning her flawless complexion a shade of crimson that almost matches her pristine Birkin bag.

"Just ... just take it away," she says, flustered, her palm sprawling her glassy, Botoxed forehead.

Nodding, I take the 'cake back to the kitchen, only I stop when I reach the galley, grabbing a stack of cloth napkins and hiding the plate beneath it. As soon as my military patron finishes his first pancake, I'll run this back to the kitchen and claim he accidentally dropped it on the floor.

"Order up!" one of the line guys calls from the window, and I head over to see my military man's breakfast is hot and ready—though I may have accidentally moved it to the front of the ticket line when no one was looking because I don't have the energy to deal with him freaking out if his breakfast is taking too long.

Grabbing his plate, I rush it out to him, delivering it with a smile and a sweet, "Can I get you anything else right now?"

His gaze drops to his food and then lifts to me.

"I know," I say, palm up. "Just ... trust me. I'll take care of you."

I wink, partially disgusted with myself. He has no idea how difficult it is for me to be accommodating to him when he's treating me like this. I'd love nothing more than to pour a steaming hot pitcher of coffee into his lap, but out of respect and appreciation—and *only* respect and appreciation—for his service, I won't resort to such a thing.

Plus, I work for tips. I kind of *have* to be accommodating. And lord knows I need this job. I may be living in my grandmother's gorgeous guesthouse, but believe me, she charges rent.

Free rides aren't a thing in the Claiborne family.

He peers down his straight nose, stabbing the tines of his polished fork into a chunk of fluffy scrambled egg.

He doesn't say thank you—not surprising—and I tell him I'll be back to check on him in a little while before making my way to the galley where another server, Rachael, is also seeking respite.

"That table with the screaming kids," I ask, "that yours?"

She blows her blonde bangs off her forehead and rolls her eyes. "Yup."

"Better you than me," I tease. Rachael's got three of her own at home. She's good with kids and she always seems to know the right thing to say to distract them or thwart a total meltdown.

"I'll trade you," she says. "The family for the dimples at table four."

"He has dimples?" I peek my head out, staring toward my military man.

"Oh, God, yes," she says. "Deep ones. Killer smile, too.

Thought maybe he was some model or actor or something, but he said he was an army corporal."

"We can't be talking about the same guy. He hasn't so much as half-smiled at me and he's already told you what he does for a living?"

"Huh." Rachael lifts a thin red brow, like she's wondering if we're talking about two different people. "He asked me how I was doing earlier and smiled. Thought he was real friendly."

"That one. Right there. Dark hair? Golden eyes? Muscles bulging out of his gray t-shirt?" I do a quick point before retracting my finger.

She takes another look. "Yeah. That's him. You don't forget a face like that. Or biceps like that ..."

"Weird." I fold my arms, staring his way and wondering if maybe he has a thing against girls like me. Though I'm pretty ordinary compared to most girls out here. Average height. Average weight. Brown hair. Brown eyes.

Maybe I remind him of an ex?

I'm mid-thought when out of nowhere he turns around, our eyes catching like he knew I was watching. Reaching for a hand towel in front of me, I glance down and try to act busy by wiping up a melted ice cube on the galley counter.

"Busted." Rachael elbows me before heading out to check on the Designer family. I swat her on the arm as she passes, and then I give myself a second to regain my composure. As soon as the warmth has left my cheeks, I head out to check on him, relieved to find his pancake demolished, not a single, spongey scrap left behind. In fact, his entire meal is finished ... coffee and all.

Reaching for his plate, he stops me, his hand covering mine, and then our eyes lock.

"Why were you staring at me over there?" he asks. The

way he looks at me is equal parts invasive and intriguing, like he's studying me, forming a hard and fast opinion, but also like he's checking me out which makes zero sense because his annoyance with me practically oozes out of his perfect, tawny physique.

"I'm sorry?" I play dumb.

"I saw you. Answer the question."

Oh, god. He's not going to let this go. Something tells me I should've taken Rachael up on her offer to trade tables. This one's been nothing but trouble since the moment I poured his coffee.

My mouth falls and I'm not sure what to say. Half of me knows I should probably utter some kind of nonsense most likely to appease him so he doesn't complain to my manager, but the other half of me is tired of being nice to a man who has the decency to ask another waitress how her day is going and can't even bring himself to treat his own server like a human being.

"You were talking about me with that other waitress," he says. His hand still covers mine, preventing me from exiting this conversation.

Exhaling, I say, "She wanted to trade tables."

His dark brow arches and he studies my face.

"And then she said you had dimples," I expand. "She said you smiled at her earlier ... I was just thinking about why you'd be so polite to her and not me."

He releases me and I stand up straight, tugging my apron into place before smoothing my hands down the front.

"She handed me a newspaper while I waited. She didn't have to do that," he says, lips pressing flat. "Give me something to smile about and I'll smile at you."

The *audacity* of this man.

The heat in my ears and the clench in my jaw tells me I should walk away now if I want to preserve my esteemed position as morning server here at Brentwood Pancake and Coffee, but it's guys like him ...

I try to say something, but all the thoughts in my head are temporarily nonsensical and flavored with a hint of rage. A second later, I manage a simple yet gritted, "Would you like me to grab your check, sir?"

"No," he says without pause. "I'm not finished with my breakfast yet."

We both glance at his empty plates.

"More eggs?" I ask.

"No."

I can't believe I'm about to do this for him, but at this point, the sooner I get him out of here, the better. I mean, at this point I'm doing it for myself, let's be real.

"One moment." I take his empty dishes to the kitchen before sneaking into the galley and grabbing that kid's dirty pancake. My pulse whooshes in my ears and my body is lit, but I forge ahead, returning to the pick-up window and telling one of the cooks that my customer at table twelve dropped his 'cake on the floor.

He glances at the plate, then to the security monitor, then back to me before taking it out of my hands and exchanging it for a fresh one. It's a verifiable assembly line back there, just a bunch of guys in hairnets and aprons standing around a twenty-foot griddle, spatulas in each hand.

"Thanks, Brad," I say. Making my way back to my guy, I stop to check on the Carnavales, only their table is already being bussed and Rachael tells me she took care of their check because they were in a hurry.

Shit.

"Here you are." I place the plate in front of my guy.

He glances up at me, honeyed eyes squinting for a moment. I wink, praying he doesn't ask questions.

"Let me know if you need anything else, okay?" I ask, wishing I could add, *"just don't ask for another pancake because I'll be damned if I risk my job for an ingrate like you ever again."*

"Coffee, ma'am. I'd like another cup of coffee." He reaches for his glass syrup carafe, pouring sticky sweet, imported-from-Vermont goodness all over his steaming pancake, and I try not to watch as he forms an "x" and then a circle.

Striding away, I grab a fresh carafe of coffee and return to top him off, stopping at three-quarters of the way full. A second later, he glances up at me, his full lips pulling up at the sides, revealing the most perfect pair of dimples I've ever seen ... as if the past twenty minutes have all been some kind of joke and he was only busting my chops by being the world's biggest douche lord.

But just like that, it disappears.

His pearly, dimpled smirk is gone before I get the chance to fully appreciate how kind of a soul he appears to be when he's not all tense and surly.

"Glad I finally gave you a reason to smile." I'm teasing. Sort of. And I gently rub his shoulder, which is still tight as hell. "Anything else I can get you?"

"Yes, ma'am. I'll take my check."

Thank. God.

I can't get it fast enough. Within a minute, I've punched my staff ID into the system, printed his ticket, shoved it into a check presenter, and rushed it to his table. His debit card rests on the edge when I arrive, as if I'd taken too long and he grew tired of holding it in his hand.

He's just as anxious to leave as I am to get him out of here. Guess that marks the one and only thing that puts us on the same page.

"I'll be right back with this," I tell him. His card—plain navy plastic with the VISA logo in the lower corner and NAVY ARMY CREDIT UNION along the top—bears the name "Isaiah Torres."

When I return, I hand him a neon purple gel pen from my pocket and gather his empty dishes.

"Thank you for the ..." he points at the sticky plate in my hand as he signs his check. "For that."

"Of course," I say, avoiding eye contact because the sooner I can pretend he's already gone, the better. "Enjoy the rest of your day."

Asshole.

Glancing up, I spot our hostess, Maddie, flagging me down and mouthing that I have *three* new tables. Great. Thanks to this charmer, I've disappointed the Carnavales, risked my job, and kept several tables waiting all within the span of a half hour.

Isaiah signs his check, closes the leather binder, and slides out of his booth. When he stands, he towers over me, peering down his nose and holding my gaze captive for what feels like a single, endless second.

For a moment, I'm so blinded by his chiseled jaw and full lips, that my heart misses a couple of beats and I almost forget our little exchange.

"Ma'am, if you'll kindly excuse me," he says as I realize I'm blocking his path.

I step aside, and as he passes, his arm brushes against mine and the scent of fresh soap and spicy aftershave fills my lungs. Shoving the check presenter in my apron, I tend to my new tables before rushing back to start filling drinks.

Glancing toward the exit, I catch him stopping in the doorway before slowly turning to steal one last look at me for reasons I'll never know, and it isn't until an hour later that I finally get a chance to check his ticket. Maybe I'd been dreading it, maybe I'd purposely placed it in the back of my mind, knowing full well he was going to leave me some lousy, slap-in-the-face tip after everything I'd done for him. Or worse: nothing at all.

But I stand corrected.

"Maritza, what is it?" Rachael asks, stopping short in front of me, hands full of strategically stacked dirty dishes.

I shake my head. "That guy ... he left me a hundred-dollar tip."

Her nose wrinkles. "What? Let me see. Maybe it's a typo?"

I show her the tab and the very clearly one and two zeroes on the tip line. The total confirms that the tip was no typo.

"I don't understand. He was such an ass," I say under my breath. "This is like, what, five hundred percent?"

"Maybe he grew a conscience at the last minute?" Her lips jut forward.

I roll my eyes. "Whatever it was, I just hope he never comes here again. And if he does, you get him. There isn't enough tip money in the world that would make me want to serve that arrogant prick again. I don't care how hot he is."

"Gladly." Her mouth pulls wide. "I have this thing for generous pricks with dashing good looks."

"I know," I say. "I met your last two exes."

Rachael sticks her tongue out before prancing off, and I steal one last look at Isaiah's tip. It's not like he's the first person ever to bestow me with such plentiful gratuity—this is a city where cash basically grows on trees—it's just that it doesn't make sense and I'll probably never get a chance to ask him why.

Exhaling, I get back to work.

I've worked way too damn hard to un-complicate my life lately, and I'm not about to waste another thought on some complicated man I'm never going to see ever again.

2

ISAIAH

"YOU DOING OKAY, *MAMÃE*?" I step into my mother's bedroom in her little South-Central LA apartment after grabbing breakfast and running a few errands. I'd have eaten something here this morning, but all I could find in her cupboards were dented cans of off-brand soup, a loaf of expired white bread, and a couple boxes of Shake-n-Bake.

I intend to hit up the grocery store here soon, and after that, I'll remind my piece-of-shit siblings that this is their job in my absence.

"Ma?" I ask, drowning in the pitch blackness of her room. "You awake?"

The sound of police sirens wailing down the street and the neighbor kids above us stomping up and down the hall has become the common soundtrack in these parts. Ironically enough, it all blends together into some kind of white noise, making it easier to tune out.

She rolls to her side, and the room smells like death

despite the fact that Alba Torres is still kicking. The doctors have been attempting to diagnose her for years, saying she has Chronic Fatigue Syndrome or Fibromyalgia one minute, then saying she has Lyme disease the next. Other doctors claim to have ruled those out in favor of doing more testing. More lab work. More MRIs. More examinations. More referrals.

And still ... we know nothing—just that she's always tired, always hurting.

"Isaiah?" she asks with a slight groan, attempting to sit up.

I go to her side and flick on the dim lamp on her pill bottle-covered nightstand. Mom's face lights up when she sees me, reaching up to hold the side of my face with a thin, shaky hand.

"*Que horas sao*?" She reaches for her glasses on the table next, knocking over a tissue box. Despite the fact that she's lived in the states since she was twenty, she tends to revert to speaking Portuguese when she's especially exhausted.

"Almost four."

"PM?" she asks.

I nod. "Yes, Ma. PM."

"What'd you do today?" She takes her time sitting up before patting the edge of her bed.

I have a seat. "Had breakfast at a café. Ran a few errands. Caught a movie."

"*Sozinho*?" She frowns.

"Yes. Alone." I don't know why she acts disappointed or heartbroken that I do things alone. I'm twenty-seven and despite the fact that I have more siblings than I can count on one hand and I've lived in enough states to have accumulated hundreds of friends and associates over the years, I've always preferred to go about things my own way—by myself.

Life's a hell of a lot less disappointing that way.

"I'm so glad you're home, Isaiah." She offers a pained smile, reaching for my hands. She places them between hers, her palms warm but her fingers like ice. "Please tell me you'll be staying a while?"

"I leave next week," I remind her. "In nine days, actually."

My mother shakes her head. "I don't know why you keep going back there, Isaiah. It's a blessed miracle that you make it home each time, but one of these days it's going to be in a box in the belly of an airplane."

She makes the sign of the cross, mouthing a short Catholic prayer under her breath.

I pinch the bridge of my nose before resting my elbows on my knees. I can't look at her right now, not when her dark eyes are getting glassier by the second. I hate seeing her in pain, and I especially hate seeing her in pain because of me.

"This is my job," I say, knowing full well it won't make any of this easier for her. "My *career*."

"Couldn't you have been anything else?" she asks. "What about something with computers? Or fixing cars? Or building things? You were always so good with your hands."

"Still am," I say.

"Remind me, when can you retire?" she asks.

"You know I re-enlisted last year." I exhale, steadying my patience. We've been through this a hundred times, but I shouldn't get frustrated. Her medications fog her memory.

Ma clucks her tongue. "I always thought you and your sisters would open a restaurant someday."

"Yeah, well, they went ahead and did that without me,

but that's all right. You've tried my cooking before." I smirk, thinking about the time I made the family tacos but forgot the seasoning. For years they refused to let me live that down. I never stepped foot inside the kitchen again after that. "I brought you some dinner. You hungry?"

Rising, I head to the kitchen, grabbing the hearts of palm salad I ordered from her favorite Brazilian steakhouse down the street as well as a bottle of water, her evening meds, and a tin TV tray.

When I return to her room, she's situated in her corner chair, flicking through TV stations on the thirty-inch TV perched on top of her hand-me-down dresser. After a minute, she settles on *Jeopardy*, and then her eyes flicker. Ma struggles to stay awake but she fights through it.

"Thank you, *meu amor*," she says when I situate her dinner before her. Lifting her hand to my face once more, she smiles. "You're so good to me, Isaiah. I don't deserve you."

"Ma, don't say that. You deserve *tudo*. You deserve everything."

Once upon a time she was a vibrant woman who couldn't sit still for more than two minutes and taught her American-born children every Brazilian lullaby she could remember. With a contagious laugh, long dark hair down her back, and a wardrobe full of bright, happy colors, Alba Torres was the loudest person in the room, literally and figuratively. Her enthusiasm for life was nothing short of infectious and her five-foot two frame could barely contain her enormous personality.

And then she got sick.

But someone's got to take care of her, and it sure as hell hasn't been my siblings. They only do shit when they have to—which is when I'm gone.

I'll admit my oldest sister, Calista, tends to carry the brunt of the load in my absence, but she's also raising four kids while her husband works two jobs, so I tend to cut her some slack.

"What are you doing the rest of the week?" she asks. "Anything special?"

I shrug. I'll mostly be biding my time. "A little of this. A little of that."

Ma rolls her eyes, returning her sleepy gaze to Alex Trebek. "Always so secretive, my Isaiah."

"No secrets here. Just trying to stay busy."

"With women and booze?" she asks, lifting a dark brow.

"Is that what you think I do in my spare time?" I pretend to be offended, though we both know she isn't wrong. I had every intention of hitting up the sports bar down the street tonight ... tomorrow night ... and the next.

Maybe even the night after that.

That's the beauty of being a lone wolf. Your life is one-hundred percent yours and you can do whatever the hell you damn well please.

"I'd like to think you're volunteering at a homeless shelter or cleaning up litter on the highway, but I know you." She reaches for a fork before glancing at her salad. "Maybe one of these days you'll meet someone nice and then you'll finally stop playing around and wasting the best years of your life on strangers who don't deserve you."

"You worry too much." I lean down, kissing the top of her head, which smells like stale, unwashed hair. I'll have to call Calista over to help her shower soon. "I'm going to the grocery store. Your cupboards are empty."

Her frail hand lifts to my cheek and her full mouth bends. "Don't tell the others, but you've always been *meu favorito*."

I smirk. "I know."

MY CART IS OVERFLOWING, filled mostly with organic non-perishables. Unlike my siblings, I decided not to be a cheap ass. She deserves good quality food that's not going to make her sicker than she already is, which is why I drove all the way to the Whole Foods in Brentwood instead of hitting up the discount grocer with the bars on the windows down the street from her apartment.

I count forty cans of soups and vegetables, twenty boxes of all-natural rice and pasta dinners, eight loaves of bread I intend to stick in the freezer, ten cartons of shelf-stable milk, and a few other necessities; mostly soaps and shampoos and paper products. Passing through the candy aisle, I grab a few bars of her favorite Mayan chocolate.

I didn't earn the title of Alba Torres' favorite child by accident.

Fifteen minutes later, I'm loaded up and headed back to her place, waiting at an infinite red light. Two green arrows light, allowing the left two lanes to go, but the rest of us are stuck waiting.

Checking my phone, I fire off a text to an old army friend who lives nearby, asking if he wants to get drinks later, but before I get a chance to press 'send' a metallic crunch fills my ears and my car lunges forward several feet, stopping the second it smashes into the back of a cherry red Mercedes Benz.

"Motherfucker." I pound my hands on the steering wheel before stepping out, and by the time I head back to examine the damage, the driver who caused this mess is already there, crouched down with her hand grazing a section of her dented Prius bumper.

"The fuck is the matter with you?" A man in a gray suit is shouting at the two of us, his phone plastered against his face as his tawny complexion turns fifty shades of red.

"I'm so sorry, sir." The girl rises, her hands cupping her face. "I saw the green light and I hit my gas. I didn't realize it was only for the turn lanes. I wasn't paying attention."

I lift a finger to silence her. Clearly she's never been in an accident before or she'd know not to accept the blame.

"Great. Now I'm going to miss my reservation." He shakes his head, jaw clenched. "Hope you're happy."

"Man. Come on," I say, tossing my hands in the air. "It was an accident. She apologized. Let's do what we need to do here so we can all get on with our lives."

Returning my attention to the bumper of my vintage Porsche 911T, I examine the deep scratches and blue paint remnants littering her once-pristine Carrara White bumper. As much as I, too, would like to berate this woman for forgetting how to fucking drive and denting up my most prized possession, I take a deep breath and gather myself. Last thing I want is to look like el douche bag over there in the Mercedes.

"Here you go." The girl hands me her insurance card, and I grab my phone, taking a picture of the front and back before handing it over. Our hands graze in the process, and it's only then that I finally get a good look at her.

Jesus Christ.

It's the waitress.

From the pancake place.

The second our eyes lock, her expression suspends. She recognizes me too.

"You got your insurance card?" The huffy bastard interrupts us, practically yanking the little piece of paper from her hands. "You *are* insured, right?"

"Dude, calm the fuck down," I tell him, head cocked.

"Don't call me dude, you fucking prick, and don't tell me to calm the fuck down," he says, lips pulled into an ugly sneer. "Have you seen what your piece of shit did to my bumper?"

My "piece of shit" happens to be a 1969 Porsche 911T, of which there are only a few hundred left in the world. Actually, I found her in a junkyard years back and did the restore job myself in between deployments. She's good as new, but if it makes him feel better to berate it, that's on him.

"What an asshole," the waitress whispers, hand cupping the side of her full mouth like we're a couple of pals sharing a secret.

"You were texting and driving, weren't you?" I ask. My hands rest at my hips and my brows furrow. Just because we're both on the same page about this tool over here doesn't mean we're suddenly best friends.

She shakes her head, arms crossed. "I told you, I was looking at the wrong light."

"My gas tank is in the front of my car," I say. "You're lucky you weren't going any faster than you were."

Dragging my palm along my jaw, I watch as the Mercedes asshat approaches a squad car pulling up to the scene. Cars that pass us honk, drivers rolling down their windows and shouting profanities at us for holding up traffic. I don't blame them. It's five o'clock and people are trying to get home. It's already bad enough without some stupid collision blocking the flow.

The officer talks to the disgruntled guy for a second

before strutting our way, and I duck back into my car to grab my registration.

After statements are taken and information is exchanged, the Mercedes guy gets the fuck out of there and the waitress returns to her car and I to mine. Glancing into my rearview, I see she's texting on her phone again.

Rolling my eyes, I reach toward the ignition and turn the keys.

Nothing.

I try again.

Still nothing.

"You've got to be fucking kidding me." I press my head against the steering wheel. The second she hit me the first thing I thought about was the fact that my engine is just behind my rear axle, but when I examined the damage, it only appeared to be cosmetic.

The impact must've knocked something vital out of place.

Climbing out, I head back to the rear and pop the hood, hunching over the engine to see if anything looks amiss.

"Everything okay?" a female voice steals my attention. When I turn around, I find the waitress again.

"Obviously not." I turn away. "Won't start."

"Oh, jeez. Let me call you a tow." She grabs her phone and begins typing furiously into a search engine. "I'm so sorry."

"Yeah. You already said that. Earlier."

I examine the distributor cap, then the fuel pump relay, which could easily trip on collision. No leaks on the ground yet and the coolant level looks good. I'm probably going to have to tear shit apart just to figure out what's wrong—which is exactly how I wanted to spend the rest of my pre-deployment week ...

"You need a ride home?" she asks.

Glancing at the mountain of grocery sacks taking up my passenger side, I know they're all non-perishables, but I spent a pretty penny at Whole Foods and I'd like to get them to Mom's as soon as possible on the off-chance I get hit by a bus ... and judging by the way this day's going, that's not an unlikely possibility. I could call an Uber but I could be waiting here a while.

"Seriously, I'll take you home," she offers. "I feel awful about your car." She leans closer. "I don't feel bad about that other guy's car though, just between us."

The pretty waitress fights a smirk, but I don't return one of my own. Nothing about this is funny.

"Okay, I take it back," she says, rolling her eyes and crossing her arms. "Just trying to lighten the mood. And you have to admit that guy was a piece of work."

A few minutes later, I close my rear hood and lean against my car. "You call a tow yet?"

She nods.

Forcing a hard breath through my nose, I shove my hands in my jeans pockets and wait. The waitress takes a seat on the hood of her Prius, her Lacoste-sneakered feet resting on the dented bumper while her chin sits in her hands. Her thick, dark hair is pulled back into a ponytail and her round, deep set eyes are an intense and distracting shade of mocha.

Despite the fact that she's arguably drop dead gorgeous, she's too perky for my taste, too chatty. Too effervescent.

And I've got more important things to worry about right now, like trying to figure out what the hell she did to my car.

"Tow will be here soon," she calls out over a symphony of motors and horns. The weight of her stare is noticeable, but I couldn't care less. Turning my attention to my phone, I waste the next twenty minutes on stupid internet sites and email before the tow truck arrives.

"The groceries in my front seat," I say to her, pointing toward my car. "Grab them and put them in your trunk."

She hops down, transferring brown paper bags to her Prius one-by-one as I eye the tow truck a few blocks away and hope to God it's mine.

Five minutes later, I breathe a sigh of relief when he slows down and positions his truck in front of my baby.

By the time my 911T is loaded up and I hand off my key, the tension running through me is getting harder to ignore. It was easy to be cool about this shit an hour ago, when I assumed all I was dealing with were some scratches and paint. But now I'm fucking stranded in a city where everyone needs a car and my pride and joy wheels are going to sit in some oily mechanic's parking lot overnight.

I tell the driver to haul it to my buddy's shop in Pasadena, giving him the address, and I watch as my Porsche disappears into traffic on the back of a bright yellow truck with *Tim's Tow-n-Haul* painted across the side.

"You ready?" the waitress asks, nodding toward her car.

Saying nothing, I climb into the passenger side, realizing I have no idea what her name is and fuck if I can remember what she said it was this morning at breakfast.

I had other things on my mind then.

I didn't have time for niceties, small talk, or worrying about remembering the name of some woman I was never supposed to see again.

She flicks off her hazard lights and I retrieve my phone from my pocket, pulling up the image of her insurance card.

Maritza Claiborne.

"So where are we headed?" she asks, placing her phone in a cup holder. A palm tree air freshener hangs from her rearview and the fading scent of coconuts and pineapples fills the space.

"South-Central LA," I say, my words dry, unapologetic.

She's quiet at first, the silence palpable. Everyone around here knows you don't go to South Central unless you have to. It isn't the safest of places, but this time of day she should be fine as long as she's in and out.

"Take a right at the next light," I tell her.

It's going to be a long hour, maybe longer depending on traffic, so I close my eyes and rest my head against the cool glass of the passenger window. Fortunately, being in the army my entire adult life has taught me how to sleep anywhere, any time with comfort being the least of my concerns.

"Thank you," she says, her voice slicing through the quietude I was just beginning to enjoy, "for the tip earlier. It was really generous of you. I don't always get a chance to thank people when they do that."

I don't open my eyes, instead I mumble a quick, "Yep."

"Can I ask ... why?" The car pulls to a sudden LA stop.

I open my eyes to make sure we're not about to become minced meat. "Why *what*?"

"Why did you tip me a hundred dollars on a twenty-dollar tab?" she asks.

Shrugging, I sit up straight, accepting the fact that she's probably one of those types who are going to want to talk the whole ride home. Some people just can't handle silence. It's like they don't know what to do with it.

"Does it matter?" I ask.

Maritza turns to me, her dark eyes fanned with even darker lashes. "It's just that you were so rude to me at first. I actually expected you to stiff me. So when you went in the complete opposite direction ... it just caught me off guard."

"I don't know. Token of appreciation for bending the rules."

"Not like I had a choice." Her foot presses into the gas pedal and we start moving again. "You all but demanded I give you another pancake."

"Turn left at the next light," I tell her, changing the subject.

"For the record, I only caved because you were so damn persistent. And you're military. I have a soft spot for you guys."

People always mean well when they glorify you for serving in the military, for when they thank you for your service or offer you free things or discounts, but I'm not some saint and I don't deserve any kind of special recognition.

I've only ever done what I had to do.

No credit is due.

I check the time. Forty more minutes to go.

A *long* forty more minutes.

"So are you still in the military?" she asks. "Active duty, I mean?"

"Yep. Going back to Afghanistan next week."

"Do you ever get scared? Going there?" she asks. Her question feels way too personal to ask a complete stranger but I'm sort of stuck here, so ...

"This is the wrong line of work if going over there scares you," I say, releasing a hard breath. I'm not sure how this girl can crash into my Porsche and then act like we're suddenly best friends having a heart-to-heart.

"How do you do it?" she asks, glancing my way for a second. "How do you not let it get to you?"

I'll admit the first time was a little unnerving, not

knowing what to expect, but a guy gets used to it, especially when he has no other choice.

"You block out the parts that make you feel the shit you don't want to feel," I say, shifting in my seat.

"Ah," she says, hands gripping the steering wheel. "You're one of *those*."

"One of *those*?"

"Yeah. A macho-macho man," she says, sinking her perfect teeth into her full lower lip as she fights a teasing smirk. "No emotion. No cares. Personality of steel."

"You say that like it's a bad thing."

"It *is* a bad thing. We owe it to ourselves to feel. To allow ourselves to be angry or sad or scared or whatever," she says. "There's beauty in feeling an entire spectrum of emotions in a world where everyone else is trying to numb themselves with drugs or alcohol or sorry excuses for love."

If I allowed myself to feel everything all the time, it might send me on my own personal warpath and that wouldn't be good for anyone. Been there, done that. Can't do it again. I hurt way too many people—people that I cared about more than anything in this world.

"Take a left," I say.

"I dated this one guy for, like, three years. Took me that long to realize he was always going to love his garage band more than me." Maritza chuckles. It says a lot about a person who can laugh about wasting some of the best years of her life on some self-centered prick. She clicks on her turn signal and cuts off a BMW.

"I'm sorry—why are you telling me this?"

"I'm just elaborating," she says. "On the whole letting-yourself-feel thing. If I would've just numbed myself off, I'd probably be knee deep in some new, shitty relationship, repeating all my old mistakes. Negative emotions have a purpose, you know?"

"Sure." I try to shut her out but her voice is so soft and soothing, annoyingly pleasant. She's like a real life podcast that I'm being forced to listen to but secretly think it's not all that bad.

"I told my roommate I'm swearing off relationships for at least a year," she continues. "I just want to find myself—which I know is completely cliché, but I don't care. I want to say 'yes' more and do things I wouldn't have done before, meet new people, make new friends. That sort of thing. You probably think I'm insane, but it just feels like the timing's right. I kind of just want to be solo for a while, you know? Party of one."

My lips press together. If I were in a chatty mood, I could tell her how much I appreciate that we share many of the same sentiments. There aren't a lot of girls, especially girls who look like her, who aren't throwing themselves at every man they meet, desperate to try to pin them down so they don't have to spend another New Year's, spring break, or wedding season alone.

"You said you deploy next week?" she asks. "What are you doing until then?"

My nose wrinkles and for a second, I wonder if she's using some kind of reverse psychology or bait-and-switch tactic on me. I've seen girls do that before ... acting disinterested or anti-love one minute because they think it makes you want them more, and the second they have you exactly where they want you, they make a move.

Too bad for them that's the kind of shit that doesn't work on me.

In fact, it usually tends to do the exact opposite, leaving

me turned off and disgusted. Insulting my intelligence is one of the worst things a woman can do.

"Don't worry—I'm not asking you out. I just feel bad about your car," she says. "I'm sure you had plans and stuff. I'd hate for you to be stranded all week. If you need any rides anywhere, let me know. My number should be on that paperwork the cop gave you."

Adjusting my seat, I pull in a deep breath. It's the least she could do for me—driving me all over LA like my own personal chauffeur, but I refuse to rely on anyone, especially not some chick I don't even know.

"I'll manage," I say.

Ma has an old Mercury Sable in storage—granted, I have no idea if it still runs—but I've got my fingers crossed pretty damn hard. I'll probably spend the rest of tonight tinkering around with it and once I get that running, I'll head to Pasadena to start fixing my Porsche.

"You think your car will be okay?" she asks.

"Hopefully." I'm ninety percent sure it'll be fine, but I won't know until I take a closer look. Until then, she can continue feeling bad about it for all I care.

"It's a cool car. Love that it's not flashy. It's understated," she says. "Very classic."

That's exactly what I love about it, too. "Thanks."

I spout off the next direction and we linger in silence for a solid ten minutes—a new record—before she points to a billboard above a Taco Bell.

"Oh, look! Panoramic Sunrise is playing at The Mintz tomorrow night," she says, bouncing in her seat. "How did I not know that? I *love* them."

I chuff. Me too.

"Really? I swear whenever I talk about them people act

like I'm speaking a foreign language. It's like no one's ever heard of them."

I neglect to tell her the lead singer just so happens to be my brother-in-law's cousin. "Look, can we stop the small talk? It's nothing personal. I'm just not a fan."

Maritza turns to me, expression falling. "Oh. Sure. I was just about to ask if you wanted to go to the concert with me but—"

I don't have to think twice before answering her. "I'm busy."

"Busy ..." Maritza speaks slowly. She doesn't buy it, but I don't particularly care.

"I've got a car to fix," I clarify my statement, not that I need to prove anything to her.

Her hands grip the steering wheel as she sinks into her seat and stares ahead. "All right, that's cool. Whatevs."

When we finally pull into my mother's apartment complex after an enjoyable bout of silence, I step out of her Prius and begin gathering grocery bags in my arms. It's going to be at least three trips up and down two flights of stairs, maybe four.

"Let me help," she says, loading bags before I have a chance to tell her no.

Maritza the Waitress follows me to apartment 3C and I tell her to place everything on the kitchen table once we're inside. We get the job done with one more trip, only this time she lingers in my mother's doorway, her hands slipping into the back pockets of her shorts.

I realize now she's still in her work uniform, her white button-down shirt and little black shorts. Formal but not too formal, the kind of California cool the locals eat up in droves.

Lifting a brow, I shrug. "You need something?"

"Go to the concert with me," she says. "I'll buy your ticket."

I frown. "No. And no."

"Why not?"

"Told you. I'm busy." I keep my voice down. If Ma is sleeping and she wakes up to the sound of some strange woman's voice in her apartment, I'll never hear the end of it. She'll let me have it with her last fighting breath.

"My home is not a brothel," she'd say, teasing but also serious. "Go have your *fun* somewhere else."

"Fine. It's just that you're the only other person I know who's heard of this band. Thought it might be fun. And I feel like I owe you after I smashed into your car today."

I draw in a slow breath, studying her in the fading evening light.

She's pretty with curves in all the right places, a sexy smirk, silky hair, and dark eyes that light up in the most fucking adorable way when she gets excited ... but she's not the kind of girl I'd want to spend one of my last nights with.

For one, she talks way too fucking much.

And she's too philosophical.

Too optimistic.

Too opinionated.

No amount of pretty can make up for the fact that she's not my type. Not even close.

"What, you think I'm trying to ask you on a date?" She huffs. "Please. I don't even remember your name. What was it again?"

Exhaling, I drag my hand through my hair. "Isaiah."

"Right. Isaiah." She cocks her head to the side. "Anyway, don't flatter yourself because even if I were looking for someone to date, you're not what I usually go for, so ..."

"Likewise."

"Wow." Maritza throws her hands up, turning to leave. "Okay, well ... I ... I don't have anything else to say to you then. Congratulations. You've rendered me speechless twice in one day, and that's a first."

Thank. God.

But just when she's almost finally gone, she stops in the doorway, turning on her heel to face me.

"You know ... I meant what I said in the car. I say 'yes' to a lot of things now. To new people. To new experiences. Maybe you thought I was hitting on you, but I swear on my life, Isaiah ... I wasn't. I just wanted to have fun at a concert on a Friday night." Maritza shrugs. "That's what I get for forgetting some people are content being miserable assholes."

With that, she's gone, pulling the door closed behind her.

Pinching the bridge of my nose, I exhale.

"Who was that?" My sister, Calista, asks.

Shit.

I had no idea she was here and now I'm about to get the Spanish fucking Inquisition.

I shake my head and begin unpacking groceries. "No one."

She emerges from the dark hall next to Mom's room. "That's not no one, Isaiah. You brought a girl here and you've *never* brought a girl here. Who was it?"

"What are you doing here?" I change the subject.

"Brought Ma dinner."

"A text would've been nice," I say. "I brought her dinner a couple of hours ago."

Calista waves her hand. "Oh, well. The woman needs more meat on her bones anyway."

That's one thing we can both agree on.

"She seemed nice—that girl," Calista says, taking a seat on Mom's weathered sofa and finger-combing her dark hair into a ponytail. "And she totally called you on your shit, which was hilarious."

I grab another grocery sack.

"Ma needs her hair washed," I say.

"Some nice, pretty girl asks you to go to the concert of a band you *love* and you turn her down like she was some kind of leper." My sister chuckles, refusing to lay off the subject. "You would've had a nice time together, I bet."

"Doubtful."

"I love you, but she was right. You're a miserable asshole," Calista says. "That girl could've balanced you out a bit. Maybe made you a little more likable."

"I couldn't give two shits about how likable I am."

Calista rises, coming to help me with the provisions. She takes a can of Pepper Pot soup and examines the label. "Yeah. I know. And that's your problem."

"You can go now," I say, brushing her aside. "Unless you want to stick around and give Ma her bath."

"We actually just finished up before you got here," she says.

"All right then. I've got this. You can go home."

Calista's mouth curls into a smart-mouthed snarl and she raises her hand, curling it like a tiger's paw. "Who pissed in your cornflakes today?"

"Oh, I don't know. Maybe the *nice* girl who rear-ended my Porsche."

She covers her mouth, fighting a laugh. "Is that why she gave you a ride home?"

"Yup."

Calista shrugs. "Well, I still think she seemed cool."

Her phone lights with a text, her fingers gliding across

the screen at warp speed before she grabs her purse off a nearby console. One of her kids must need something. Or her husband. I can't imagine what it would feel like to be needed like that, constantly.

Just the thought of it makes me feel as if I'm suffocating, and I've spent my entire life just trying to breathe.

"All right. Looks like you're getting your wish. I'm getting out of your hair," Calista says, sliding her phone back into her bag.

I give her a quick finger wave and stack the last can of non-genetically modified corn on the shelf before me.

"Text if you need anything," she says on her way out. And then she stops. "And Isaiah?"

Glancing up, our eyes meet. "Yeah?"

"Stop being a miserable asshole and go to the fucking concert."

3

MARITZA

"NEXT." The woman at The Mintz's will-call window waves me forward Friday night. "Name?"

"Maritza Claiborne," I say, reaching for my ID before sliding it across the counter.

The woman, whose arms are covered in vibrant tattoos of naked women and whose pixie cut is dyed the prettiest shade of lavender checks my driver's license before rifling through a stack of tickets to her left.

A moment later, she's frowning ... like it's not there.

I bought the ticket online yesterday—it *has* to be there.

"I have the confirmation in my email if you need to see it," I say, searching for my phone in the bottomless pit of my vintage Goyard tote—a hand-me-down gift from my mother before she and my father moved to New York City last year because apparently they'd lost their minds and grown were tired of the sunshine. My breath quickens. If I can't see Panoramic Sunrise I'm going to cry—and I'm not a crier.

"Found it." She holds up a lanyard, examining the name on the plastic badge. "It was in the VIP pile."

My chin juts forward and I press my lips together. I didn't buy a VIP ticket. Those were five hundred bucks and included a special section in the front, a private bar, an all-access behind the scenes meet and greet, as well as a chance to have a beer with the band after the bar closes.

I bought a seventy-five-dollar general admission ticket.

I *know* I did ...

"Here you go." She slides the pass across the counter along with my ID and smiles before glancing over my shoulder. "Next!"

Grabbing my lanyard, I place it around my neck before anyone has a chance to declare this a grave mistake and yank it away from me. Making my way to the ticket taker, I'm fully expecting to have my bubble popped any second, only he scans my pass and waves me toward a less crowded area designated for VIPs, and as soon as I'm in, I find a spot at an empty high-top table for two a mere six feet from the front of the stage.

My pulse quickens and I can't help but wear the dorkiest grin when I see the band's guitars and mic on stage. Panoramic Sunrise is my drug. It soothes and comforts and relaxes and reinvigorates me all at the same time. Everything about their low-key, indie, folk-rock tunes resonates with the deepest part of my soul in a way I could never fully explain or even understand. Plus the lead singer looks like an even hotter version of Adam Levine, so there's that.

"Can I grab you a drink?" A pretty cocktail waitress with a high ponytail and orange-red lipstick approaches my table.

"Amaretto and Coke would be amazing. Thank you."

They always open with their number one hit, Flipside,

which is my favorite song in the history of songs. It's sad in parts, funny in others, but mostly it's angsty and ironic.

"This seat taken?" A man asks, standing behind me.

I glance over my shoulder to follow his voice, only by the time my gaze focuses on his chiseled face, he's already taking the spot beside me.

"You again," I say, sitting up straight.

Isaiah Torres' fingers are wrapped around the neck of a Corona.

"You're welcome for the VIP pass," he says, taking a swig and letting his stare penetrate.

My head cocks as I try to wrap my mind around this. Minutes ago, I'd convinced myself the VIP thing was some kind of happy mix-up.

"How'd you know I was going to be here tonight?" I ask.

"Lucky guess," he says. "And I know people who know people who could find out."

The cocktail waitress returns with my drink, and I hand her my card to start a tab before returning my attention back to Isaiah.

"All right then. Thank you for this," I tell him, clutching at the lanyard around my neck. Sliding off my chair, I eye a spot near the front of the stage as the opening act begins to take their places.

"Where are you going?" he asks.

"I'm going to enjoy the concert. That's where I'm going."

I leave him at the table-for-two. Fun and relaxation is my only objective for the night. If he thinks I'll overlook the fact that he was nothing but a rude asshole yesterday just because he does one nice thing, then he's clearly smoking something.

From the corner of my eye, I catch him watching me.

I don't understand him, but it's okay because I really don't need to.

THE HOUSE LIGHTS come on three hours later and some six-foot-seven muscle head in a black t-shirt stands behind a velvet rope, telling us VIP pass holders to follow him.

Herded down a hallway with about fifty other people, I somehow wind up in the front of the line, waiting outside a dressing room with a heart that won't stop thrumming and a breath that won't steady.

I've seen them in concert at least a dozen times since high school, but never once have I seen them up close and personal. I'm not even sure what I'll say or if I'll end up foaming at the mouth, unable to form a coherent sentence, but the second the door opens and an older, gray-haired man steps out and meets my gaze, I clear my throat and straighten my spine.

"You first?" He points at me, speaking in an East Coast accent.

I swallow the lump in my throat and nod, silently reminding myself to be cool.

"Get your phone ready if you want pictures." The man swings the door open. "You've got one minute in there. Make it count."

Case Malbec. Landon Spencer. Kieko Ayoshi. Alec Bastion.

I know all of their names. Their birthdays. Their Wikipedia life stories. I've seen every documentary, every music video, every interview.

And now they're here, in the flesh, seated before me.

A few other people are in here as well, makeup artists, groupies, roadies ...

But all I see is them.

Case, the lead singer, sits shirtless, a white towel wrapped around his shoulders. He smiles when he sees me, and while I'm sure he smiles at all his fans, his stare pierces through me, like he's curious and studying me.

"I'm Case," he says, reaching for me. He slips his arm over my shoulder like we're just a couple of old friends who go way back. The rest of the band assumes their practiced, photo-ready positions around us. "And you are?"

"Maritza," I manage to say, proud of my voice for not squeaking, cracking, or cutting out.

Case takes my phone from my hand. "Isaiah, can you take our pic?"

Glancing up, I watch as Isaiah Torres takes my phone from Case Malbec's hand and points it at the two of us. I force a smile, my mind running a million miles a minute as I try to piece this together.

"You two know each other?" I ask, my finger pointing between the two of them once the picture is over.

Isaiah hands my phone over. "Yep."

"You didn't tell me you knew them," I say.

"You didn't ask." Isaiah hooks his hands on his hips, towering over me.

"Is this the girl?" Case asks.

"What girl?" My gaze narrows at Isaiah.

Case smirks. "He called me this morning, asked me if he could get a VIP pass for some girl."

This is all happening so fast it's hardly comprehensible.

"Time's up," the gray-haired man says, motioning for me to head to the door.

"Dude, it's okay," Case says, "she can have more than thirty seconds with us."

The man presses his chin against his chest. "You see that line of people at the door? It stretches down the hallway then around the next. Sorry, Case. We gotta be out of here by two AM. I don't make the rules." He turns away, calling, "Next!" and a group of giggling girls shove their way inside the already cramped space. "When you're done, just head out to the bar. The band will be out in about an hour. You each get *one* beer on the house. *One*."

I'm ushered out of the room, my head spinning, and I head to the bar to find a place to wait. Never really been much of a beer enthusiast, but I'll be damned if I miss an opportunity to have a drink with Case Malbec.

The bartender delivers a glass of ice water while I wait, and a staffer runs a wide broom across the floor, sweeping up remnants of tonight's show, I wait in a quiet, lit bar, spinning a cardboard coaster between my fingers while simultaneously scrolling through my phone.

Minutes later, the screech of the bar stool beside me grinding against the concrete floor pulls me out of my moment. "Never got a chance to apologize for yesterday."

It's Isaiah. For the millionth time.

"You get your Porsche to start?" I ask.

His brows furrow. "Yeah. Why?"

I lift a shoulder. "It explains why you're being so nice now."

"All due respect, you don't know me." His jaw tightens and he adjusts himself in his seat.

"Thank God for that." I say. "I may not know you, but I do know you were perfectly fine being rude to a complete stranger yesterday—not once but twice—and that says a lot about you as a person. So yeah, thanks for the ticket tonight, but your apologies aren't needed because they won't change the fact that you're a miserable asshole."

My face turns numb. Shock? Disbelief maybe? I've never gone off on anyone like that before, but I had to say those things. He needed to hear them. People like that need to hear words like this.

"Jesus." He exhales. "You're, uh, you're kind of intense when you're angry."

"Now you're just being offensive."

"Offensive?" He jerks away, fighting a smirk.

"Yes. I'm trying to be real with you and you're not taking me seriously," I say. "And now you're laughing at me."

His lips press together, like he's stifling another grin, and I have half a mind to slap him and I've never slapped anyone before.

"I'm sorry," he says. "It's just hard when you're trying to be so angry and all I can think about is how you're kind of sexy when you're angry."

My jaw hangs.

Somewhere in the past five minutes we clearly took a wrong turn.

Or he's severely under the influence.

Yeah. Alcohol. It's got to be the alcohol talking.

"You ever get tired of being like this?" I ask him. "So ... douche-y?"

"You ever get tired of being so perfect all the time?" he asks. "Clearly you never do anything wrong or have a bad fucking day in your life because if you did, you wouldn't be so quick to write off someone's apology."

"I'm not perfect, Isaiah. I'm nice. There's a difference. I treat people the way I want to be treated." I stand, my finger pointed in his face, and while I'm trying not to raise my voice, I can't help it. My blood is boiling, my skin on fire, my palms aching to smack him across his impossibly gorgeous face. "I'd rather be nice than a fucking prick like you."

In an instant, I lose it.

I just want him out of my space.

I lose all control and I do something I've never done in my life.

And by the time I open my eyes, I confirm that I have indeed thrown my ice water in his face.

Oops.

The two of us are wearing matching horrified expressions and Isaiah looks like he's two seconds from uttering some kind of profanity in my direction when a man's voice booms in our ears, "Enough!"

We both turn to find the six-foot-seven behemoth standing over us, his arms folded across his barrel chest as he peers down his aquiline nose.

"You guys are done," he says, pointing toward the door with a meaty finger. The muscles bulging out of his black "security" t-shirt are enough to make me not question his authority. "You're out of here."

Isaiah and I exchange looks and despite the fact that his gray t-shirt is drenched and his hair is ruined and I still have the urge to smack him across his arrogant mouth, he's still annoyingly attractive.

"We're fine," he tells the security guard. "She just got a little worked up, but we're cool now. Right, Maritza?"

"Yep. We're cool," I say, forcing my voice steady despite the fact that my entire body is trembling with little adrenaline-fueled aftershocks.

The giant's expression doesn't soften or budge and he moves behind us, herding us toward the exit.

"Are we really being kicked out?" I ask.

The man doesn't answer. Isaiah stays quiet, respectful. Hopefully with his connections he can get us back in ... then again, he doesn't exactly owe me any favors and we're not exactly on pleasant terms right now.

The second we're outside, the door slams behind us. Isaiah checks it, pushing on the handle but with no use. We're locked out.

"Hope it was worth it," he says under his breath. Pulling his phone from his pocket, he makes a call, then sends a text, then shoves it back in.

"What are you doing?" I ask.

"Trying to get us back in, but Case isn't answering." He runs his hand through his dark hair before staring toward a traffic light in the distance. "He probably doesn't have his phone on him. Great. This is really fucking great."

"How was I supposed to know calling you a prick would get us both kicked out? What the hell kind of archaic rule is that?"

"You didn't just call me a prick. You yelled and pointed your finger in my face and then *dumped your water* on me. The situation was escalating. They just did what they had to do before it got out of hand."

Shaking my head—at him, at the situation, and at myself—I dig into my tote to locate my phone so I can order an Uber and get the hell out of here ...

... only I don't feel the familiar glassy screen or smooth plastic case.

Stepping beneath a street lamp, I dig deeper, unearthing my wallet and various lip balms and travel-sized perfumes—but no phone.

"Shit. I left my phone in there." I rise on my toes, staring at the blackened windows of The Mintz and the closed sign on the door. A moment later, I'm pounding on the glass. I wait before pounding again. And again. And again. They're either ignoring me or they can't hear me.

Isaiah stands back, quiet and contemplative.

I'm sure he doesn't want to give me a ride home any more than I don't want to ask him for one, but right now I'm stranded.

"Is there someone you can call?" he asks, yawning.

Exhaling, I shake my head. "I don't have anyone's numbers memorized."

"Seriously?"

I wave my hand at him. "Now's not the time."

Digging into his pocket, he retrieves a set of keys, lifting them. "I'll take you home."

Eyes wide, I lift my brows. "You sure? I live an hour from here. And you live an hour from me. You won't get home until after three AM."

"I'm not going to leave you here, stranded in downtown LA," he says. A Yellow Cab whirs past us and we both steal a glance. "You're not taking a taxi. It'd cost you an arm and a leg to get home from here. Come on."

He looks both ways before darting across the street, and I follow, keeping a few steps behind.

"What about my phone?" I ask.

"I'll text Case and see if he can have someone look for it."

His white, dented Porsche stands out amongst the flashier cars in the parking lot, but in a good way. Painted in warm moonlight under a starless sky, we hit the road with windows cranked and tunes playing softly from his old speakers. Sinking into the worn, buttery leather passenger seat and decide that maybe ... just maybe ... he's not *all* that bad.

4

ISAIAH

"I DON'T WANT you to get the wrong idea. And I still think you're a miserable asshole," she says as she leans over me and punches in a code to a gate outside a sprawling Brentwood estate. The smell of her citrus perfume mixes with the sweet tang of liquor, filling my lungs until she returns to her seat. The gate swings open and I pull ahead. "But you were yawning every five minutes the whole way here and I can't, in good conscience, let you drive another hour home. You're crashing on my couch tonight."

"No."

"*Yes*." She points to the left. "Around back there's a guesthouse. You can park out front."

Passing a circle drive and a bubbling fountain and rounding the rambling hacienda-style mansion, I spot a smaller version of the main house positioned next to a turquoise pool lit up like Christmas for no other reason than to look pretty. First impressions are everything out here amongst the rich and fabulous locals.

I have no idea how some diner waitress can afford to live in a guesthouse next to an estate like this, but I've seen crazier things in LA, and to be honest, it's none of my damn concern anyway.

I let the engine idle as she climbs out but when she realizes I'm not following, she crouches down, sticks her head back inside the car, and reaches for the ignition, yanking my keys out.

"Come on," she says, not giving me a choice.

My eyes are heavy and a cool pillow sounds like heaven right about now, so I surrender and follow her inside.

The place is dark, window shades pulled. There's a faint light from the kitchen leaking toward the entryway and living room, as if someone left a bathroom light on, but other than that I can't make out much besides outlines until my eyes adjust.

"There's the couch." She points toward the living room as I kick off my shoes. "Let me grab you a pillow and blanket."

The gentle tinker and click of nails on hardwood precede some small furry critter trotting toward me.

"Oh, that's Murphy. My roommate's dog," she says.

I glance down at what appears to be a little pug with a smooshy, alien-like face and eyes round as saucers. He pants, head tilted like he's confused as to why I won't pick him up.

"Come here, Murph. Let's go back to Melrose's room." She swoops down to grab him before telling me she'll be right back, and I hear her open and close a couple of doors.

I take a seat, running my palms along what feels like velvet. The tick of some clock in another room echoes in the dark, quiet space. Several minutes later, Maritza returns, a folded blanket in her arm topped with a white pillow.

"Thanks." I take them from her and begin converting her sofa to a makeshift bed. All I need are a few hours of shut eye and then I'll be out of her hair before the sun comes up.

Maritza saunters toward the kitchen a second later, opening the fridge to retrieve two bottles of water, and it's only then I notice she's wearing a skimpy, damn near transparent pink tank top with matching shorts. She must have changed when she grabbed my bedding. How I missed this, I have no idea, but now I can't stop staring at her long legs, the curve of her lower back, and the way her top clings to her perfect tits.

I shake myself out of it when she returns and hands me a bottle of Fiji water.

It's funny ... an hour ago she was ripping my head off and spitting down my neck and now she's doing everything she can to ensure that I'm comfortable and can get home safely.

"Why are you being so nice to me?" I ask.

"Don't get it twisted. The pillows and blankets are so you don't drool all over my velvet sofa cushions and the water is so you don't wake me up in the middle of the night stumbling through my kitchen just because you're thirsty."

"Thank you," I say, silently admiring her comeback. I deserved that.

"Sorry about your shirt," she says a second later. "You want a different one?"

I shake my head. "It's dry now."

My eyes adjust enough that I can see the velvet I'll be sleeping on tonight is a vibrant shade of what appears to be emerald green. I've slept a lot of places in my life—buses, airports, pup tents, floors ... but never on the emerald green velvet sofa of a complete stranger who served me pancakes and rear ended me and then threw a glass of water at me after I so generously secured her a VIP pass to see her favorite band perform.

"Thanks again for the ticket," she says, one hand resting on her hip. The hem of her tank top lifts up just enough to expose a hint of soft skin. "I had a good time. All things considered."

I smirk. "All things considered meaning ... me."

Maritza rolls her eyes. "Basically."

"You still mad at me?"

"I can't be mad at you, Isaiah. I don't know you." She exhales, head tilting and dark hair curtaining the side of her face.

Part of me can't help but wonder what would've happened had this night gone in a different direction and she hadn't blown up at me. Maybe I had her all wrong. Here I thought she was this doormat, this Pollyanna ray of sunshine but it turns out there might be more to her than meets the eye.

Not to mention the best sex I ever had was with a girl who hated my fucking guts.

Talk about fire and ice.

"Why are you looking at me like that?" she asks, shifting as she adjusts the fallen spaghetti strap on her left shoulder.

I don't answer, I simply shrug. What am I supposed to tell her? I'm looking at her because she's standing there in sheer pajamas and I'm a fucking red-blooded American man who gets instantly aroused by the fact that she *doesn't* want me?

Maritza rolls her eyes. "What are you thinking about?"

"You don't want to know." I release a held breath and

my gaze falls to her full mouth for a fraction of a second. But I'm baiting her. You tell a girl she doesn't want to know what you're thinking and it's only going to make her want to know that much more.

Reverse psychology 101.

"Try me." Her head tilts and I decide it's adorable as fuck.

Yeah. This girl is sexy. I'll admit it. When I first saw her in the restaurant two days ago, I silently appreciated her finely crafted exterior, the curves and the lingering glances, but a couple of interactions with her and I knew she wasn't the kind of girl I was in the market for, so I pushed the thought from my mind.

But this ... this is a pleasant little twist in our strange little story.

My fingers form a peak as I blow a breath through them and our eyes catch. "I was thinking about how if you were any other girl and you didn't make it crystal clear that you despise me, I'd have kissed you by now."

The silence between us is palpable until she swallows and clears her throat and breaks eye contact. Her hand reaches for her neck as she focuses on the rug between us.

"Look. I don't want to make you uncomfortable in your own home," I say, resting my elbows on my knees. "So ... I guess this is goodnight."

She doesn't leave, doesn't so much as move a muscle.

"I don't despise you, Isaiah," she says, voice half broken. "Actually, I was thinking earlier ... that I might have misjudged you."

She has my full attention. If she's saying what I *think* she's saying ... I think I just found my second wind.

"It's funny." Her lips bend upward for a second before she lowers her chin and looks away. "There was a moment tonight when I wasn't thinking about slapping you across the face, and instead I was thinking about what it'd be like to kiss you."

I smirk, like a lion who has his prey exactly where he wants her. "I bet you were."

"What's that supposed to mean?"

"I feel like you were overcompensating all night," I say, shrugging.

"Overcompensating for *what*?"

"The fact that you can't stand me but you're crazy attracted to me."

"Cocky much?"

"Nope. Just perceptive."

"Anyway, you're right. I'm attracted to you and I can't stand you." Her arms fold across her chest.

I rise, slow and careful, coming toward her, bringing my hand toward her face and cupping her pointed chin, I angle her mouth into the perfect position. "All loathing aside, do you want to know what's it like? Or do you want to spend the rest of your life wondering?"

Her cherry lips twist and she exhales through her nose.

"You infuriate me," she says, our eyes holding. "But at the same time ... you kind of turn me on. And that makes it really hard for me to walk away from you right now."

"Then don't." I twist a strand of her dark hair around my fingers before letting it fall to her soft shoulder.

Her perfect teeth rake across her lower lip and she drags in a slow breath, a wordless surrender of sorts.

"For the record, sex with you is going to mean absolutely nothing to me," she says, head cocked and eyes playful.

"As it should."

"And this is a one-time thing." She lifts a single, manicured finger.

"Perfect."

Dragging in a ragged breath, she tilts her mouth toward mine, waiting ... almost hesitating, as if I'm some fire she might burn her finger on if she isn't careful.

Smart girl.

My hands drop to her hips, pulling her body against mine, and I crush her full lips as her body melts against me.

I've been told I have that effect on people—I can make them love me or hate me. Sometimes both at the same time. It's a blessing and a curse, but mostly a blessing of the convenient variety. Most of the time I can use it to my advantage.

The taste of toothpaste on her tongue mixes with a hint of the sweet liquor she was sipping on all night, and when her hands lift to the back of my neck and her nails trace against my scalp, my cock strains, growing harder with each graze of our mouths.

Sliding my palms down the sides of her thighs, I lift her, wrapping her long legs around my hips as I carry her to the sofa and lower myself, keeping her straddled in my lap.

Her mouth presses against the underside of my jaw, peppering hot kisses into my flesh as she trails down my right shoulder, her nails digging into my skin. Maritza's hips rock against mine, grinding on my cock, tempering the ache.

Taking the flimsy hem of her tank top between my fingers, I lift her top over her head before cupping two of the most perfect tits I've ever seen in my life. I twist a single pink bud between my thumb and forefinger before lowering my mouth and giving it a taste.

Maritza tosses her head back, slow and intentional as she offers her body to me. When she sits up and our eyes meet, she reaches for my shirt, tearing it off before running her palms down my chest and abs, her fingers tracing the grooves and ridges of each muscle.

"You're so ... hard," she says, bending forward and tracing the tattoo above my heart with a single finger. "What does it mean?"

"Nothing," I say, sliding a finger beneath the waistband of her shorts. "It means absolutely nothing."

Tugging them down her thighs and letting the scent of her arousal fill my lungs, I switch places with her, letting her lie down as I grab a rubber from my wallet and unzip my pants.

"Holy shit," she says when she sees what I'm working with.

I smirk, proud. The reaction never gets old no matter how many times I see it.

Sitting up, she takes my cock in her hand, pumping the length as she struggles to wrap her soft palm all the way around it. Bringing her mouth to the tip, she swallows as much as she can fit, her tongue circling the tip before swirling just beneath the head.

Maritza takes her time. She doesn't rush like some girls do.

She enjoys it, moaning and pausing every so often to glance up at me, coyly wipe the side of her mouth, and let me take in the view as she swallows my pre-cum and goes back for more.

Gathering her silky hair in my fist, I guide my cock deeper into her mouth until I feel a tight swell that takes everything in my power to ignore.

"Your turn," I say, lowering myself between her thighs as she spreads her legs, hooking them over my shoulders.

Dragging a finger along the seam of her wet pussy, I

tease her clit and her tight, sweet hole before letting my tongue take over. Circling her swollen clit and devouring her sweetness, my cock throbs each time she moans and sighs and wriggles against me.

When she's had enough, she reaches for me, pulling me over top of her and kissing her taste off my lips.

Grabbing the gold foil packet on the sofa cushion beside us, I sheathe my cock before slipping my fingers between her silken folds and massaging her clit.

"On your knees," I tell her, guiding her before positioning myself behind her perfect apricot ass.

Dragging the tip of my cock along her slick seam, I tease her before impaling her with one hard push. She gasps and I wrap my arms around her, pulling her body against mine as my hips thrust harder, faster, finding the perfect rhythm.

Cupping her breasts and filling her to the hilt, I squeeze my eyes and lose myself in the moment, appreciating the way her body molds to mine and relents to my every wordless command. It's like we're finally speaking the same language, even if that language consists of breathless gasps and whispered compliments in the form of sacrilegious profanities.

"Don't stop," she pleads, her arms reaching behind her and cupping fistfuls of my hair.

Brushing her dark hair aside, I kiss the side of her neck. "I won't."

I can go all fucking night long.

MY PHONE VIBRATES, pulling me out of my sex-induced coma. Maritza's naked body rests on top of mine and the living room is still dark, though the slightest hint of pre-dawn peeks through the blinds.

Moving her gently to the side, I slide out from under her and cover her up with the blanket we shared the past several hours. Stepping into my jeans, I tug on the zipper while scanning the room for my shirt.

"What time is it?" Maritza's groggy voice cuts through the silence. "Why are you up right now?"

"I have to go," I say. I place an apologetic tone in my voice, but it's genuine. Sex with Maritza was good last night. Really fucking good. So good that I'd be willing to break my one-and-done rule and go for round two, but Mom needs her morning meds and her coffee, and if I stay too long Maritza might offer to cook me breakfast and I don't want to do that whole awkward, morning-after-sex routine. I've done enough of those to last me a lifetime.

"You're deploying next week, right?" She sits up, brushing her dark hair out of her pretty face.

"Yep."

"What are you doing until then?" she asks.

I locate my t-shirt hanging off the back of an armchair and tug it over my head, trying to buy time so I can think of the best way to imply that this is the end of the road for us.

"We should hang out." She sits up, leaning over to click on a lamp, illuminating the living room with gentle light before lifting her palm. "And before you go jumping to conclusions, I don't mean we should hang out like *that*. Or because of what we did last night. I just mean ... I had fun with you. And you should have fun before you leave. We could do, like ... I don't know ... a week of Saturdays or something."

"A week of Saturdays?"

"Yeah. A week where we treat every day like it's a

Saturday and we pal around the city and do fun, stupid stuff," she says. "Not dates. Nothing romantic. Just a couple of ... dare I say ... friends."

I smirk, adjusting my shirt into place. "I don't know."

It's hard enough to be friends with a woman and harder still to be friends with a woman once you've fucked her.

Maritza stands, wrapping the blanket around her naked body, and ambles toward me. "I don't want to date you, Isaiah, if that's what you're afraid of. You're not my type for one and for two, I really, *really* like being single."

I slip my phone and keys into my pockets and eye the door.

"What do you say?" she asks. "One week. No romance. No lies or bullshit or games. Just a couple of people hanging out and having fun."

I'll admit she's dynamite in bed and maybe "hanging out" a few more times with her before I leave would be better than finding some fast and loose girl at the sports bar down the street from Ma's, but I don't know.

Once you sleep with someone a few times and get to know them, shit changes and sometimes you have no control over how it's going to change—if it's going to be better or worse or complicated or the kind of thing you'll spend the rest of your life trying to recover from.

I'm leaning toward the inclination that no good can possibly come of something like this. Someone's going to catch feelings and get hurt and more than likely it's not going to be me.

"I don't know if it's a good idea," I say.

Her expression doesn't waver. "I'm not taking 'no' for an answer."

I exhale. I just want to get the fuck out of here, get

through the rest of the week, and get my ass overseas where I belong.

"I can get some of my shifts covered for the week," she says, stepping closer and wrapping the blanket so tight the tops of her breasts practically spill out. It's a silent bribe, I fucking know it is. "Come on. We could have fun."

"No romance or dates?" I ask.

"None." She makes an 'x' across her chest.

"No bullshit or lies?" I ask.

I can't believe I'm even considering this. It's got to be those eyes. Those big brown eyes. She's luring me in, casting a spell or some shit. I don't know. For some reason, I feel almost powerless around her. Or maybe it's nothing more than curiosity and an amazing sex hangover that left me wanting more.

"Zero." Her full lips turn up at the sides, like a girl who knows she's about to get what she wants.

Running a hand through my messy hair, I exhale, locking eyes with her. "Fine."

This marks the first time in the last ten years that I've been defeated by a woman, that I've given up control of a situation when every fiber of my being is screaming at me to walk away, to say no while I still can, before this gets messy.

She wraps her arms around my shoulders, bouncing before pressing her body against mine. "Go home. Get some sleep. Saturday number one is tomorrow."

I just hope I won't live to regret this.

And I hope she won't either.

5

MARITZA

Saturday #1

"I never realized how small Miley Cyrus was," I say as I pull Isaiah toward her wax likeness Sunday morning. "I think I was twelve last time I looked like this."

Isaiah doesn't seem amused and he doesn't seem to care.

"Hey, look, you're the same height as Ryan Gosling," I say, pointing.

Yesterday morning a courier delivered my phone from The Mintz at approximately seven AM, and I can only imagine Isaiah arranged that.

This morning I texted him as soon as I woke up and told him to meet me at 6933 Hollywood Boulevard by 9:30 AM. I met him with two coffees in hand—two creams and a half of a sugar pack for him—because somehow I remembered.

"You don't find this shit creepy?" he asks.

"I find real celebrities creepier than their waxy counterparts." I take a sip of coffee. "They're so ... all over the place. You never know if they're going to be nice or rude or in a good mood or a bad mood or if they're nothing like the last fifteen movie roles they played. These wax people are more real than any celebrity, and I speak from experience."

He doesn't ask, but he doesn't have to. When you live in LA, people just assume you run into famous people on a daily basis. And sometimes you do. Depends on where you work or where you spend most of your time.

These days, living in my grandmother's guesthouse in her Brentwood estate on the same street where Marilyn Monroe took her final breath, I don't tend to get out much. Most people in Brentwood keep to themselves and the flashier stars stick to Beverly Hills and those places. A few of the B and C listers who've pseudo-retired and started families have been migrating to Encinitas and Temecula, but for the most part, I might see someone I recognize from TV *mayyyyybe* once a month.

"Oh, full disclosure," I say, placing my hand on his arm as I catch him checking out waxy J. Lo's booty. "We were talking about not being fake and stuff yesterday?"

"Yeah?"

"My boobs are fake. Just putting it out there in the interest of full honesty and sticking to our agreement."

He smirks for a split second, dimples flashing, and his honeyed eyes land on my rack.

"That wasn't an invitation to check them out," I say, pointing at him with two fingers and then pointing at my eyes. "Up here, Corporal."

"How'd you know I was a corporal?" he asks.

"Rachael told me that day at the diner. I don't forget a thing." I point to my head and give him a wink.

He sniffs, like maybe he's impressed. "Anyway, that was a natural reflex. Forgive me."

"Forgiven," I say, pressing my palms against my full C-cups. "I've had them since the month I turned eighteen. At the time, all my girlfriends were getting new boobs as graduation gifts, and my friend's dad was a plastic surgeon who offered a buy-one-implant-get-one-free deal to all her friends. In retrospect, having her dad do my surgery was kind of creepy, but at the time, all I could think about was how nice it was going to be to finally fill out a bikini top for the first time in my life."

"Priorities of an eighteen-year-old."

"Exactly." I grin, head tilting, and I nudge his shoulder with mine. "See, you get it."

We make our way into the next room, which is set up like some fancy nightclub. Will Smith is perched on some futuristic-looking seat, Jada standing beside him. Across from them is Edward Norton—random—and then of course Brad and Angelina.

"Whoever runs this place needs to read an Us Weekly. Brangelina broke up, like, a year ago," I say.

"Who?"

"Never mind."

He slips his hands into his jeans pockets, and I watch the subtle flex of his triceps before following the round curve of his shoulders. Isaiah is pure muscle. Hard, steely muscle.

Shaking my head, I snap myself out of it.

"You're not into this celebrity stuff, are you?" I ask. "You seem bored. If I'm being honest. And I am. Always."

He drags his hand down his full mouth. "Yeah. This isn't my thing."

"Then why do you live in LA?"

"I don't. My mom is here. I stay with her between deployments."

"So, where's home then?" I ask.

Isaiah shrugs. "Nowhere."

I follow him to the next exhibit, which is full of historical replicas of people like Benjamin Franklin and George Washington. He lingers in here a bit longer. Maybe history is more his thing?

"My cousin, Eli, is a huge history buff," I say. "He's in the army, too. I think that's partially why he joined. He wanted to be in command, he wanted to lead, but more than that, he wanted his name printed in a history book. True story."

He shakes his head. "Yeah, I've met a lot of those."

"Can you believe I've lived in LA my entire life and this is the first time I've ever been here?" I muse. "Here, take my picture next to this guy. I like his hair."

"Thomas Edison?" He lifts a brow.

"Yeah." I strike a pose, flashing a peace sign and sticking my tongue out of the side of my mouth a la Miley. Fuck trying to look cool. I'd rather be memorable, even if it means looking like a dork.

Isaiah lifts his phone and snaps a picture, texting it to me a second later, and we head toward the exit.

"So, uh ... Before I knew you didn't like this stuff, I kind of, sort of booked us this celebrity tour-of-homes sightseeing excursion." I wince, eyes squinting hard as I shrug my shoulders. "But we don't have to go."

Even though I already paid the eighty bucks to hold our spots ...

"Nah, it's fine," he says, glancing toward the distance. "I'll try anything once."

"Just don't get your hopes up, okay? You strike me as the adrenaline-seeking type, and this is going to be more like Midwestern tourists and little old ladies asking where Clark Gable used to live."

Looping my hand into the bend of his elbow because

I'm an unapologetically touchy-feely kind of girl, I pull him toward Sunset Boulevard where we're supposed to wait for some hot pink topless bus type of vehicle with the words CELEB VIP TOURS painted across the sides.

By the time we round the corner, the open-top bus contraption is pulling into a reserved parking spot and a herd of little old ladies are climbing on.

"Sure you want to do this?" I ask. "I'm giving you an out right now, so if you want it, you better take it."

"I told you, I'll try anything once," he says.

"Good. Because I wouldn't want you violating rule number one on our first day," I say, winking.

"Did you say day or date?" he asks, face pinched.

"*DAY*," I say, loud and clear, enunciating each and every letter.

"All right. Just checking."

Elbowing him as we climb on board, I say under my breath, "You'd be so lucky."

I swear he fights a smirk.

Retrieving my phone, I pull up our tickets in my email and the driver scans the barcodes. We find a seat in the back row, left side, and he gives me the outside which clearly has the better view.

"Okay, are we ready for our *Homes of the Stars* tour?" The driver-slash-tour guide speaks into a microphone, his enthusiasm way too extreme for a weekday morning. The women around us smile and half-clap, and he takes his seat, buckling up.

We pull into traffic a second later, and while I feel like an enormous dork, I'm secretly pleased because this is always something I've wanted to do, but my friends always acted like they were too cool for shit like this.

The first stop is the Holmby Hills neighborhood, where

the guide rambles on about the Playboy Mansion, spouting as much trivia and fun facts as he can as we pass by the gated drive. Next we approach the old Spelling Manor, which now belongs to some international gazillionaire whose name I couldn't understand because the guide's mic was all crackly and an onyx Maserati was honking at a baby blue Aston Martin.

Ten minutes later, he approaches the Holiday Palms neighborhood, which he proudly spouts was *the* place to live in the sixties, with Raquel Welch, Farrah Fawcett, and Gloria Claiborne all living door to door at one point in time.

"It's true," I lean into Isaiah. "Grandma said Farrah was sweet as pie. Raquel was the one to watch out for. Wasn't her fault though. Men couldn't resist her exotic beauty and sensual charm."

"Grandma?" He lifts a brow.

"Yep. Gloria Claiborne is my grandma," I say. It's better that I get it out now because sooner or later, I find myself accidentally working it into conversation. And it's not that I'm trying to brag or name drop—because let's be honest, most people my age have no idea who she was back then—but my grandma is one of my favorite human beings on the planet, so I talk about her more than most people probably talk about their grandmothers.

He scratches the side of his nose, brows furrowed. "Wasn't she in that movie ..."

I nod. "Davida's Desire."

"Yeah," he says.

"You've seen it?"

"No. But my dad had that famous poster in his garage growing up ... the one with the white bikini."

I laugh. "Yeah, I know exactly which poster that is. My grandma has a room full of all her old movie posters."

Over the years, her poster for Davida's Desire has gained cult status, kind of like Farrah's red swimsuit cover. People recognize it instantly—Grandma's thick, chocolate girls, round, babydoll eyes, elegant pointed nose, bee-stung pout, and curves spilling out of a tiny string bikini as she lies in the sand next to a turquoise ocean.

"Huh." Isaiah's palm drags across his jaw and I feel him staring at me, looking at me through a new lens. "You kind of look like her now that I think about it."

Rolling my eyes, I say, "Yeah, I get that."

I don't like to make it into a thing, but my entire life people have pointed out how much I resemble my grandma in her younger days. And it's true. We have the same abundant, coffee-brown mane. The same round-as-saucers, coffee-hued irises. The pinched nose and the full lips are another Claiborne trademark.

The only thing I didn't inherit from her were her exaggerated curves.

My father (her son) saw it fit to marry a 90s runway model with straight hips, long legs, and no boobs. From the neck down, I'm all my mother ... minus the breast implants of course.

The tour lasts a long and sometimes fascinating two hours before the bus returns us to Sunset Boulevard. Isaiah stands, letting me out first, and then I swear I feel his hand graze my lower back as he follows me.

A zing of something—not sure what—zaps through my middle, but it's gone by the time I climb down the bus's steps and hit the pavement.

Checking the time, I bite my lower lip.

"What is it?" he asks.

"We should probably call it a day," I say, eyes flicking to

his as my words are laced in an apologetic tone. A tepid Californian breeze kisses my skin.

"Really?" He checks the time on his phone.

"Just realized I forgot to feed my Murphy this morning," I say. "He hasn't eaten since last night."

"Wow." His hands rest at his hips and he takes a step back, glancing down the packed street.

"What?"

"If you don't want to hang out, just say so. Don't make up some bullshit excuse about your roommate's dog."

I laugh. "Wait—you think ... no. I'm not making this up, Isaiah. I seriously need to feed her dog. She's out of town and I'm supposed to be taking care of him. He's probably starving by now, and I feel awful."

His head tilts, like he still doesn't believe me.

"I'm being honest, I swear. Rule number two, remember? No bullshit, no lies," I remind him.

Isaiah exhales, lips pressed flat as he studies me for a moment. "All right. I believe you."

"Good. You should. And I'll see you tomorrow," I tell him, cinching my purse strap over my shoulder. Mouth drawn into a smile, I say, "I had fun with you today."

He nods. "I did too."

"Liar."

"I would never violate your rules, Maritza," he says, rebelling against a hint of a smile. His gaze keeps dropping to my mouth then lifting back to my eyes. And while I didn't give it much thought before, there were a few small moments today when I caught him staring at me ... almost like he was wondering what would happen if he kissed me again.

And truth be told, I caught myself thinking that I kind of wouldn't mind if he did ...

... in the name of fun, of course.

"Text me tonight," I tell him. "Tell me where to find you tomorrow and I'll be there."

With that, I turn, walking away, feeling the weight of his stare and wondering what the hell I've gotten myself into.

6

ISAIAH

SATURDAY #2

"SANTA MONICA PIER, EH?"

She finds me on a bench next to a churro vendor, and her hands rest in the back pockets of her cutoff shorts. A white, v-neck tee shows off her tanned skin and a hint of the pale pink lace bra she's wearing underneath.

Maritza the Waitress is a stunning work of art and the proud recipient of the Claiborne genetic lottery, but I have to remind myself to keep my eyes where they belong. Far too many times yesterday, I caught myself checking her out, letting my gaze linger on every square inch of her every time I knew she wasn't paying attention.

Despite the fact that we christened our non-relationship that night at the concert, I've got no business turning this into any kind of a thing.

Aside from the fact that her bubbly and effervescent personality tends to grate on my skin half the time, I respect the hell out of the fact that she has no qualms about calling things the way she sees them, and she isn't trying to impress anyone—certainly not me. Maritza is simply Maritza. She isn't hiding behind layers of makeup, nervous giggles, or agreeable opinions.

But I would never tell her that.

She might get the wrong idea.

She might think that I *like* her.

"What made you pick this place?" Maritza takes the spot beside me, her thigh brushing against mine. The scent of fried dough, cinnamon, and sugar fills the salty air, and I'm immediately taken back to my younger days.

"My parents used to take us here when we were younger," I say. "They'd let us run around, buy us anything we wanted."

The memories of the better times are the only thing I really hold onto from my earlier days.

"Sounds nice," she says, exhaling with a gentle hum. "So, you grew up in Santa Monica then?"

"Nah." I shake my head and crack my knuckles as I stare toward the ocean. "Riverside mostly."

"When was the last time you came here?"

I blow a heavy breath through my lips, shaking my head. "I wouldn't even know. Ten, twelve years ago?"

I'm guessing I was sixteen or seventeen the last time he took us, which makes sense because that was right before he died, which was right after he walked out of his life and left behind his disabled wife and their six children.

"You're quiet," she says a few beats later, nudging my arm. "What are you thinking about?"

"Nothing worth sharing," I say. And it's true. She

doesn't need to know about my past. It has nothing to do with the here and now, with our week of Saturdays. It's a part of me I no longer discuss and that's *all* that it is.

"Everything is worth sharing."

I shake my head. "Not this."

Maritza leans forward, elbows on her knees and chin resting on her hands, watching the crowd. "Do you ever people watch?"

"Sometimes. Why?"

"When I was younger, my cousin Melrose and I would always people watch and we'd make up these stories ... like we'd pick someone and then whip up their whole life story in thirty seconds," she says. "See that guy over there? Posing by that Route 66 sign?"

Maritza casually points toward a man in jean shorts and a black t-shirt, a Santa Monica Pier hat on his head and a thick blond beard covering the lower half of his face.

"Yeah. I see him," I say.

"His name is Collin Burke and he's from Denver, Colorado," she says, licking her lips as she studies him. "He's the baby of the family, which is why he's comfortable posing for pictures and being the center of attention. He's a computer programmer by trade, and for fun he gets together with his friends and does some live action role playing stuff. And despite the fact that he's clearly in his mid-thirties, he has a Star Wars comforter on his bed at home and a dog named Yoda. Also, he has a girlfriend. Her name is Samantha Robbins and she's the one taking his picture. She doesn't know it yet, but he's going to pop the question this year at his family's lake house on the Fourth of July, just as the fireworks begin."

"Nerdy *and* romantic," I say. "Killer combo."

Maritza sighs. "And that's exactly why she's going to say yes. She's crazy for him. Wants to have *alllll* his babies."

I chuckle. "You're so random."

And I kind of like it ...

"Okay, your turn. Pick someone and give me their life story," she says, sitting back against the bench, her arm against mine and her hand patting the top of my knee. Normally I like my space, but for some reason being this close with another person isn't giving me that grating, nails-on-a-chalkboard sensation that makes my teeth grind and my breath quicken.

Scanning the pier and examining my options, my gaze lands on a woman in the distance, wearing nothing but a peach bikini and sitting all alone on a green towel on the beach.

"Her," I say, nodding in her direction. "The girl in the bikini, sitting by herself."

"The one in the straw hat?"

"Yep," I say, pulling in a deep breath. "Her name is Cadence."

"Pretty name."

"And she recently broke up with her boyfriend because he was screwing her best friend," I say.

"Damn. You're taking this in a Maury Povich direction, but okay. Keep going," she says.

"She grew up in New Hampshire but she always felt like more of a west coaster, hence the bleach blonde hair and skin cancer tan."

"Judge much?"

"Okay fine. It's a spray tan and she's extremely diligent about wearing sunscreen. That better?" I ask.

"Much."

"Anyway, she dumped her boyfriend and came out here

because she wanted to be alone with her thoughts but surrounded by people. She's complicated like that, but that's most women. They're always wanting two completely different things at the same time and they have no clue why half the time."

Maritza laughs. "Hashtag truth."

"She's also secretly hoping that some random, attractive guy will hit on her, give her his number, and make her forget about the guy who screwed her over," I add. "But at the end of the day, she's going to go home empty handed, call up some girlfriends, and head to their favorite bar for some drinks so they can talk about how fucking stupid men are. And it's true. We're stupid as hell when it comes to women ... and half of it is because we're designed that way and the other half of it is because you guys are so complicated we can't even begin to figure you out."

"Whoa, whoa, whoa, Corporal. Don't lump us all together," she says, head cocked and eyes squinting. "I pride myself in not being complicated ninety-nine percent of the time. I'm a bona fide what-you-see-is-what-you-get kind of woman—except at work, of course. I have to be sweet and accommodating there or else I won't be able to pay my rent."

"Your grandma charges you rent?"

She nods. "Of course. What, you thought I was some freeloader?"

"I don't know what I thought." I lift a hand. "Anyway, so that's peach bikini girl's story."

"You didn't even go into her past. Like does she have siblings? What kind of car does she drive?"

"You're taking this way too seriously," I say. "Does it matter what car she drives? Her heart was just obliterated. Everything else is secondary at this point."

"Fair enough." Maritza exhales, and I'm relieved that my 'turn' is over. "Hey, are you hungry?"

I check my phone. It's nearly noon.

"Do you want to get sushi or something?" she asks. "Do you like sushi? What do you like?"

"Sushi's fine."

She stands. "Everything's always 'fine' with you."

I rise, shrugging. "So?"

"Is anything ever not fine?"

I frown. Lots of things aren't fine, but those things aren't in the here and now. "When you've seen what I've seen, let's just say it gives you a little perspective as to what's fine and what's not."

She links her arm into mine and we head up the pier.

"That's deep, Corporal. I like when you go deep." Her hand cups her mouth. "I didn't mean it like that," she says. "I just mean, you're so quiet all the time. I think it's cool when you say something meaningful. You're a man who only really talks when he has something to say, and I like that about you."

"Anyway." We head past vendors slinging corn dogs and popcorn and weave through yoga-pants wearing moms and squeeze past two bicyclists and not once does she let go of me. "Are you always this hands-on with people you hardly know?"

"Oh, sweetheart, I think we're a little past that, aren't we?" she asks, lashes fluttering as her lips bunch in one corner. "Anyway, does it bother you? You can tell me if it does."

"Not yet," I say. "But I'll keep you posted."

Maritza points to a place called SUGARFISH and leads us that way. The hostess tells us the wait is at least forty-five to fifty minutes, so we head to the bar to kill time.

"There's only one stool," she says. "You want it?"

"I'm insulted that you'd even ask me that." I take a step back, pointing at the seat. "It's yours."

I'll be damned if I'm some selfish tool who makes a woman stand while he gets to sit.

A minute later, we order drinks. The place is loud and packed as hell for a weekday afternoon, but I decide to enjoy this because this is heaven compared to where I'm going to be a week from now.

"I'm starving," she says with a sigh, her full lower lip pouting. "I forgot to eat breakfast. At least I remembered to feed the dog before I left."

My phone buzzes in my pocket, and I slide it out to find my sister Calista's name on the screen. She only ever calls about Mom, so I lift a finger. "I'm sorry. I have to take this."

"Of course." She smiles, turning to face the bar.

"Calista," I answer. "What's up?"

"Hey, I was supposed to bring Mom dinner tonight, but Evangeline's got a fever and Grayson has basketball and Rod's working a double." Her voice is a mixture of exhaustion and surrender.

"It's fine," I say. "I'll swing by and grab her something tonight."

"Thanks, little brother. I owe you."

"You owe me nothing," I say.

"What am I going to do when you're gone?" she asks, exhaling into the phone.

"You'll do what you always do," I say. The sound of rattling toys and a blaring TV in the background disrupts our moment and she tells me she has to go.

As much as the two of us butt heads, Calista hates that I'm in the military. She's made that crystal clear from the day I enlisted. And it's not that she has something against the army—she's scared for me, that's all. She's scared to lose me. We were always so close growing up. Then she got married and had kids and I was overseas. Now our interactions are relegated to short phone calls about Mom and silent "love yous" that are never said but always somehow felt.

It's really the closest I allow myself to get to actually feeling something.

Slipping my phone back into my pocket, I turn toward Maritza, only to find some emaciated jackass with a sleeve of tattoos and an ear full of piercings leaning up against the bar, wearing a jerkoff's smile and looking at her like a shark about to devour chum.

I have to intervene.

She'll thank me later.

Returning to her side, I slip my arm over her shoulder and give that tool a good, hard stare. He doesn't get it at first. Almost scoffing and then laughing, like he thinks it's some kind of joke.

"This guy bothering you, babe?" I ask.

She glances up at me before gently removing my arm from her shoulders. "Isaiah, stop."

The guy scratches his temple, glancing around, fidgeting almost.

I make him nervous.

"Find someone else, all right, bud?" I say, flashing a pearly white 'fuck off' smile. "This one's mine."

"Isaiah." Maritza says my name harder now, her brows meeting.

The guy's shoulders slump, his confidence taking the shape of a deflated Mylar balloon, and he ambles away, disappearing into the crowd.

"Why did you do that?" She punches my arm. I think she's actually mad.

"I was doing you a favor."

"No, you were acting like a jealous asshole. Need I remind you that *we* are not a thing? That *this* is not a date? That you have no claim over me?"

"No need to remind me at all," I say because we're still very much on the same page. "I saw a situation that required an intervention and I delivered."

Maritza rolls her eyes. "Un-fucking-believable."

Our drinks arrive and she reaches for hers so quickly she nearly knocks it over.

"He just wanted a piece," I tell her.

Her back is to me, and she lifts her martini glass to her full lips. "And you knew that how? Because you sized him up for all of three seconds?"

"I know men," I say. "I know how we think, how we operate. I've spent the last damn near decade of my life around sex-starved men who treat bars like some kind of fucking feeding frenzy and that guy was fishing hard."

She says nothing, only takes another sip. But I wish she'd reply because now *I'm* starting to feel like the jackass.

"Maritza," I say.

A moment later, she finally turns to me. "You know, honestly? I'm offended right now. I'm offended that you think I'm too stupid to not know the difference between a man who's genuinely interested and a man who just wants a piece. That guy was nice and we were talking about Aerosmith because he was wearing an original t-shirt from their 1993 Get A Grip tour, and you made him feel about 'this' tall."

She pinches her fingers together before turning back around.

"I'm sorry," I say, scraping my hand across the gritty stubble that peppers my jaw.

"What if he was supposed to be my future husband? What if he was the one?" she asks, back still toward me. "What if we were supposed to get married someday? And have two point five kids and live in a beautiful house in Temecula? But now I'll never know." Maritza turns back to me. "I just hope you can live with yourself after this."

"What?"

"You'll have to live with the fact that you basically killed my future children by intervening in destiny," she says, lifting her glass. "That's some Back to the Future level shit, Corporal."

I'm so fucking confused.

And then she bursts out laughing. "I'm fucking with you."

Exhaling, I take half a step away. She got me. She got me good.

"I had no interest in that guy," she said. "He was nice but not my type, so thanks for saving me."

Our buzzer goes off, our table must be ready early.

"You're so fucking dramatic," I tell her, wearing a half-smirk. If I knew her better, I'd give her ass a good pinch right now. Instead, I shamelessly let my gaze drop as I follow behind her, considering this her atonement, her penance.

"It's in my blood," she says. "Literally."

A moment later, we're seated in a cozy corner booth and given two menus printed on linen paper. It's broad daylight outside, but in here it's dark and intimate, candles everywhere. And while this is the furthest thing from a date and getting attached to this woman is the last thing I need to be doing, the smallest—and I mean the most minuscule—part of me finds myself wishing I wasn't leaving next week, that I could stick around and get to know her a little better.

Something tells me I could like her.

And that's saying a lot because truly, I don't like anyone.

"WHAT DID YOU DO TODAY, ISAIAH?" Mom asks as she settles behind a TV tray that night and reaches for her remote.

"Just palled around."

She glances at me. She might be tired and her brain might be foggy every now and then, but she knows me.

"Don't get smart with me," she says, chin tucked against her chest. "What'd you do?"

"Went to the Pier."

Ma mutes the TV, lips pressed flat. Some days she doesn't remember much, but she surely remembers the pier.

"Alone?" she asks.

Taking a seat on the edge of her bed, I shake my head. "With a friend."

"Which friend?"

Drawing in a heavy breath, I rise. "It's hot in here. You want the fan on?"

"No. Sit." She waves for me to return to my post. "Which friend?"

"Just ... this girl I met a few days ago."

Ma's face doesn't light. She knows I'm not one for commitment and I haven't brought a girl home in almost a decade, so anytime I merely mention hanging out with a woman, she assumes I'm referring to some piece I picked up at the local sports bar.

"She's nice," I say, only to reassure her. "You'd like her. She's funny."

My mother's face softens. "Can I meet her?"

"Nope."

Her head tilts and she crosses her legs, angling her body toward me, examining me. "You like her? This girl?"

"Ma, your food's getting cold." I point to the Styrofoam container she hasn't touched since I delivered it to her five minutes ago. "You know steak's not good when you microwave it."

Sitting up, she reaches for a knife and a fork and begins sawing her meat, muttering in Portuguese under her breath.

"She's a good girl," I say. "Respectable. But we're just friends."

If you can even call us that ...

"You enjoy spending time with her?" Ma asks.

"I do."

She takes a tiny bite, chewing, contemplating. "All I want for you is to have a nice girl to spend time with. Someone who puts a smile on your face. My dying wish, Isaiah."

"Ma, don't talk like that."

"What?"

"Don't talk about dying wishes," I say. "You're not dying."

Ma's mouth curls into a bittersweet smile. "*Meu amor*, you live in the land of denial and you have for quite some time. If you deny death, you're denying life. Just promise me you'll never deny your feelings."

Rising from her bed once more, I offer a humoring chuff before bending to kiss the top of her forehead. "I'll be in the next room if you need me."

7

MARITZA

SATURDAY #3

"LET ME GET THIS STRAIGHT." My cousin-slash-best friend-slash roommate, Melrose, leans against my bathroom doorway as I get ready to meet up with Isaiah. "I'm on location for three days and I come back and you're spending a week with a complete stranger?"

Her jaw hangs as she gathers her messy blonde waves into an even messier top knot, gazing at her reflection via my mirror.

"You're crazy," she says. "Not that you didn't already know this. Do your parents know?"

"Nope."

"Does Gram?"

"Nope."

"Good God, Maritza, what if something happened to you? And no one would've known who you were hanging out with?" She clucks her tongue. If Isaiah thinks *I'm* dramatic, wait until he meets her.

If he ever meets her.

Which he probably won't.

"He's in the army," I tell her, as if that automatically makes him safe.

"Lots of people are in the army."

"He's a good person," I add, because anyone who's willing to sacrifice their life for complete strangers qualifies as "good" in my book even if they're not exactly the warm, personable type.

"And you know this because you've known him for a hot minute?" She pushes past me, taking a seat on my toilet lid and resting her elbow against my vanity. "I thought you were insane when you fostered those stray dogs last year. And then I thought you were even crazier when you changed your major to Gender Whatever Studies because up until then, you'd never so much as expressed a single interest in that topic, but this ... this takes the cake, my love."

"We're having fun," I say, shrugging off her concerns.

Melrose is an actress, trying desperately to follow in our grandmother's footsteps. So far her IMDB is just small stuff. Minor roles. She's still taking acting classes and looking for her big break, but last year she was in an episode of Law and Order: SVU and ever since then she's become obsessed with shows like Dateline and anything related to creepy, twisted crimes and she's suddenly adamant that everyone has an ulterior motive at all times.

I decide to take her dramatic concerns with a grain of salt.

Besides, I have pepper spray and a whistle in my purse should he try anything stupid, and I taught women's self-defense classes my sophomore year at UC-Berkeley. Plus, if he were a serial killer, I feel like he would've had ample opportunity to murder me Friday night when he stayed at my place—a little detail I have no intention of sharing with Mel in the immediate future.

Twisting my hair into a low chignon, I check my reflection one last time before reaching for a bottle of my Kai perfume and spritzing my pulse points.

"We're going to the Brentwood farmer's market today," I tell her.

She makes a face.

"What?" I ask.

"Since when do you do shit like that?"

"Since never," I say. "But we're trying new things this week, things neither of us have ever done before. It's a week of 'yes.'"

Melrose sticks her finger down her throat, pretending to gag herself. Always so judge-y, this one. But I don't take offense to it. Her idea of spending time with a man involves one at least twice her age, a sexy sports car, and a reservation at an exclusive LA eatery.

She may be my best friend, but we couldn't be more different.

"All right, well ... while you're hanging out with your serial killer friend, I'm going to be lunching with Gram at The Ivy," she says, teasing like I should be jealous. And then she cracks a smile. "Wish you could join us ..."

"Next time." I hit the bathroom light and head to my room, grabbing my things and stepping into a pair of comfy sneakers. The farmer's market is only six blocks from here, so I'm walking. But before heading out the door, I text Isaiah and tell him I'll see him in ten minutes.

He says he's already there.

I smirk.

Those military boys and their punctuality ...

"YOU STAND OUT LIKE A SORE THUMB," I tell him when I find him.

"Why do you say that?" he asks.

"I don't know. Can't put my finger on it. You just do. You're not a farmer's market person, I can tell."

"Should I have worn my flax pants and straw hat today?" he asks. We begin to walk, our arms bumping into one another every few steps.

"Smart ass." We pass a flower stand and a bouquet of blue hydrangeas steals my attention. "Hold up. I want to buy some of these."

"Want or need?"

"Blue hydrangeas are always a need."

A minute later, I walk away with a beautiful bouquet wrapped in brown paper and Isaiah stops at a breakfast burrito stand for some wrap made with local, cage-free eggs, organic cheddar sourced from Northern California, and free-range chicken sausage.

We find an empty table next to a wine vendor's booth and steal a couple of spots.

"So what is a farmer's market person?" he asks.

I laugh through my nose. "I don't know ... maybe a Volvo-driving, organic-obsessed, Pilates-loving mom of four? Not to be, you know, stereotypical. I'm just going off of what I see here. There definitely seems to be some consistencies around us."

He glances toward a parking lot behind us and I count at least eight Volvo XC-90s, most of which are polished black or glimmering white. A woman pushing a double stroller and wearing $90 yoga pants yells at her two older kids, telling them not to run off.

"See?" I point toward her. "Am I right or am I right?"

"You're right." He inhales his last bite of burrito and wipes his hands on a napkin. "So what kind of person am I?"

"What?"

"If I'm not a farmer's market person ... how would you categorize me? What box would you place me in?" he asks.

Sucking in a deep breath, I mull over my response. I promised him honesty, so honesty he's going to get.

"You're still a question mark, Isaiah," I say. "At first glance, I'd put you in some kind of military category because you're so serious and clean cut and stoic. But these last few days, I don't know. I think there's more to you than you're letting on. You're closed off. So closed off I haven't even attempted to figure you out. I tried, too. Laid in bed one night replaying our day together, trying to see if there were any things I missed. Then I got a headache, so I went to sleep."

He sniffs, shaking his head. "A question mark, eh?"

I nod. "Yup."

"That's a fair statement."

"You ever going to open up? You know you can tell me anything. We're still basically strangers. You probably don't even remember my last name, so your secrets are safe with me."

"I don't really tell anyone anything," he says. "It's

nothing personal. And I do remember your last name because I had to submit a claim to your insurance for the damage you did to my car."

I exhale. He's going to be a tough one to crack, but I feel like he'd be worth cracking. Only problem is our days are numbered, our time together dwindling by the second, and I don't see myself making much progress with him before he goes.

"It's okay." I rub his arm. "Just know that if you ever want to vent about anything, I'm your girl."

"I don't vent."

His full mouth lifts at one corner and he leans back in his seat, staring at me in a way he's yet to stare at me until now. I'd give anything to know what he's thinking, good or bad.

"Should we do a little more exploring?" I ask, rising. He breaks his gaze and stands beside me, stretching his arms over his head. His shirt lifts just enough that I spot the chiseled muscles pointing down the sides of his hips as well as the hint of a rippled six-pack.

My heart hiccups and I lose my train of thought for all of three seconds. I don't remember fully appreciating those things that night at the concert.

"I heard there's a killer cinnamon roll stand here," I tell him, scanning the booths. "First one to find it wins."

"Wins what?"

"Wins at life, Corporal. Cinnamon rolls are everything, duh."

He follows me into the crowd, and it isn't until we're at the far end of the farmer's market when I realize I left my hydrangeas back at the wine stand.

"Shit," I say.

"What?" He frowns. "What is it?"

"I left my flowers."

His gaze drags the length of me, like he needs to personally confirm that I did in fact lose my flowers, and then he exhales. "You want to go back and get them?"

"I'm sure they're long gone by now. Trust me, these farmer's market ladies see an abandoned bouquet of hydrangeas and they're going to be more than happy to give them a good home." I swat my hand. I hate dwelling on negative shit for too long. It makes me crazy. "Oh, well."

Isaiah glances back from where we came, his hands resting on his hips.

"Don't," I say. He turns toward me, feigning ignorance. "You're thinking about doing the chivalrous thing and buying me some replacement flowers. Don't do it."

"What are you talking about?" His nose wrinkles, but I don't buy it.

"I don't want flowers from you," I say. "Even if you're replacing the flowers I bought for myself."

"I would never buy you flowers. That'd be breaking rule number one."

My head cocks to the side, and I examine his handsome face. "Don't lie to me, Corporal. Don't break rule number two just so you don't break rule number one."

"For the record, I was thinking about getting another burrito," he says.

"Mm hm." I'm still not sure if I believe him. "All right, whatever. Let's get you another burrito."

I slip my hand into the crook of his elbow and we head back into the crowd, just a couple of SoCal salmon swimming upstream and stopping at the cinnamon roll booth on the way.

After this, I'm taking him to the Vista theatre, a glorious, nearly century-old tinsel town fixture.

Today we're seeing Casablanca.

Which is kind of fitting ... because of all the pancake joints in all the towns in the world, he walked into mine.

And no matter what happens after this week, we'll always have Brentwood.

8

ISAIAH

SATURDAY #4

"YOU NEED ANYTHING BEFORE I GO?" I peek my head into my mom's room, surprised to find her awake this early in the day.

Rubbing her still-closed eyes, she shakes her head 'no.'

"I'm okay, Isaiah," she says. "Though I'd love a cup of coffee if you have the time."

"Of course, Ma." I head to the kitchen and return a few minutes later with her favorite hazelnut coffee, placing it on the coaster on her nightstand.

"What are you dressed like that for? You going to the gym?" she asks when her eyes focus on my gym shorts and sneakers.

"I'm going for a hike," I say.

"Oh, yeah? Where?"

"By the Hollywood sign. Brush Canyon trail."

She chuckles. "No kidding?"

I nod, but I don't elaborate. She doesn't know about Maritza and really there's nothing to tell her. Maritza's just a distraction. I wouldn't even call us friends despite the fact that I kind of, sort of secretly enjoy her company.

"I'll be back later. Call if you need me, all right?" I wait for Mom to sit up and get situated, and then I head out.

"SIX AND A HALF MILES. Race you to the top?" Maritza assumes a makeshift starting line position before a sly smirk claims her pink lips. Her posture relaxes and she bends at the waist, stretching before glancing up at me. "I'm sure six and a half miles is nothing for you."

"Why would you say that?"

Her eyes widen. "Um, have you looked in the mirror lately? You're jacked. Ripped. Whatever people call it these days. Clearly you know what the inside of a gym looks like."

"Kind of you to notice."

"I don't run," she says. "And the number of times I've hiked, I can count on one hand."

"So why'd you agree to go hiking today?" I study her face, willing my gaze not to fall to the hot pink sports bra that hardly contains her cleavage or the black shorts that leave very little to the imagination.

Maritza shrugs. "Because I've never hiked this trail before and we're doing all these quintessentially Hollywood touristy things. It fit the theme."

I chuckle. "All right."

"Don't you mean 'fine'?" she teases.

"Fine." I stretch out for a minute before doing a quick

jog in place. Taking a swig from the water bottle I brought, I eye the trail sign ahead and watch as a skinny, blonde-haired woman jogs by with a fit and lean yellow Lab.

We head up the trail, and I stay a bit behind her because it's the proper thing to do ... and the *view* is killer. It isn't until we're a good mile and a half into our hike when Maritza stumbles over a boulder sticking out of the ground and goes flying.

I try not to laugh despite the fact that it was fucking hilarious.

"Don't laugh." Maritza reaches for her foot and moans.

"Oh, shit." I drop to her side, examining her left ankle.

"Don't touch it." She swats me away.

"I'm not going to touch it, I just want to look at it." With gentle hands and barely any pressure, I examine her ankle the way I would an injured soldier's on the battlefield. "You think you can stand on it?"

"Um, no." Her eyes brim with tears and she glances away. "And for the record, I'm not crying. It's just ... the pain is making my eyes water."

"Here. Let me help you up. If you can't stand, I've got you." I don't give her a chance to refuse, instead I slide my forearms under her arms and slowly bring her into a standing position.

With her left knee bent, she taps her toe on the dirt before attempting to stand.

"I can't," she says. "I swear, Isaiah, I'm not being a baby. It just really fucking hurts. I don't think it's broken, I think it's just ... really twisted."

"Fine," I say, placing myself in front of her. "Hike's over."

Draping her arms over my shoulders, I then reach for the backs of her thighs.

"What are you doing?" she asks.

"Climb onto my back. I'll carry you back to the car."

"You're going to carry me on your back for almost two miles?"

"I don't suppose you saw any wheelchair rentals on your way up the mountain, did you?" With her legs wrapped around my hips, I hook my hands behind her knees.

"Smart ass."

She's leggy but light and this is going to be a piece of cake. I've carried grown men farther distances than this before.

Twenty minutes later, we arrive back at the street parking, and she carefully slides down my back, leaning against the passenger door of her blue Prius for support.

"You going to be able to drive home?" I ask, examining her ankle, which is already starting to swell like a son of a bitch. "Damn. You got yourself pretty good."

Crouching down, I give it a closer look. Maybe she could drive herself home just fine, but she's not going to be able to get out of the car once she gets there, not without some help.

"We need to get some ice on that," I say, frowning. "Give me your keys."

"What? Why?"

"I'm taking you home. Unless you want to ride in my car ... I just figured you'd feel safer in yours. You know, since we're strangers."

Digging into a little zippered pocket in her tiny shorts, she hands me a valet key, which I use to unlock her passenger door. Helping her in, I get her seatbelt and tell her to keep her ankle elevated. Rounding the front of the car, I climb into the driver's side.

I'll have to Uber it back here to get my car later.

Pressing the "home" button on her GPS, we turn ourselves around and head down the steep hills that led us to this mountain trail, coming to a stop just before a busy road filled with lunch hour traffic.

"You doing okay?" I ask, glancing at her while we wait for the light to turn green.

Biting her lip and wincing, she nods. Her ankle is resting on her dash and I swear it's growing bigger by the second.

The radio plays some cheesy pop song and I keep an eye on the GPS, focusing on getting her home. Twenty minutes later, we pull up to the familiar iron gate outside her grandmother's sprawling, hacienda-style mansion. Reaching into the console, Maritza retrieves a remote, pressing a black button.

The gate swings open and I pull through.

"Just ... drive around back to the guest house. I don't want my grandma to see you. She'll ask too many questions and then she'll invite you in for tea and that's going to turn into her showing you her Oscar and making you watch Davida's Desire."

"I see your sense of humor's back. Feeling better?"

"Kind of."

I come to a stop outside her little white guest house, and by little, I mean only in comparison to its big sister out front. This place, which looks different in the daylight, is still massive and it's positioned just outside a sparkling teal-blue pool with trickling fountains and a Grecian-style cabana. There's a lot of different styles going on here, but somehow it all fits in an eclectic, crazy famous person kind of way.

Killing the engine, I step out and move around to her side, getting her door. Placing her arms around my shoulder,

I help her out and she hobbles to a side entrance where she punches in a key code. A second later, the lock beeps, and we're in.

"Couch?" I ask. She nods, and I help her toward her emerald green velvet sofa. We prop her left ankle on a pillow I've placed on her gold-and-glass coffee table covered in fashion and lifestyle magazines, all of which are addressed to Melrose Claiborne. "All right. I'm going to grab you some ice."

I head to her kitchen, which is the most eighties-looking thing I've ever seen, complete with yellow appliances and carpet on the floor, but judging by the kitschy accessories, it seems she and her roommate have completely embraced the vintage theme and made it their own.

Yanking the top door of the little yellow fridge, I grab an ice tray and check a few drawers until I find a spare hand towel.

"Here." I return to her side, taking a seat next to her and placing the makeshift ice pack on her ankle. She breathes in through her teeth. "You okay?"

Maritza nods, leaning forward to place her hand over the towel, brushing mine in the process. "I've got it now."

Reaching for the far end of the coffee table, I grab her TV remote. "Anything else you need?"

Her brows meet as she thinks. "Nope. I should be good for now."

Pulling out my phone, I tap my Uber app.

"What are you doing?" she asks.

"Getting a ride back to my car."

Glancing up at me through long dark lashes, she chuckles. "You're welcome to stay here if you want. We can ... I don't know ... watch Netflix or something? The day doesn't have to be a total bust."

Sitting my phone aside, I drag my thumb and forefinger down the side of my mouth.

"I'd like you to stay," she says, point blank. "Honest."

I pull in a hard breath, giving it some more thought. Sightseeing and Saturday-ing is one thing. But hanging out on a couch watching TV and trying to fight this bizarre attraction between us is something else entirely.

It's almost reckless.

"Don't make me beg, Corporal," she says with a teasing tone. "I just feel bad that I ruined our hike. And also, I don't want to sit here and be bored the rest of the day ..."

"Fine. I'll stay for a little while. But only if I get to pick what we watch." If I'm going to stick around, it has to be on my terms.

"Oh, now that might be a deal breaker for me. I kind of had my heart set on watching season three of Fuller House."

"Yeah, well Fuller House just so happens to be a deal breaker for me." I shrug, rising slow. "So I guess I should be on my way."

"Wait." She stops me, palm lifted in the air and head cocked. "If I let you pick ... what might we be watching?"

Dragging my hand along my jaw and inhaling the spicy floral scent of her living room, I blow a breath through my lips. "The Punisher."

She makes a face.

"Luke Cage, then," I say.

Her expression doesn't budge.

"Stranger Things?" I ask.

Her full lips twist at the side and she taps her finger against her chin. "I guess."

Taking a seat on her sofa, I ensure we're separated by at least one full seat cushion as she starts the show.

"Oh, wait. Can you do me the tiniest favor?" Maritza

turns to me just as the opening credits finish. "I should probably take something for the swelling. Can you grab me a bottle of water and some Advil from the cupboard by the sink? Oh, and help yourself to whatever you want in the fridge. I think there's some leftover beer from Melrose's last boyfriend."

"Melrose?"

"My cousin slash roommate."

"I see." Rising, I head back to the glorious eighties kitchen and grab her water and ibuprofen, helping myself to an ice-cold bottle of Rolling Rock on the way back.

"Why are you sitting so far away? That's a terrible angle for watching TV," she asks when I take my seat. She pats the cushion beside her, brows lifted. "I twisted my ankle. It's not like I'm contagious."

With my arm resting across the back of the couch, I shrug. "It's fine."

Maritza rolls her eyes. "You picked this dumb show and now you're going to sit all the way over there where you can barely see the screen?"

Groaning, I slide closer—but only because she has a point. "There. That better?"

"*Shh.*" She swats at me just as the show begins to start. "Show's on. No more talking."

Her eyes are glued and I take pride in knowing that I picked out a fucking amazing show for us to watch.

Settling into the seat back, I cross my legs wide and watch her from my periphery. She's totally into this and I love it.

By the time the first episode ends, she doesn't so much as touch the remote, letting the next one automatically play.

"I guess this stupid show is okay," she says, leaning

forward and adjusting the ice pack on her ankle. She lifts it for a second to check the swelling, but it's still pretty ugly.

"Pretty sure you just broke rule number two."

"Pretty sure you broke rule number one," she says, her dark hair curtaining her beautiful face as she turns to look at me.

"What are you talking about?"

"It was sweet what you did for me today. Romantic almost—textbook standards anyway. Carrying me down the trail, driving me home, taking care of me."

I scoff. "That's not romance. That's called being a decent human being."

Licking her lips, she tucks her hair behind her ear. "Fine. Maybe I was reading into it too much."

"Definitely. You were definitely reading into it too much," I say.

When I saw her injured, it was instinctive—I had to save her. I may do this shit on the regular with my fellow comrades, but trust me when I say I've never done anything like this for some random girl I hardly know.

Reaching for the remote, she pauses the show, drawing in a deep breath.

"Can I just say something here?" she asks. "I feel like I need to address the elephant in the room."

I lift a brow, having zero idea where she's going with this. "All right. Address away."

"You check me out all the time," she says. "You think I don't see it, but I do. And you're always looking at me like you're two seconds from devouring me. I don't even think you realize it. Or maybe you do. Maybe you do it on purpose because you think you're not going to get caught. I don't know."

Pressing my lips together, I stare at the paused show on the screen.

Fuck.

"I just ... I feel like if the situation were different ... if you weren't about to be deployed ... I think ..." she stops, taking another deep breath. "I think we have chemistry. Basically. Is what I'm trying to say. And the more we ignore it and deny it, the stronger it's going to get. So if we could just address it and kiss or fuck or whatever the hell we're inevitably going to do by the end of the week, I think we could—"

"Fuck chemistry. Fuck all that bullshit."

"So you're just going to deny that we—"

Pulling her into my lap, I silence her words with a greedy kiss, and I don't even feel bad about it. This isn't romantic and I'm not some Casanova trying to win her heart. I'm simply a man with needs, a man who's been wanting to taste those lips all over again since the night at The Mintz.

Her mouth is strawberries.

Her tongue is peppermint.

Her lips are hot, pillow soft.

Everything is better than I remember, and when her hands find my hair and her nails rake against the nape of my neck, I almost fucking lose it.

"Hi." Maritza straddles me, pressing her hips against my growing cock as she balances on her knees. Her mouth curls, her eyes light, and I crush her cherry lips all over again.

"Is your ankle okay?" I ask between kisses, my mouth grazing hers.

"I don't feel a thing, Corporal," she says, breathless and smirking just before our tongues collide.

My hands grip her hips before working the hem of her shirt, fingertips trailing her soft skin until I reach the hook of her bra.

"This means nothing," she says, grinding harder. "Right? Tell me it means nothing. We're just ... we're just getting it out of our system."

"It means nothing," I assure her, unhooking her clasp. My hands slip beneath her bra, cupping her perfect tits. I'm so fucking hard it hurts and while I want to enjoy the hell out of all of this, I'm counting down the minutes until I'm deep inside of her, all the way in, fucking her in a way she'll never forget so long as she lives.

And I don't say that out of arrogance.

One-night stands and short-lived flings are kind of my specialty, and I've been told I'm the best, that I always deliver.

"Oh, my God!" A woman's voice shrieks and the front door slams.

Maritza climbs off me, tugging her shirt back into place and fixing her hair. "Melrose, hey. I didn't know you were going to be around today. Thought you had auditions?"

The other woman, who's easily the blonde-haired version of Maritza, stands with her mouth agape and eyes wide as saucers, shocked gaze flicking between the two of us.

"Melrose, this is Isaiah. Isaiah, this is my roommate slash cousin, Melrose." Maritza and her cousin exchange looks. I take it they've discussed me before.

She looks familiar, like a face I've seen before. Maybe on TV. Or it could just be the striking Claiborne resemblance.

"My audition ended earlier than I thought." Melrose hooks her bag on the back of a living room chair.

"Oh, yeah? How'd it go?" Maritza asks, pretending like Melrose didn't just walk in on us about to fuck.

My cock is still hard, though it's beginning to diminish thanks to the sheer fucking awkwardness of this situation.

"Fine," she says. "I read for some part in some Ryan Gosling movie. I'd be playing his snarky younger sister. It's got about twenty lines, so that's something."

"No kidding. Better than 'victim number two' on Law and Order," Maritza says with a wink.

"That role put me on the map." Melrose points. "I landed two other parts because of that role."

"I'm not knocking it," Maritza says, palms up.

"Anyway, I'm going to go for a run," her roommate says. I don't know this chick from Adam, but she seems a bit down. I imagine it gets exhausting auditioning and getting your hopes up and dealing with disappointment after disappointment. "If you two feel the need to continue to get your freak on, kindly do it in the privacy of your *boudoir*."

Maritza rolls her eyes and Melrose disappears down a hallway.

"She's always in a mood after her auditions," she tells me. "She wants so badly to be the Gloria Claiborne of our generation. Her words, not mine."

"Nothing wrong with setting goals."

"Right. I have no room to talk. At least she knows what she wants to do with her life and she's taking the necessary steps to get there." Maritza reaches for her water bottle on the coffee table, lifting it to her swollen lips, the very same ones I was claiming a few minutes ago.

But now the moment is lost.

And maybe it's for the best.

"I should go." I rise, grabbing my phone and trying not to acknowledge the disappointed look in her eyes that has no business being there. She should be fine with me staying and equally fine with me going. "See you tomorrow. I'll text you the info in the morning."

Showing myself out, I walk toward the front gate and wait for my ride.

Half of me wants to stay.

The other half of me knows it's best that I go.

9

MARITZA

SATURDAY #5

"OKAY, LET ME JUST APOLOGIZE QUICK." I hobble up to Isaiah the second he enters the main doors of the La Brea Tar Pits, maneuvering through groups of families, mothers with small children, and preschoolers on field trips. "I had no idea this was, like, a children's science center type place."

His eyes scan the lobby before dragging the length of a realistic-looking woolly mammoth.

A little curly-haired boy in a red polo plows into him, shouting sorry as he runs off. His mother chases after him, and just outside a yellow bus full of elementary schoolers pulls into the drop off lane.

This place has been open all of twenty minutes and already it's filled to the brim with tiny humans, their loud voices echoing off the high ceilings and expansive wall space.

"We can go somewhere else," I tell him, apologizing with my eyes and my voice and the placement of my hands on his broad chest.

Raking his teeth across his lower lip, he pulls in a deep breath, like he's mulling it over, and then he shrugs.

"It's fine. We're here," he says.

"You sure?" I lift a brow. "I've got some other ideas, more places we can go."

Isaiah shakes his head and hooks his arm over my shoulder, which catches me off guard for a moment. We walk to the ticket desk, the warmth of his body permeating through my cotton tee and his spicy cologne filling my lungs.

"How's the ankle?" He asks when we reach the line.

"Better. Sore but better."

Ten minutes later, tickets in hand, we begin a self-guided tour, beginning at their Titans of the Ice Age exhibit and moving on to the Fossil Lab, which seems to be popular with the preschoolers surrounding us.

We stop at Pit 91, where they're conducting a live excavation, unearthing saber tooth tiger and dire wolf fossils, and Isaiah stops to watch.

"You know, I read once that if you placed the entire timeline of the universe into a single calendar year, humans would show up on December 31st at 11 PM," I say. "I'm paraphrasing, but you get the picture."

His lips flatten. He's engrossed by the architects digging in the dirt with all of their fancy tools and brushes.

"Isn't it crazy when you think about how inconsequential we are? As a species, we're still so new and all these living, breathing creatures existed millions and millions of years ago. It blows my mind, really. Kind of makes me awestruck and depressed at the same time," I say.

"Depressed?" He turns to me.

"Well, not clinically depressed, but almost kind of sad ... because it makes me feel like someday maybe millions of years from now, we're all probably going to be extinct. Just a bunch of fossils in the ground, no legacies to leave behind, no one to tell our stories."

"I still don't see how that's a sad thing. Being extinct. If we're dead, we're not going to be around to care," he says. "And these dinosaurs and whatnot have left a legacy of fossil fuels, if you want to put it that way. They didn't live and die for nothing."

"I guess, but I just think people are always so fixated on their problems all the time, but if they could just look at the big picture—that someday they're just going to be a pile of bones in a mound of dirt—maybe they'd worry a little less? Live a little more? Try to contribute to society or leave the world a little bit better than they found it?"

"You're such an idealist." He hooks his arm around me, which marks the second time today, and my heart does the tiniest flutter without so much as asking for permission.

We spend the next couple of hours touring the garden and a few more dig sites before stopping at the lake pit on our way to the parking lot.

Hot bubbling asphalt glugs behind us as we stand next to a bunch of fake animals pretending to play in the pit.

"What do you think it'd be like if we went extinct and some future species found our bones and turned us into robotic models and placed us on display?" I ask as we watch the bubbles float to the surface and pop.

"Probably about how you'd expect." He clears his

throat, glancing down at me, and I'd love to know what he's thinking about.

"You know, my grandma in the sixties, all she wanted was to have a legacy, to be remembered forever. People were always comparing her to Marilyn Monroe, especially after Marilyn died, and my grandma would get so upset because unless you die young and your beauty is immortalized, you've got nothing to leave behind but your good deeds. But if you're simply known for your beauty, no one really cares if you're feeding orphans and adopting shelter dogs or paying for vaccines in third world nations. She wants to be remembered for her philanthropy, but anytime someone hears the name Gloria Claiborne, all they associate her with is old Hollywood glamour or that white bikini."

"Sounds like she needs a good PR team."

I roll my eyes. "Does it really count if you have to publicize it? It's like those people who donate money to places so they can get their names on a plaque on the wall as a "Gold Star Donor" or whatever the stupid name is."

"Giving is giving."

"Unless you're doing it for the wrong reasons. Some people give for others. Some people give for themselves."

"It's not really our place to judge other people's reasons for giving," he says, words terse.

"Yeah, well, you haven't met some of the elitist assholes who hang out with my parents and brag about how much money they donated to their kids' schools. One jerkoff donated a hundred grand so he could have his kid's name painted on some mural on the playground."

"It's their money," he says. "They can spend it how they want."

"Stop making me sound like an asshole," I say. "I'm just

being honest. This is a judgement-free zone. You can't judge me for judging other people."

"Seems a little hypocritical."

I wrinkle my nose. "Okay. I take back everything I said. Everyone who ever donates a single dollar to a single cause is a selfless saint."

Isaiah laughs. At me. "Why are you getting so worked up? This is such a dumb conversation to have. Who the hell cares who donates to what and why?"

Drawing in a deep breath, I let it go, crossing my arms over my chest. "I don't know. You're right. It's dumb."

He slips his arm over my shoulder—again—and gives me a side hug. "You ever heard of the phrase 'stay in your own lane'?"

"No?"

"It means mind your own. Don't worry about what anyone else is doing," he says. "Trust me, it's the only way to live. Worry about yourself. Forget the rest."

Turning to face him, I glance up into his warm gaze, studying his perfectly chiseled features and longing to brush the strand of dark hair off his bronzed forehead.

"What made you enlist, Isaiah?" I ask. "It takes a lot to sacrifice money for a good cause, but it takes even more to be willing to sacrifice your life. That couldn't have been an easy decision for you."

He releases my gaze, his expression hardening. I can practically feel him closing up.

"It's a long story. Some other time, all right?" he asks.

I bury my disappointment in a small smile. "Of course."

I know from talking to my cousin, that a lot of guys enlist for very personal reasons and it wouldn't be right to push and prod. Maybe with time, he'll open up?

Making our way around the tar pit, we stop next to a

mastodon. Isaiah reads the plaque beside it, but I try to read him.

And fail.

Miserably.

There's no denying something's there, something that makes my heart trot when he looks at me, something that makes me slick on an extra coat of lip balm or an extra spritz of perfume before dashing out the door to meet him.

And while I'm the one who made the rules—no romance and only honesty at all times—I'm the one who can't stop thinking about what would happen if we broke one of them.

Only problem is, I have zero idea if he's thinking what I'm thinking. He's so even-keeled and emotionally guarded, but they say actions speak louder than words and the fact that he's here, spending time with me doing stupid shit has to count for something ... right?

"Why are you staring like that?" Isaiah asks when he turns around.

My cheeks warm. I'd been spacing off. "No reason."

"Bullshit. You can't lie, remember? Tell me what you were thinking about." His lips draw into a playful smirk, and I can't decide if I like his mysterious side or his spirited side best. It's like trying to choose between white chocolate and milk chocolate, which are both delicious in their own ways.

"You don't want to know."

And I'm serious. He doesn't want to know that I'm thinking about him in a way that I was determined not to. Besides, he's leaving in a few days. There's no point in ruining the rest of our time together by making this situation unnecessarily complicated.

"Try me," he says, his stare boring into me. Something tells me he's not going to let this go.

Giving myself a moment, I gather my thoughts and nibble on my lower lip. "I was just thinking about connections."

"Connections?" His hands rest on his hips, his shoulders parallel with mine. I have his full, undivided attention.

"I was just thinking about how I hardly know you, but I feel connected to you," I say, cringing on the inside but fully embracing the discomfiture of this conversation.

He says nothing, which doesn't make this moment any less awkward for the both of us.

"You asked!" I remind him, throwing my hands up.

Another moment passes, the two of us lingering next to some hairy elephant-looking creature with a long-as-hell scientific name as a group of children runs past us.

"Now I want to know what *you're* thinking about." I nudge his arm. "It's only fair."

He smirks, then it fades, and he gazes into the distance. It's like there's something on the tip of his tongue, but if I push or prod too much, he'll never share it.

"Nothing, Maritza. I was thinking about nothing."

I don't buy it, but I don't press any further. I want to burn this awkward moment into a pile of ash and move on.

"Are you going to remember me after this week?" I ask after a bout of silence.

His golden irises glint as his eyes narrow in my direction. "What kind of question is that?"

"A legit one," I say. "Will you remember me? Or am I always just going to be that waitress girl that you hung out with for a week?"

"Don't think I could forget you if I tried." He speaks in

such a way that I'm not sure if what he's saying is a good thing or a bad thing. "Can I be honest right now?"

"You must. It's a requirement."

Isaiah's tongue grazes his full lips for a quick second and he holds my gaze for what feels like forever. "I don't want to make this any more confusing for either of us, but I feel like kissing you right now."

I fight a smile. I don't want to smile. I want to scoff at him and tell him to stop being such a hypocrite.

But that's only half of me.

The other half of me wants him to kiss me, wants his hands in my hair and his taste on my tongue just one more time because we'll never have this moment again and once it's gone, it's gone forever.

"I'll allow it," I say, half-teasing. "But only because we're standing in front of a fiberglass mastodon and it doesn't get any less romantic than that."

Isaiah glances around to ensure we're not in the presence of impressionable minds, and then he sinks his mouth onto mine, taking his time like he'd been waiting patiently all day and doesn't want to ruin it by rushing.

I'm light as air and grounded at the same time. Nothing else exists outside his warm, soft mouth and his steady hands. I can't even comprehend my own thoughts because my heart is pounding so hard in my chest it's the only thing I hear.

When it's over, reality is back in the driver's seat. Rubbing my lips together, savoring the sweet burn of what lingers, I tell myself it's just a kiss.

As long as there are no flowers exchanged these next couple of days, no sweet words or careless whispers, no promises made and no looking at each other like we hung the moon ... we should be fine and both of us should be able to walk away from this completely unscathed, not a single battle wound or commemorative scar.

"How's that ankle holding up?" he asks, glancing down toward my foot. "Still looks a little swollen. Hope we didn't make it worse today."

"I took, like, ten Advil this morning so I can't feel a thing."

Except that kiss.

I felt the hell out of that kiss.

He smirks, half-chuckling. "You hungry? You want to go somewhere?"

He's not ready for our "Saturday" to end just yet.

And truth be told, neither am I.

10

ISAIAH

SATURDAY #6

I MISS a lot of things when I'm overseas, but most of the time I try not to think about them. Out of sight, out of mind is a way of survival when you're thousands of miles away from the comforts of home.

It's just easier that way.

But it's what I signed up for. There are no regrets or self-pitying moments that seep into my mind when I'm tossing and turning on the nights when it's unbearably hot and sleep is impossible.

But last night, when I took Maritza back to her car after an afternoon of hanging around the city, dropping into coffee shops, people watching on Rodeo Drive, and catching the latest Marvel flick at my insistence, she asked me point blank if I was lonely.

Her question came out of the blue, but given what I know of this woman, randomness is kind of how she rolls.

"Clearly you're longing for some kind of connection with someone," she told me as I walked her to her car. "Or you wouldn't be here, spending a week with some girl you picked up at a café."

"Excuse me? Last I checked, you picked me up," I told her. "And it wasn't in a café. You fucking rear ended my car. And then you—"

"You don't have any other friends around here?" she cut me off with a question.

"Some."

"And your family?" she asked.

"We're not that close these days."

She looked at me with pity in her eyes and I shook my head, telling her not to feel sorry for me.

"I'm not a sob story," I tell her. "My life hasn't been ideal, sure. But you'd be doing me a disservice if you felt sorry for me."

"Then you're running away from something," she said, nibbling her thumbnail as she studied me. It was dark by then, the moon reflecting in her chocolate-brown irises, her creamy complexion glowing. Everything about her was soft and ethereal and I wanted to kiss her again, but I couldn't.

I'd kissed her enough that day, and for reasons I couldn't comprehend.

Of course, I swore to her they were just kisses, they meant nothing. But I couldn't explain why I kept craving them, kept finding every excuse I could to casually touch her, trailing my fingertips down her arms, brushing her dark hair out of her face, leading her by the hand when we'd cross the street.

I pull up outside her grandmother's house just past

sunset and send her a text. Today *I'm* picking *her* up—her insistence. Within minutes, the gate swings open and she strides out in a short sundress, her long legs tanned and accented in strappy sandals.

Her mouth is slicked in bright red and when our eyes meet, she smiles as wide as I've ever seen her smile. Reaching up, she holds her chestnut curls in place as the breeze blows at her skirt.

"Day six," she says with a smile while she climbs into my passenger seat, her voice tinged in melancholy.

"Yep." I shift into reverse, not wanting to dwell on the fact that after tomorrow we're going our separate ways. "How was work?"

She wasn't able to switch shifts with anyone today, which worked out because tonight I'm taking her stargazing at the Griffith Observatory. I'm sure she'll say it's romantic and I'll insist that it's not, but it's something I've always wanted to do.

There's something about feeling small that puts things into perspective for me, and no better way to do that than to gaze at billions of stars in an infinite universe.

"I lied to you last night," I say as we head down her grandmother's picturesque residential street.

"What?" Her attention whips to me as she adjusts her dress over her legs.

"You asked if I ever miss anything when I'm over there," I say. "I miss Pringles. And Starbursts. And peanut butter M&Ms."

Her fist meets my shoulder, though it hardly hurts. "Ass."

"What?"

"I thought you were being serious."

I chuckle, coming to a stop at a red light. "I am. I miss

those things. You can't get them over there. Not that easily anyway."

I know there are other things I should probably miss ... like the feel of soft lips, the smell of sweet perfume, the wash of contentedness I get when a beautiful girl looks at me like I'm something special. Soft things. Comforting things. Distracting things.

We don't have those over there.

But I try not to think about that. And I try not to think about what it might feel like to be thousands of miles away from here, missing Maritza.

If the past has shown me anything, it's that I'm a shit boyfriend. I'm terrible at communication. I'm bullheaded and rash. And I'm not quite ready to lace up my boots for the last time.

This is why I can't go deep with her.

I can tell her that I miss candy, but I can't tell her that I might miss *her* ...

We pull up to the observatory forty minutes later and find a place to park.

"Stargazing, Corporal?" She laughs through her nose, shaking her head as she checks her phone, silences it, and slips it into her purse. "Like that's not romantic."

We get out of my car and I meet her by my dented, scratched-up bumper. "I knew you'd read into it."

She walks beside me, arm grazing mine as the soles of her sandals pad the concrete sidewalk. "Just keep your hands to yourself and we should have ourselves a nice, non-romantic evening."

We head inside, and I hold the door for Maritza and the couple entering behind us. They're dressed to the nines in a navy suit and little black dress. Diamonds glint from the woman's ears and the man presses his hand into her lower back before muttering a quick "thanks."

We find an available telescope a few minutes later, and I stand back as Maritza crouches slightly, peering into the eyepiece.

"You have to look at the moon," she says, waving for me to come closer. "That's so crazy. You can see every little detail."

I take a look for myself, though it's exactly what I expected. Growing up, one of my brothers had a telescope. He'd use it to spy on the girls next door when they were outside sunbathing, but I actually put it to good use, checking out stars and neighboring plants as best I could.

The moon was always my favorite though.

Even through our cheap telescope it looked so tangible, like I could reach up and touch it, crumble it in my hands.

"What's your favorite constellation?" I ask her.

She stands straighter, gazing up at the clear sky as she blows a breath through her red lips. "I don't know? The Big Dipper?"

"Ursa major," I say. "That's the proper name."

"It's the only one I really know."

"When's your birthday, Maritza?" I ask.

"August fourteenth. Why?"

Placing my hand at her lower back, I pull her closer to the telescope. Bending, I peer through the eyepiece and locate the Leo constellation.

"We're in luck," I say. "Take a look."

She bends, squinting as she glances in. "What am I looking at?"

"See that cluster of stars that kind of looks like a clothes iron with a little hook coming out of it?"

"Yeah?"

"That's Leo. Arguably the easiest constellation to find, but there you go."

Maritza stares at it a bit longer before backing off, and when she looks at me, she clasps her hand over her heart. "Isaiah, that was really sweet what you just did."

"I wasn't trying to be—"

"Hush." She swats my arm. "When's your birthday? I want to see your constellation."

Dragging my thumb and forefinger down the sides of my mouth, I chuckle. "April first. Fool's day."

"You're joking."

"Yeah, no." I roll my eyes, like I haven't heard that a million times before.

"So that makes you, what ... an Aries?"

I nod. "Yeah, but you can't really see the Aries constellation this time of year. It's easier to find in the winter, right around Christmas."

Maritza stands in awe of me, quiet, eyes wide. "Seriously, Isaiah."

"What?" My brows meet.

"There's so much more to you than you let on," she says. "All week I thought maybe I was scratching a little bit of that surface of yours, and then you spring this on me."

"I'm not springing anything on you."

"You know stars and constellations and that's just so ... deep," she says. "And so cool. You're not just some handsome, muscle-bound soldier."

I laugh. "Right. I'm human. With interests. Just like anyone else. Doesn't make me special."

Her head cocks. "It does in my book. You're special, Isaiah. And weird. And complicated. And wonderful."

"Anyway." I wholly disagree with all of that, but I'm not

in the mood to argue with a girl who thinks she's right about everything all of the time.

"I hope you never change."

"I don't plan to," I say.

"But if you do change, you know, I hope it's for reasons that make your heart happy," she says, sighing.

"Can you not?" I ask.

Her expression fades. "Can I not what?"

"Get all mushy and sentimental."

She laughs. "Trust me. You haven't seen mushy or sentimental. Anyway, just being out here with the stars and everything just makes me feel philosophical or something. I blame you. You brought me here. This is your fault."

"Right. Because I control what comes out of that mouth of yours." My eyes drop to her cherry red lips and my breath catches in my throat. I've never craved anything so badly in my life as I crave her strawberry taste on my tongue right now.

"Excuse me. You two finished with your telescope?" A surfer-looking guy with his two surfer-looking sons stands behind us, expression eager as his hands rest on their shoulders.

Great timing, dude.

"It's all yours." Maritza slips her arm into mine and leads me away, only several steps later and she's yet to let me go. In fact, she's holding on tight, and I don't even know if she realizes it.

Everything about the way she touches me is so natural.

"We should pick a star," she says as we walk.

"What? Why?"

Her eyes widen as she gazes above and her mouth curls into a cheesy grin. "I don't know. So anytime you're over there and you feel alone you can look at the star and remember this night."

"Stop." I scoff. "Only lame asses do shit like that. And I kind of feel like you're starting to break your own rule ..."

Maritza shrugs. "Tomorrow's our last Saturday together. I guess it's kind of hitting me in a way I didn't expect. It went by so fast."

"It did." We walk side by side, slow, silently savoring our dwindling time together.

As soon as we return to my car, she folds her arms, leaning against the passenger door. "I'm not tired. Are you?"

My gaze falls to her mouth before lifting to her glinting eyes. "Nope."

"Want to get a drink?"

"WHY ISN'T this stupid thing working?" It's almost two in the morning and Maritza is pressing the remote to the gate so hard I think the stupid thing is going to fall apart in her hands.

"Maybe the battery's dead."

Glancing past my dash, she squints. "Think we can climb that? Maybe if you just hoisted me over ..."

"You're drunk off your ass. I'm not letting you climb a nine-foot iron gate. You'll fall and hurt yourself." I massage my temples.

I'm exhausted.

She's wasted.

And all the flirting she did these last several hours did nothing more than gift me with a raging case of blue balls.

"Let me see if Melrose is up." She grabs her phone, dropping it on the floor. Maritza giggles before finally managing to dial her cousin's number. "Mel! Can you come outside? My remote's not working and we need in ... yes, I said *we* ... Isaiah, who else? ... I know ... just come get us."

I'm half able to make out what sounds like her cousin lecturing her about bringing strange men home, but at this point I couldn't care less. After tomorrow, I'm never going to see Maritza or her cousin again and I've spent the better part of the past two hours convincing myself for the millionth time that I'm okay with that.

"Thanks, sweets." She hangs up. "Mel's coming. It'll just be a minute."

We sit in my idling car for what feels like a decade before the gate slowly opens and her cousin stands before us in a see-through tank top, red plaid shorts, a messy blonde bun, and a mint green face mask. Her arms are folded and she's glaring at me, as if it's my fault Maritza got so hammered.

Truth be told, I have no idea how this happened.

I paced myself. I thought she did too.

"God, I'm starving," Maritza moans as I pull through the gate. "I should've had dinner earlier. I haven't eaten since breakfast."

Oh, there we go. That's how this happened.

"Want to order a pizza?" she asks, her face lit like it's the best idea she's had all night.

"You go ahead, I'm just walking you to your door then I'm taking off."

Her hand rests on my forearm. "You're not staying?"

I park in her grandmother's circle drive, beside a trickling fountain surrounded by strategically placed up-lights.

"Why would I stay? I just wanted to make sure you got home safely."

"What's with you all of a sudden?" She unfastens her

seatbelt, angling her body toward me. "I thought we were having a good time tonight?"

"We were," I say. "We did. But the night's over."

"Am I annoying you? Is that what this is? You can be honest," she says. "I swear, Isaiah, I only had, like three drinks, you saw me. I didn't mean to get like this. It's just, I was so busy at work today and then I had to come home and get ready and I guess I forgot to eat?"

"It's fine."

"No." Her full lips press together. "It's not fine. I should've stopped hours ago or switched to water or something. I'm sorry. I hope I didn't ruin your night."

I reach for the ignition and kill the engine. "I'll walk you in."

Climbing out of the car, I meet her around front, by the hood. She's quiet, studying me as she attempts to keep her balance. The front door of the guesthouse is cocked open. Guess Melrose beat us back.

"Come on. Let's get you inside." Hooking my hand into her elbow, I pull her against me and lead her inside, trying not to breathe in the way the warm Southern California breeze mingles with her grandmother's flowers and Maritza's citrus perfume.

Stopping outside the door, she stands to face me, squaring her shoulders with mine.

"I had fun stargazing tonight," she says. "Thank you for showing me Leo."

I nod. "Of course."

Maritza lingers, like she's waiting for me to cap the night off with a kiss, but I refuse. It was fun earlier this week, but somewhere along the line, shit threatened to get real and now I have to draw a hard line.

"Tomorrow's our last Saturday," she says. It's got to be

the second or third time she's brought it up tonight, as if I could possibly forget. But as much as I want to spend another day with her, part of me thinks it might only make this harder ... and it might defeat the entire point of spending the week with a girl I thought I could walk away from in the end.

After getting to know her and spending day in and day out with all of her idiosyncrasies, I've realized she's funny and witty and sarcastic. She's genuine and honest and kind. She's unapologetic and charismatic.

If I were the committed type, I'd lock her down in a heartbeat.

I'd make her mine and never let her go.

But it doesn't work that way. I'm leaving and she'll be here. We'll be worlds apart. And commitment was something I longed for a lifetime ago. It doesn't mean a damn thing to me now.

"I had fun with you this week," she says, voice soft and low. "I'm kind of sad for it to end."

"Goodnight, Maritza." Forcing a quick smile, I leave before it gets too deep.

Returning to my car, I fire up the engine and get the hell out of there before I say or do something I might regret.

It's only when I'm several blocks away that I glance at my phone for the first time all night and find seven missed calls in a row, all of them from my sister.

11

MARITZA

SATURDAY #7

"NOT HANGING out with lover boy today?" Melrose is lying by Gram's pool, removing the two cucumber slices from her eyes when I take a seat beside her. "Where's your bikini? Why are you dressed like that?"

She squints at my getup, one of our grandmother's vintage Pucci cover ups and an oversized, floppy hat.

"Does Gram know you raided her closet?" she asks.

"Haven't you heard? The sun causes wrinkles." I cross my legs. "I'm surprised you're not more concerned. Your skin is your canvas, right?"

"Sweets, I've been using retinols since sixteen and getting Botox since twenty-one. Nothing's going to crack this glass." She reaches for an issue of Elle magazine and pages through it, skipping all the ads, and her oil-slicked skin glistens in the sunlight. "Anyway, why aren't you with Isaiah?"

I bite my lip, trying to ignore that sunken-in feeling in my chest that's resided there since he texted me this morning and told me he wasn't sure he'd be able to see me today.

"Something came up," he texted me several hours ago, nothing more, nothing less.

But I don't know what to believe.

There's not much about last night that I remember up until the time he took me home. And now, all I keep picturing is that look on his face as he stood across from me by the front door. It's like he was placing this extra distance between us, and I'm not talking physical.

It was emotional.

And he didn't so much as try to kiss me. Maybe part of that reason was because I was pretty freaking tipsy, but still. There was just something different in his eyes last night, something stiff and armored about his tone.

I grab a spare magazine and lean back on the rattan lounger. It's a balmy eight degrees without a cloud in sight, weather that all but demands a good mood. But I'm nothing but sullen, riddled with emptiness. I wanted to see him today. I wanted our last Saturday to mean something. I wanted to go out with a bang.

Instead, he blew me off.

Like I mean absolutely nothing.

There's a chance he's telling the truth. And he should be. That was the agreement. But at the end of the day, I really don't know him. And at the end of the day he doesn't owe me a damn thing, not even the truth.

Maybe I'm naïve. Maybe he was looking for a week of sex and debauchery only to find himself sorely disappointed. Maybe he was hoping one thing would lead to another and I would be a crazy fling that he could walk away from, but somewhere along the line I think he realized that in a perfect world we would be good for each other.

Not that I'm in the market for a boyfriend.

But if the stars aligned and the opportunity was there and he wasn't about to leave the country, I might have been willing to explore the possibility of something more.

"So what are you going to do today?" Melrose asks. "I mean, you took the day off. I guess that's what happens when you drop everything for a stranger with a pretty smile."

Today of all days I'm not in the mood for her side comments and signature snark.

"What are you going to do if he calls you and changes his mind? Like do you really think something came up or do you think he's just blowing you off?" she asks a moment later, tossing her magazine aside.

"I don't know what I think."

"I don't know why you're feeling sorry for yourself. You knew he was just some charismatic ass like the rest of them." She sighs. "Maritza, I hate to be the bearer of bad news, but he just wanted a piece."

I exhale. Melrose and her lack of compassion are getting on my nerves and I'm two seconds from going back inside the house, changing into sweats, and watching Netflix by myself.

"I don't need a lecture, Mel. Believe it or not, I don't regret the time I spent with him. I told him from day one I didn't want a relationship, that I didn't want romance or attachment of any kind. If he's done with me, I have no right to be upset with him—and I'm *not* upset with him. Just disappointed."

Melrose exhales, grabbing a Vogue next and flipping it open before reaching for a bottle of Fiji water on the table beside her. "All lecturing aside, he is really fucking hot and it would've required superhero strength to turn down the chance to spend a week with him. Anyway, I'm not judging you. I'm just protective of you. And I hate to see you sad."

I stand, eyeing the house.

"You going back inside?" she asks.

"I don't know. I just don't want to sit around being annoyed. I need to do something. I thought I'd feel better if I sat by the pool and relaxed, but I'm just sitting here stewing."

"You're upset."

"I'm not upset," I say.

She laughs. "Yes, you are. And it's fine. You should be upset. He's a jerk for cancelling your plans."

"I'm going to head inside and see what Gram's up to." I toss a magazine on the lounge chair and head toward the sliding glass door just off my grandmother's kitchen.

"Maritza!" Seated at her kitchen table, dressed in a Versace caftan and sipping her signature oolong from a floral tea cup, she lights up when I walk in the door. "I haven't seen you all week, love. Come have a seat."

I take the chair beside her, feeling the weight of her stare as she examines me.

"Something's off," she says, taking a sip, eyes focused in my direction. She's always been good at picking up on non-verbal cues and nuances, which is probably why she's had a decades-long career as an Oscar winning actress. She's always said much of how we communicate has nothing to do with what we're saying. "You seem ... blue. What is it?"

She rests her taut jawline against her smooth hand. My grandmother in all her self-assured glory has refused to age gracefully. Instead, she has a top Beverly Hills plastic surgeon on her payroll to keep each and every wrinkle and age spot at bay. As much as she talks about not wanting to be known solely for her beauty, she has a hard time walking away from something that's become so imbedded into her identity.

You can take the screen siren out of Hollywood, you can't take Hollywood out of the screen siren.

"I made a new friend this week," I tell her, reaching for a single white rose in the elaborate bouquet that anchors her table, running my fingertips along its velvet petals. "At least, I thought we were friends."

"What happened? Did she say something crass?"

"He, Grandma. It's a *he*." Our eyes meet. She doesn't flinch.

"Oh? A gay friend?" she asks, eyes fluttering. In her day, it was uncommon for a straight man and a straight woman to simply be friends, though it's starting to seem like nothing's changed.

"No, Gram."

"I see." Her brows lift. "All right, then. What happened with this man?"

I shrug. "He's an army corporal and he leaves for deployment tomorrow. Today was going to be our last day together and then he just ... cancelled. Said something came up."

Her red lips press together and she exhales. "Maybe he didn't want to say goodbye?"

Maybe. But it's pointless to analyze it now. At the end of the day, this—whatever it was—is over and it makes no difference why he cancelled.

I shake my head. "I don't want to talk about this anymore. Honestly, we spent six days together and I'd rather not invest any more of my time or energy into thinking about someone I'm never going to see again."

"Smart girl." She smiles, eyes crinkling at the sides. "A true Claiborne doesn't wait around for anyone. Either they love us or they don't. We accept either fate and we don't dwell if things don't go our way. You know there once was a time I was head over heels with Richard Burton."

Her lashes bat in slow motion and her hand lifts to her heart. I've heard this story a million times, but I let her continue as I always do.

"I thought that what we had was real, and then I realized his heart would always belong to Elizabeth," she says, referring to her older arch nemesis and violet-eyed stunner, Elizabeth Taylor. "I had to give him up. I had to let Richard go. But in doing so, I met your grandfather."

My chest squeezes when she mentions him. It's been six years since he passed, but there isn't a day that goes by that I don't miss his infectious laugh or the ornery twinkle in his blue-gray eyes. Even in his eighties, he was the definition of a charismatic people pleaser.

"Anyway, if he isn't going to make time to see you, he isn't worth your time," she says.

"I know."

Grandma tilts her head, studying me. "I know you know. I just wanted to remind you."

I hate that I'm letting this get to me more than it should. He was never supposed to mean anything to me. I was never supposed to so much as flirt with the idea of getting attached.

"I'm going to head back and throw some laundry in," I say, getting up from the table. After that I'll text my friends and see who's around today. The last several times I've tried getting together with them, it hasn't panned out.

Chelsea is obsessed with her new boyfriend and can't be bothered to be without him for more than an hour at a time, Meg is shooting some Benicio del Toro film on location in Spain for the next two months, Vivienne is still at UC-Berkeley finishing the degree we both started at the same time, and Honor got a job interning for some stylist-to-the-stars and is putting in sixty hour weeks on the regular.

But I can try.

Wrapping my arms around my grandmother, I squeeze her tight, inhale her signature Quelques Fleurs perfume, and head back to the guesthouse.

By the time I've rounded up all my dirty clothes and shoved them in the wash, I head back to my room, passing my phone on the way. It's been sitting on my nightstand all morning—since Isaiah first texted me.

But now I see that I have four missed calls ... all of them from him ... which is odd because we've always only texted.

Perching on the seat of my bed, I hold my phone, staring at his name, drawing in deep, slow breaths. Pressing my lips together, I debate whether or not to call him back, only the decision seems to be made for me the second my screen lights.

My heart kick starts, my mouth dries.

He's calling.

Clearing my throat, I sit up tall and press the green button after the fourth ring. "Hello?"

"Maritza." His voice is smooth, unrushed.

I pause before saying, "Yes?"

"Been trying to get a hold of you the past hour. Wanted to see if you're still going to be around today?"

I catch my reflection in my dresser mirror on the other side of the room, and it isn't pretty. My face is twisted, brows furrowed and lips turned down at the sides. Disappointment is never a good look on anyone.

"I thought something came up?" I ask, trying to keep my inflection normal so he doesn't see how annoyed I am that he cancelled on me earlier and all of a sudden expects me to pick right back up where we left off.

"Something *did* come up," he says. "But everything's okay now."

"I don't know." I exhale. I could tell him I made other plans and it wouldn't be lying ... I made plans to do laundry. But I've never been one to play games.

"Ah. All right. I see." Isaiah exhales into the receiver. He doesn't hide his displeasure.

For a minute, we both linger on the phone, neither one of us speaking, neither one of us saying goodbye.

"If you didn't want to hang out before, all you had to do was say something." I'm pacing my room now. If this were the nineties, I'd have a phone cord wrapped around my finger and the receiver in my other hand. "I was looking forward to seeing you today. I had this whole, big day planned for us, reservations and everything. And you just texted me this morning with the most generic excuse and now that you've changed your mind, you expect me to drop everything again and act like it didn't bother me?"

He's quiet.

Which is good.

I hope he's letting this sink in.

"You don't get to treat people like this. You don't get to treat them like a toy and put them back on a shelf the second you decide you're done playing," I lecture him, still making my way around my room. Stopping by the window, I peer outside where Melrose is still soaking up the sun.

That's what I should be doing right now, catching some

rays, listening to some trashy pop music, and reading the latest issue of Us Weekly without a single care in the world.

No, actually, what I should be doing is *working*.

I took today off to spend it with him. I forfeited a day of earnings so he wouldn't have to be alone on his last day in LA. I've sacrificed hundreds if not thousands of dollars in tips this week and for what?

But it probably doesn't matter to him. He probably assumes that since I'm the granddaughter of Gloria Claiborne, everything I could ever want is just gifted to me without a second thought. If he would've actually taken the time to get to know me this past week, he'd have realized it couldn't be further from the truth.

My grandmother has always been tight with her pocketbook, but only because her intentions are good. She saw far too many of her rich and famous friends give birth to beautiful babies who grew up not knowing how to function in the real world because they'd never had to get real jobs or manage money or do anything for themselves.

Money ruins people, she always said. And she spoke from experience. Money almost ruined her marriage to my grandfather back in the sixties when they were some "it" power couple in Hollywood.

But I digress. To this day, the fact that her two sons are successful professionals is her greatest accomplishment. It means more to her than any Oscar or Academy Award she's ever received.

Anyway, I threw away hundreds of dollars, like a damn idiot, just to spend a week with a handsome stranger with warm eyes and a dimpled smile that made my stomach hit the floor.

"My mom wasn't feeling well," he says. "She ... has some medical issues. When I left your place last night, I had some missed calls from my sister. She'd gone to check on Mom while I was with you and when she arrived, I guess Mom was barely responsive. She had a fever of one hundred and five. Anyway, Calista took her to the ER and I spent the night at the hospital with them."

My heart burrows deep in my chest. I'm at a loss for words, the air sucked from my lungs.

All I did was think about myself this morning, assuming the worst and letting my bruised ego assure me that Isaiah was just like the rest of them.

"Oh, God. I'm so sorry," I manage to say a moment later. Sinking into my bed, I draw my knees against my chest. I catch my reflection in the mirror, only this time I look like a girl who's just eaten a heaping serving of crow. "I ... I just assumed you didn't want to hang out and you were just giving me some generic excuse because that's what guys do when they get bored. I ... I thought you were bored with me. Isaiah ... I'm sorry."

I could apologize a hundred times and it'd still barely put a dent in just how remorseful I am in this moment

Exhaling, I admit, "I spent all morning writing you off."

"I didn't mean to be so vague," he says. "It's just, we hadn't talked about my mom and I didn't know what was going on. Also, I hadn't slept in over twenty-four hours. I just wanted to go home and get some sleep. The last thing I want is for you to assume I was blowing you off. I'm not that callous. And I didn't get bored with you."

Maybe a part of me wanted to believe he was some jerk —if only because it'd make saying goodbye and letting him go and knowing that I'm never going to see him again ... that much easier.

Fuck.

I bury my head in my hands when I realize the worst part about this entire situation.

I'm falling for him.

And I know this because I wouldn't have gotten so worked up today if I wasn't.

"You still want to hang out?" he asks. His words blanket my hard feelings.

I can't say no.

So I don't.

12

ISAIAH

SATURDAY #7

I'M SO TIRED I can hardly function, but I didn't want to miss our last Saturday together. I'm nothing if not a man of my word, a man who respects obligations.

"Hey." She answers her door in sweats and a cut-off t-shirt, her dark hair piled on top of her head and her full lips glistening with a fresh coat of chapstick.

On the phone earlier, I told her I needed to go back to sleep for a few hours, and that I'd be fine with staying in tonight. With her. She volunteered her place and I promised I'd be there no later than seven.

"I'm so sorry about earlier," she says, apologizing yet again.

"I told you it's fine." I close her door behind me,

glancing at the TV screen in her living room, which is paused on the opening credits of Stranger Things.

I want to kiss her. I want to press her against the wall, peel her clothes off of that taut body, and devour every inch of her.

"Melrose is gone tonight," she says, biting back a smile that can only mean one thing.

"And your point?" I tease, feigning ignorance. I can beat around the bush with the best of them.

She shrugs. "I'm not trying to make a point, Corporal. Just stating a fact."

"If you want me, just say so." My cock strains in my jeans. I wasn't expecting to walk into this straightaway tonight. I thought maybe it'd take a little flirting, a little liquid courage.

"All I want is to have a little fun." She winks before slipping her hand into mine and leads me to the sofa, pulling me down beside her. A second later, she's reaching for a bottle of red wine and two stemless wine glasses.

"I don't know if you drink wine," she says. "But you're drinking it tonight."

She hands me a glass before clinking hers against mine and taking a sip.

Twenty-four hours from now, I'm going to be halfway across the world. Forty-eight hours from now I'll be a world away from this ... from her. But I try not to think about those things. Nothing good can come on fixating on shit you can't control, and I'm actually looking forward to getting out of the States for a while.

I kind of like being a world away sometimes. I wouldn't have reenlisted if I didn't.

"I had fun this week," she says, head tilted as her pretty eyes rest on mine.

"Same." I take a sip of the wine, which is sweet and goes down with a smooth, easy finish.

"Do you ever write letters when you're gone?" she asks. "Like letters back home? To friends or family?"

I shake my head. "Nah."

"Why not?"

"Not much of a letter writer," I say. "Some of the guys sign up for these pen pal services, but that's not something that's ever appealed to me."

"Can I send you letters?" she asks. Her question catches me off guard and I need a minute.

"Why would you want to do that?"

She shrugs. "Doesn't it get lonely over there? Don't you want to know someone's thinking about you?"

Laughing, I say, "I've served almost ten years now. Haven't been lonely but maybe once."

"You act like that's some badge of honor or something."

"Where I'm from, it is," I say. "You see guys who miss funerals or the births of their children. You see guys missing birthdays and holidays and shit like The Super Bowl and things that civilians take for granted. It's just easier if I keep those things out of mind."

Her gaze lowers and her lower lip juts forward before she takes a drink. "Makes sense, I guess."

"It's nice that you want to do that though."

"It's going to be so weird saying goodbye to you." Her voice is breathy and wistful and she flashes a pained smile.

"Yeah, but this is what we signed up for."

Maritza nods, drawing her legs onto the couch. "No, I know."

"Come on." I reach for her face, cupping her chin and angling her face until our eyes meet again. "Let's have fun tonight. If you get all sad and mopey it's going to completely defeat the entire purpose of this week."

She pulls in a hard breath, lets it go, and softens her expression. "All right. Sad and mopey Maritza is gone in three ... two ..."

Snapping her fingers, she plasters the most ridiculous grin I've ever seen in my life across that pretty face of hers.

I can't help but laugh at her.

"You're such a fucking dork," I say, pulling her into my lap. My palms graze her outer thighs, working their way to her hips as our stares hold steady. She smells like sweet almonds and feels like cashmere and right here, right now is the only place I want to be.

Her hands caress my face, her mouth sinking onto mine. A moment later, her lips part and our tongues meet and her hips grind against the rock-hard throb forming in my jeans.

Grabbing the hem of her shirt, I lift it over her head only to reveal she wasn't wearing a bra to begin with.

"You came prepared," I say, breathing her in.

Her lips curl against mine. "You have no idea how badly I wanted this to happen again."

Pushing her sweats down her hips, I slide them down her long legs, followed by her lacy black thong. The sweet scent of her arousal fills the tight space between us. When I stand, she reaches for my zipper, freeing me.

Her dark eyes are wide as she stares up at me, pumping my hardened length in her hand with a devious smirk. A second later, she takes me into her mouth, her full lips velvet soft against my shaft as her tongue circles the tip.

Groaning, I bury my fist in her dark hair, her messy bun coming undone as she swallows my length over and over.

Yanking my shirt over my head, my heart pounds in my chest. I want her skin on mine. I want her warmth, her heat, her breathless sighs in my ear. I want her biting her lip and screaming my name and riding my cock so hard she won't be able to walk straight for a week.

But first things first.

Pulling myself away, I guide her to the sofa, positioning myself between her thighs as she leans back against a throw pillow.

Maritza exhales when my tongue drags the length of her seam and she moans when I slip a finger inside. Aided by her arousal, I add another until the tension between us aches with an impatient fervor.

My hands are greedy, my touch generous as I explore every peak and valley of her nubile body as she writhes beneath me, her breath growing quicker the closer she gets to the edge.

I can't take it anymore.

I've waited long enough. I have to have her.

Reaching for my jeans on the floor, I grab my wallet and retrieve a rubber, ripping the foil packet between my teeth before sheathing my girth. Maritza watches, her full tits rising and falling as she waits, and the second I'm ready, I take her hand, pulling her up and telling her to get on her hands and knees.

Her cherry ass beneath my palm is pure fucking gold, and I slide my fingers between her thighs until I reach her swollen pussy. Guiding my cock inside, pushing it as deep as I can go, she releases the softest sigh before gripping the pillow in her tight fists.

My hands steady her hips, pulling them back to meet my every thrust. Her pussy forms to my cock, each plunge tight and slick, charging the two of us with insatiable energy. Bringing her body against mine harder, faster, I squeeze my eyes and lose myself in the distracting euphoria of this moment.

Running my hands down her hips, toward her belly, and then between her breasts, I bring her closer to me, pressing my body against her back as I drive into her. My palm wraps softly around her neck, my fingers just beneath her jaw as I bury my face in her hair.

My focus is her.

Her surrender is mine.

There's a frenzied race to the finish as her body melds against mine, but I won't let her go until we're both spent, collapsed, and barely able to utter a single coherent phrase.

Her left hand lifts, her fingers reaching for my hair as I caress her breasts, pumping my length into her again and again. The rapid, shallow breaths are a sign she's getting closer and the moment she presses back against me, taking me to the hilt, I fucking lose it.

She rides the wave, her body warm and pliant, mine wild and reckless, and when we're done, I sink back, gathering her in my arms, her back pressed against my chest. We're a sticky, breathless mess of unrestrained exhaustion, but already I could do this again.

I could do this all fucking night long.

Maritza turns to face me, a smiling claiming her full lips, and she cups my face in her hands, saying nothing.

"Let me write you letters," she asks a moment later. "Let me see you again, when you come home."

"Maritza ..." I need to shut this down.

The idea of having someone to come home to has never appealed to me before, but I could see myself coming home to her.

But I force that away.

This is how it has to be.

It'll be better this way.

For me.

For her.

"I know what I said a week ago," she says. "And I meant it. I don't want a relationship. And the last thing I should be doing is falling for some guy who's going away for ... how long are you going away?"

"Six months this time," I say. "If I don't volunteer to stay longer."

"Let me write to you," she says, head tilted. Her fingers trace my mouth and she kisses me hard. "I don't want to fall in love with you over letters. I don't want some cheesy pen pal arrangement. I'm just not ready to watch you walk out that door when there's still so much about you I want to know."

Exhaling, I drag my hand along my jaw. "Listen, I'm a shitty boyfriend. I'm the last person you should be pining away for."

"Who said anything about pining?" she asks. "I guess ... I guess I just want to keep you in my life. One way or another. In whatever capacity you desire. We're friends, you and me. Right? You'd call me a friend?"

Pulling in a lungful of sex and perfume-scented air, I hold her stare, finding it nearly impossible to say no to her sweet request.

"I'm not trying to fall in love with you, Corporal," she says. "I'm not trying to be your girlfriend. I just want to be ... *something* ... to you. I don't even know what."

Pressing my lips together, I mull over my options. "I don't understand what you want, Maritza."

"You fascinate me. You're complicated and quiet and strong and determined and intelligent and—"

"How can you know all those things when you've

known me a week?"

Her eyes roll and her head tilts back. "I don't know. I just ... I feel them. I can't explain it. I just know that if you walk out of here tonight and I never hear from you or see you again ... I'm not going to like that. And if you don't feel the same? Fine. I'll accept that. But I had to put it out there while I had the chance."

We're still very much naked and I'm still very much ready to devour her again, but this changes things.

Lifting my hand to her pointed chin, I run my thumb along her lower lip. "I don't want you to get your hopes up."

And I don't want to hurt her.

I respect her too much to do that.

"I'm not going to fall in love with you," she says, though I don't entirely believe her. "I told you that. I just want to hear from you, that's all. And when you come home, if you want to see me, we can make that happen."

I exhale. It's so fucking hard to say no to her when she's looking at me like this—like she thinks I'm some kind of wonderful.

"How about this," she says, "so that you know I'm not trying to fall in love with you, I'll write 'P.S. I hate you' at the end of each and every letter."

I make a face. "A little extreme, don't you think?"

"Come on. Just go with it. It can be our thing," she says, with a chuckle before booping my nose.

"Who says I want to have a *thing* with you?" I tease. Kind of.

She gives my chest a playful jab. "This could be fun."

"You're not going to let this go, are you?"

"I wish I could, Corporal." Her full mouth pulls wide, framing her perfect smile as she tilts her head. "But I don't think I can."

13

MARITZA

HE LEFT before the sun came up but those still small hours lying in my bed, our bodies melded, I'll never forget as long as I live. He kissed the inside of my palm, his touch gentle and his gaze soft. I wasn't sure if it was a silent apology or a surrender of his ironclad heart.

Whatever our time together meant, I just know I'm never going to forget my week of Saturdays with Corporal Isaiah Torres—and I'd like to think the same for him.

Curled up in an arm chair in the living room sipping a coffee, I clutch the piece of paper with his address in my hands, torn from the same sheet of paper I used to write mine earlier this morning, before watched him fold it into halves and tuck it in his wallet.

He kissed me goodbye after I walked him to the door—laughing through his nose as he told me not to read into it, that he was kissing me for purely selfish reasons that I'd never understand. I promised him it was not romantic, though in retrospect, it kind of was ...

I swear when I closed the front door and watched through the window as he made his way back to his car, there was a cannon-sized hole in the middle of my chest.

He's not my boyfriend.

And I'd hardly call us good, close friends.

But he's special.

Our week was special.

I finish my coffee and hit the shower, reluctantly washing him off of me. My body is filled with aches and I trace the parts of me his mouth and tongue caressed mere hours before. By the time I'm finished, the delicious soreness between my thighs is all that remains, a fleeting memento of our final night together.

An hour later, I trek across my grandmother's back yard and head into her kitchen where she and her best friend, Constance, are eating the breakfast Gram's chef prepared.

"Morning, sunshine," Grandma says, pointing her spoon at me.

My stomach rumbles when I spot the layout of exotic fruits and Greek yogurts and artisan bagels, and I help myself to a plate before joining the two of them.

"Morning," I say. Each minute that passes is a reminder that I'm firmly planted back in reality whether or not I want to be.

As I sit here, spooning cinnamon granola into a dish of vanilla Greek-style yogurt, somewhere Isaiah's boarding a bus to get to a plane that's going to take him to a dangerous place for the better part of a year.

"Constance and I have lunch reservations at Mr. Chow," Grandma says. "One o'clock today. Would you like to join us? Her grandson, Myles, is going to be there."

The two of them exchange looks and ward off sheepish grins.

They've been trying to hook me up with Myles for years, and while I admit he's cute, he just isn't my type. He's one of those film-school types who takes everything entirely too seriously. People like that just can't sit back and enjoy things. They have to pick them apart until there's nothing left but a few threads and crumbs, and that's just not my thing.

"He's been asking about you," Constance says. "I'm not supposed to tell you that though."

She giggles, lifting her finger to her lips.

"Oh, Maritza, you should come!" Grandma says, an oversized smile taking up half of her face. As much as I'd love to keep her happiness afloat, I can't.

And for several reasons.

The biggest of which is the fact that I'm scheduled to work today.

"Have to be at work in an hour," I say, taking a spoonful of yogurt. "Thanks for the invite though."

"It's fine, sweetheart," Constance says. "Poor planning on our part. We shouldn't have sprung it on you last minute. I'll talk to Myles today and see what his schedule's like these next few weeks. Maybe the two of you could have another little date?"

Ugh.

Please don't.

I smile out of politeness. Constance is sweet as pie and cute as a button and she means well, but the first time I got roped into going on a date with Myles, I vowed to myself it would be the last time.

We don't speak the same language, and by that, I mean he uses words like "cinematic universe" and "framing" and "bridge shot" and "aspect ratio" and "revisionistic" and the only language I speak is plain English.

And don't even get me started on the fact that he made me see some artistic French movie with subtitles. Longest night of my life.

And then he tried to *kiss* me after all of that.

I turned and gave him my cheek like a proper girl would do in one of those black and white movies Gram is always watching. He smiled, pushing his thick-framed glasses up his nose, slightly embarrassed. And then he made a comment about how this felt like an awkward scene in some Reese Witherspoon romantic comedy.

The fact that he's still interested in me years later blows my mind and proves how out of touch he is with reality. And why wouldn't he be? He lives and breathes movies and things that simply aren't real.

I prefer real.

Real is flawed men with complicated personalities who do brave things like fight wars.

War is real.

The newest Darren Aronofsky film? Not real.

Afghanistan? Real as fuck.

Finishing breakfast, I kiss Gram goodbye for now and give Constance a wave before heading back to the guesthouse to grab my keys and apron and hit the road before I get stuck in traffic.

Forty minutes later, I pull into the parking lot and hang my permit from my rear-view mirror. Heading inside, I punch in and tie my apron around my hips. The scent of cinnamon pancakes and fried bacon fills my lungs and the sound of dishes clinking and cooks shouting and patrons conversing all blurs into the background.

Everything is gray.

And I feel his absence already.

I feel it in my bones, in the hollow of my chest. The twist of my stomach, the ache in the deepest part of me. The void of his touch on my skin, the nonexistent comfort of his low whispers in my ear.

I miss him.

It wasn't supposed to be this way.

14

ISAIAH

"HEY, CORP. LOOK AT THIS." One of my guys flags me down, pulling up a picture from his email.

"What's this?" I ask, hunched over him.

"She's seven weeks," he says, beaming from ear to ear. Private Nathaniel Jansson is young, fresh faced, and the kind of guy who works hard and does what he's told without giving any flack, but he's naïve as hell.

He's me about ten years ago.

"Congrats." I give his shoulder a squeeze, glancing at his ring finger. He's babyfaced and unmarried and I've seen this song and dance before. Woman find themselves a man in uniform, get knocked up because they want a baby or someone to support them, and once they get hitched, they're golden, only playing the part of a doting, loving spouse between deployments. When their man is gone? All bets are off.

Not all women are like that, of course, but I'm pretty

sure a guy like Jansson is ripe, low-hanging fruit for a woman looking for the perfect opportunity.

"I should be home in time to see my kid being born," he says with a dopey, delirious smile. "How perfect is that?"

"Everything happens for a reason." I offer him the kindest words I can muster before heading back to my desk, an empty pad of paper catching my eye.

We've been here all of two weeks now, and I've sat down a dozen times and tried to write Maritza a letter worth receiving, but so far every single one of them have landed in the circular file.

I've never written letters to anyone before.

I don't even know what to say.

Or if she'll even be able to read my handwriting.

And it's not like I can share what we're doing here. Everything is classified. And even if it weren't, she wouldn't understand half of what I'm talking about or it'd bore her to death.

Glancing over my shoulder, I make sure no one's watching and I grab a pen, trying again.

She's probably wondering why I haven't sent her anything and with mail taking a good week or two to be delivered, it could be next month before she gets anything. I tried to get her to exchange emails, telling her it'd be quicker that way, more convenient and efficient, but she wanted paper letters.

She said emails weren't the same, that she wanted something she could hold in her hands.

Pressing my pen against the paper, I try for the thirteenth time, first scribbling the date, then her name and some generic bullshit line that sounds way too formal.

Ripping the paper off the pad, I crinkle it in my hands.

Fourteenth time's going to have to be a charm.

I have work to do and I can't sit here penning letters like some teenage girl lying on her bed listening to the latest Ed Sheeran album.

Putting ink to paper, I manage to come up with a letter that doesn't actually suck, and when I finish, I fold it into thirds and slide it into an envelope, ignoring the fact that my heart is racing a little bit more than it should.

I tell myself she means nothing, that this stupid letter exchanging thing means nothing, and then I get back to work.

15

MARITZA

"THERE'S some weird letter on the table for you," Melrose says when I get back from work. "It's got foreign-looking stamps on it or something."

My breath catches and the ache in my feet from running around for the last eight hours suddenly subsides. He left three weeks ago. And while I didn't expect to hear from him immediately for rational and logistical reasons, I didn't think it'd take nearly this long.

Rifling through the stack of mail on the kitchen table, I find a yellow envelope with my name on it. The return address is an APO. Ripping the side of the envelope, I let his letter slide out, landing in the palm of my hand, and I head back to my room, spreading out on my bed as I unfold it.

MARITZA,

I'm here. I made it.

Sorry to keep you waiting. It's been busy around here, but mostly I've been settling in, prepping for missions, and keeping my guys from getting out of line.

I wish I had something more exciting to share with you, but there's nothing exciting about where I am. It's hot and dry and sometimes it's too loud and other times it's too quiet.

Anyway, I told you I suck at writing letters.

Hope you're doing well back home.

Regards,

Corporal Isaiah Torres

P.S. Send pancakes.

"He finally wrote you?" I glance up to find Melrose leaning in my doorway, arms crossed and a mischievous smirk on her heart-shaped face. "What'd he say?"

She saunters to my bed, taking the spot beside me, and I clutch his letter to my chest.

"His letters are not your personal entertainment," I tell her. Out of respect, I'm not going to share them with anyone. His letters are for me only, even if they're boring or ridiculously formal.

"Whatevs. Be lame like that." Melrose gives me a thumbs' down before standing. "Anyway, about damn time he wrote you a letter. I was beginning to think he was just telling you what you wanted to hear."

"He deserves the benefit of the doubt," I tell her.

Ever since I wrongfully assumed he was casting me off the day his mother was sick, I've felt horrible. From what I can tell, Isaiah seems to be a man of his word, and until I have verifiable proof that he isn't, I've promised myself to give him the full benefit of the doubt.

"Plus, it takes weeks for these letters to go back and

forth," I say. "They're routed to army post offices and then sorted and it's this whole process."

"I don't get why you two just didn't exchange email addresses. Instant gratification is the way of the world. Join us."

"When was the last time you got something in the mail that wasn't a bill or a flyer for a pizza place or a box of beauty product samples?" I ask. "This might be the only time in my life I'll be able to get actual letters from an actual person. Anyway, he suggested the email thing, but I thought it might be nice for him to have something tangible too."

"How romantic."

I roll my eyes. "There's nothing romantic about a couple of friends exchanging letters. Stop trying to make it into something it's not."

"But you like him."

"Right. He's a nice person."

She laughs. "No, you *like* him."

"Don't you have somewhere to be? An audition or an acting class or something?"

"That's cool, that's cool." Melrose ambles to the doorway, her socks gliding on the carpet as she wears a smirk on her face. "I can take a hint. I know when I'm not wanted."

"Close the door behind you," I say.

She makes a weird face but obliges anyway, and as soon as she's gone, I read the letter twice more and tuck it into the vintage jewelry box on top of my dresser before grabbing a notebook and a pen of my own.

16

ISAIAH

"CORPORAL. YOU'VE GOT MAIL." Private Sanchez slaps a letter on my desk before strutting away. The return address belongs to one Miss Maritza Claiborne of 57322 Laguna Siesta Drive in Brentwood, California, mailed almost a week to the date she would've received mine.

Giving the envelope a careful tear, I find a quiet corner and unfold her letter.

CORPORAL TORRES,

My good sir, I received your letter on the eighteenth of May, year of our Lord two thousand eighteen. I'm pleased to hear you're doing well and I entrust that your soldiers are in the best of hands.

Also, can we stop with the lame, formal letters? I'm just going to go ahead and nip them in the bud right now.

For the record, I'm simply Maritza.

You're Isaiah.

And for the love of God, do not sign off with "regards" okay? Give me a "truly" or a "sincerely" but do not insult me with a "regards."

Anyway, now that that's out of the way, thanks for the letter. And for the record, I was only slightly worried about you. It's not like I expected you to unpack your bags and get cracking on a letter your first night there. I know you're working. I know you're doing important things. But I do appreciate the mail. It was a nice treat.

Oh, and Melrose tried to read it (surprise, surprise), but I wouldn't let her.

It's none of her business and she thinks this letter writing stuff is dumb, so I refuse to let her be so much as slightly entertained by our exchanges.

So what do you do over there when you're not working? Or are you always working? What kind of food do you eat? Do you have a favorite meal? What's the weather like this time of year? (That's such a Gloria Claiborne thing to ask, I'm sorry).

I've just been slinging pancakes and trying to nail down a new major to try. My father has to approve of it or else he won't pay. That's the agreement. It has to be a "useful" degree ... whatever that means. I'm not really a business-minded person and I'm not into computers or coding. Blood makes me queasy so that's a big "no" to any job in the medical field.

HALPP.

I'm twenty-four and I have no idea what I want to do with my life.

What does it feel like? Knowing exactly what you want to do with your life at such a young age? I envy people like you, the ones that have it all figured out.

All right. My hand is cramping up so I should probably go.

Always,

Maritza the Waitress

P. S. I hate you ... just kidding.

P. P. S. I'd totally ship you a pancake—but only ONE*—if I could.*

WITH A SMIRK ON MY FACE, I fold her letter and tuck it inside my shirt for safekeeping.

I'll write her back tonight, first chance I get.

17

MARITZA

"MARITZA, YOU READY?" Rachael calls from my living room, where she and Melrose are sharing a bottle of Riesling before we paint the town tonight.

"Just a second," I yell back, tearing into a letter that arrived today. I wouldn't admit this to anyone, but I'd been checking the mail every single day for the past two weeks waiting for his response.

DEAR MARITZA THE WAITRESS,

It's a good thing you're cute because you're sure as hell not as funny as you think you are. And did you seriously ask me about the weather? Have you ever heard of this thing called Google? You should try it sometime.

And glad you were only slightly worried about me, though you should do yourself a favor and not worry about me at all. My mother does enough of that for all of us.

Anyway, to answer your question, I didn't so much as know what I wanted to do as I knew what I needed to do. There's a difference there.

You should listen to your father. Sounds like he's got a good head on his shoulders. I'd tell my kid—if I had one—to do the same thing, especially if I was footing the bill.

Glad you're keeping busy with work but hope you're making time for the important stuff like touring wax museums and tar pits.

Off to shove my face full of shit food and play cards for the hundredth time this week.

Sincerely,

Corporal Torres

P.S. I hate you too.

P.P.S. But only because your letter didn't come with the pancake I'd requested.

I FOLD his letter and tuck it away inside my jewelry box before spritzing a cloud of perfume into the space in front of me and walking through it—an old trick Gram taught me back in the day.

Giving myself one last look in my full-length mirror, I smooth my hands down the black, strapless Herve Leger bandage dress I "borrowed" from my mom's closet before they moved to New York and then step into a set of killer Jimmy Choos—also "borrowed."

I don't get the chance to dress up that much these days so when I do, I tend to go all out. Plus, Melrose picked the club tonight and she's got Cristal taste, which means we're not going to some dive bar in South-Central.

"About damn time." Melrose takes a giant gulp of her white wine when she sees me. "Look at you, little mama.

God, I wish I had your legs. It's so not fair. Those should have been mine."

Rachael's eyes move between us and her wine glass is as frozen as her expression.

"My mom dated her dad before she married my dad," I explain, waving my hands around as I talk. "My mom is super tall."

"I bet the wedding was super awkward." Rachael winces.

"That's what we've been told," I say. "Apparently Melrose's dad almost no-showed and he had the ring. They made up though. He actually ended up hooking up with one of Mom's bridesmaids that night ... and that was Mel's mom. Everyone got a happy ending."

"We're meeting some of my girls at Willow House in an hour," Melrose changes the subject, tossing back the rest of her drink before setting it aside and gathering her phone, keys, and the satin Chanel clutch she claimed was a thank you gift from a producer last year.

"Which girls? Have I met them?" I ask.

Melrose shrugs, like she doesn't know and she doesn't care. I've never seen someone make so many friends she can't keep them straight. I tried looking someone up in her phone once and counted at least six "Taylors," eight "Joshes," and twelve "Megans," each of them with descriptions like, "Taylor BLUE HAIR CHATTY" and "Josh DIRTY CONVERSE BAD KISSER" and "Megan CRAZY DO NOT ANSWER." There must be at least eight hundred people in there, if not more.

"Come on girls," my cousin glances at her phone screen as she ushers us out the door. "Ride's here."

PROFESSIONALLY DJ'D MUSIC PUMPS.

Top shelf liquor flows.

Gorgeous people surround us.

And yet, I'd rather be anywhere but here.

Not that I'm not having a good time—Rachael is always a blast and Melrose has the most outlandish and eclectic group of "friends" providing ample entertainment. One of them is a Swedish pop star who came to America to try to "make it big." Another is the heiress to a Spanish oil fortune. The tall brunette in the corner is from some reality show that was really popular a few years ago. And the redhead beside me has been fighting with her boyfriend on the phone all night and airing *allllll* his dirty laundry in the process—which I'm pretty sure she's going to live to regret in the morning when they get back together.

But while I'm physically here, mentally I can't stop thinking about Isaiah. What he's doing. If he's comfortable. If he's happy. If he's having a good time. I can't imagine there's much for them to do in Afghanistan on a Saturday night.

"Why are you so quiet tonight?" Melrose moves her redheaded friend out of the way and squeeze between us. "You have cramps?"

I almost spit my drink out. "No, I don't have cramps."

"You've had, like, four drinks," she says, glancing at me with unfocused eyes. "You should be dancing on the table by now."

"When have I ever danced on a table?" I pride myself on being a good time girl, but certain things just aren't my style.

"Figuratively," she says, trying not to slur.

"I think this is only my second anyway," I say, lifting my martini.

"Okay, don't look now, but there's a guy standing at the bar in a navy-blue suit with a blue gingham tie and he's been staring at you for the past hour," she says, leaning close.

I don't look because it doesn't matter. I'm not looking to be picked up tonight. I'm not looking for a one-night stand. I just wanted to have a good time with my girls.

"Oh, my God. He's coming over here," Melrose flaps her hands, making it overly obvious that we're talking about him. I know he's arrived when she crosses her legs and bats her lashes and cups her hand under her chin. "Hi, stranger."

I turn to face him, eyes locking with a set of the bluest irises I've ever seen, tawny skin, and sandy, too-cool-to-care hair that makes some kind of casually defiant statement against his impeccable Tom Ford suit.

The man ignores my cousin. He ignores all the girls at our table. He's completely and unapologetically fixated on me.

"I'm Ansel," he says, lifting a tumbler of amber-colored liquor to his Cheshire grin. "My apologies for staring at you all night. I have a weakness for beautiful women."

Out of politeness, I don't roll my eyes.

Plus, Ansel doesn't seem greasy or skeevy. There's an air of class about him and his apology seems genuine from what I can tell.

"Do you mind if I ask your name?" He hasn't looked away from me yet. Not once. And I detect some kind of non-American accent, though I can't quite place it. German, maybe?

"Maritza," I say.

"That's a very beautiful name," he says. "Would it be all right if I bought you a drink?"

I hesitate, looking for a way to turn him down without hurting his feelings.

He's exotic and gorgeous and polite and I'm sure it took a lot for him to come over and introduce himself in a society where most people hide behind their dating apps, but when I look at him ... I feel ... nothing.

Melrose nudges me in the ribs and Ansel chuckles.

It's just a drink, I guess.

"Yeah. Sure," I say. "That'd be nice."

Ansel's mouth pulls wide and he extends his hand, helping me up. Everything about him is formal, his mannerisms, his way of speaking, the way he walks beside me as if we're Prince Harry and Meghan Markle.

But at the end of the day, beautiful Ansel is beautifully boring.

And I can't ignore the fact that for some completely insane reason, I wish it were Isaiah buying me this drink.

18

ISAIAH

DEAR CORPORAL TORRES,

I was thinking a lot about what you do for fun over there. Do you have much downtime? What do you do to kill the time? I imagine the days and nights get pretty long sometimes. How do you distract yourself?

I've been thinking about what you said about picking a practical major and I know you're right. I know my dad is right. I guess I'm just torn between following my head or my heart and I've been dragging my feet for so long that I feel I'm running out of time to decide. I suppose no one ever says you HAVE to have a college degree by a set age, but I'd personally like to have my shit figured out before I turn thirty. I don't want to be that friend still floundering around not knowing what to do with herself and serving pancakes because she's spent her twenties too afraid to make a fucking decision.

Anyway, I'm just rambling at this point. Sorry.

Melrose dragged Rachael and I out last weekend to this fancy bar where drinks were thirty dollars. Some really hot German guy hit on me and I suffered through an hour of small talk because he offered to buy me a drink.

I need to get better at saying no.

In a world filled with self-centered assholes, is there such a thing as being too nice? I like to think I'm cancelling out some bad with some good but maybe my logic is off.

Wait. Don't answer that. I already know what you're going to say.

All right. Time to get ready for work.

Yours,

Maritza the Waitress

P.S. I hate you ... in case you've forgotten.

P.P.S. Believe it or not I miss you but in the most NON-ROMANTIC *way humanly possible.*

19

MARITZA

THE ACHE in my feet from working a double dissipates the second I find his letter mixed in with a stack of junk mail on the kitchen counter. I imagine if I were to see myself right now, I'd find a dopey grin on my face, but I don't care. All that matters is I can't tear into this thing fast enough.

I meant what I said in my last letter—I miss him.

And in a non-romantic way.

The time we spent together before he left, however short it was, meant something to me, even if I don't exactly know what that is. All I know is I enjoy my time with him. And I hope I get to see him again. Soon.

MARITZA THE WAITRESS,

I'm not sure where you get the idea that I have "free time" over here, but I'd like to set that record straight. I work twelve-hour days six, sometimes seven days a week. When I'm not working, I'm doing laundry, shining my shoes, eating, or sleeping. We fit the occasional game of cards here or there but mostly we're working.

And let me get this straight, some hot guy hit on you and you "suffered" through small talk with him? Either you're lying to make me feel better or you're trying to make me jealous, both of which would be a huge waste of time because you're not my girlfriend.

I know you know that.

Just wanted to remind you.

So please, I hope you're having fun and not holding back because you're waiting for some jackass soldier to come home. And I hope you got that German dude's number because you sound kind of tense and you need to get laid.

Oh, and stop putting so much pressure on yourself to pick a major. It's not like you're making some life or death decision. What kinds of things are you interested in? What lights your fire?

Back to work.

Sincerely,

Corporal Torres

P.S. I hate you

P.P.S. Don't say that you miss me. Shit like that are nothing but land mines. Dangerous territory. If you're looking for a reaction from me, send me a pic of your tits but for the love of God, don't say you miss me. That wasn't part of the agreement.

FOLDING HIS LETTER, I roll my eyes and grab a pen, my hand twitching to get the thoughts in my head onto paper before they scatter like fall leaves to the wind.

20

ISAIAH

DEAR CORPORAL TORRES,

Just got your letter ...

If you only knew how badly I want to throw ice water in your face right now ...

If my handwriting is a little hard to decipher it's only because I'm so angry with you right now I'm shaking. The fact that even from thousands of miles away you feel the need to make it crystal clear that you don't want to date me does nothing short of infuriate me. It doesn't matter how much I told you the feeling was mutual, it's like you're convinced I'm lying.

I'm not one of those girls who play mind games, who pretend they want nothing and tell you what they think you want to hear to keep you around.

I say what I mean.

Always.

And we had a no-bullshit agreement that I take very seriously.

I'll tell you this one last time: I don't want to date you either.

Which leads me to my next order of business: we are friends.

I know you don't want to believe it, but we are. We're friends. Say it out loud: Maritza Claiborne and Isaiah Torres are friends.

And because we're friends that means I'm allowed to miss you and I'm allowed to tell you that I miss you. So stop being this tough, cold, callous distant man because that shtick might work on every other girl you've ever met, but it won't work on me.

Embrace the fact that I miss you, Isaiah, because it isn't going to change. In fact, it seems to be getting worse with each passing day if I'm being honest.

You're cool as shit and you're fun and I feel like we're on the same page with a lot of things. I'm fascinated by you and sometimes annoyed by you and other times turned on by you but at the end of the day, I fucking love that you're in my life.

I hope you feel the same and that someday, you might be able to actually admit it.

Best Friends Forever,

Maritza the Waitress

P.S. I hate you.

I READ her letter twice before tucking it into my pocket and pulling in a hard breath. I'd be lying if I said it didn't bother me to think about some smooth German dude hitting on her and buying her drinks—and I *hated* that it bothered me.

Hated.

So I overcompensated.

"Corporal, you got a package." Private Johnston places a large brown box on my desk. This marks the first time in my entire military career that anyone has sent me anything more than a letter or card. Before he struts off, I examine the return address.

Maritza.

Grabbing a box cutter, I slice through the packing tape and feast my eyes on package after package of Pringles, Starbursts, and peanut butter M&Ms.

I smirk, unable to help myself.

She remembered our conversation that night we went to the Griffith Observatory.

A note written in purple pen on a small piece of lined stationery reads:

Isaiah,

Let me know if there's anything else you want (besides pancakes—not happening, dude). I'll do my best to accommodate any (reasonable) requests. Also, I've placed a few goodies at the bottom of the box for fun.

Maritza

P.S. I hate you.

P.P.S. But I don't want you to starve or be bored while you're over there doing brave and scary things.

DIGGING THROUGH THE COLORFUL, junk food loot, I come across what resembles a summer camp care package. She appears to have tossed in a pack of UNO cards, a triple pack of her signature strawberry mint shea butter lip balm, two expensive-looking bottles of body wash that smell like a million fucking bucks, sunscreen, half a dozen bottles of Frank's Red Hot, a jumbo pack of individually wrapped beef jerky in various flavors, a few men's health and fitness magazines, and an assortment of James Patterson and Clive Cussler paperbacks.

"Hey, look at you. Finally got a package." Private Conroy stops into my doorway, leaning against the jamb, hands in his pockets. "And look at that smile on your face. Your girlfriend send that to you or your mom?"

I close the flap on the box. "Neither."

If she were here right now, I'd tell her that yes...

... there is such a thing as being too nice.

21

MARITZA

MARITZA,

Thank you for the package that you didn't have to send. Let me remind you that we agreed to letters and letters only.

And yes, there is such a thing as being too nice.

Anyway, I won't be able to write for a while. I'll be headed to the Syrian border after today. Not sure how long I'll be away.

Take care,

Isaiah

I STUFF his letter back into the envelope, smile fading and hot tears welling in my eyes, and check the date. He sent this two weeks ago. Every part of me knows I shouldn't read into this letter but it's just ... different. There was no "Maritza the Waitress," no playful "P.S. I hate you" at the end. And he signed off with a cold "take care."

Biting my lip, I place the letter aside and sink back into my bed, dragging my palms along my floral velvet duvet.

It's almost like he was intentionally distancing himself ...

Maybe I came on too strong? Maybe he read into the care package thing and took it as I *like* him and I'm trying to move things to the next level? I don't know. I don't know what was going through his head because he's a closed effing book and I knew him for all of nine days or whatever.

I allow myself to overanalyze for a solid ten minutes before snapping out of it and giving him the benefit of the doubt. Rising from my bed, I peel off my pajamas and head to the shower. I have to be at work in a couple of hours.

When I'm finished getting ready, I trek over to Gram's to grab breakfast, only the second I slide the back door open, I find myself face to face with Constance's grandson, Myles, seated at my grandmother's kitchen table.

"Oh. Hi." I stop in my tracks.

His thin lips curl. "Maritza. Hey. Haven't seen you in a while."

Yeah ...

"How have you been?" he asks, pushing his thick-rimmed glasses up his long nose. Nothing has changed since the last time I saw him. With a plaid shirt cuffed at his elbows, black skinny jeans, and white chucks, he's rocking the quintessential film studies major uniform.

"Good. You?" I head to the coffee bar off the butler's pantry and he careens his body, tracking me with his narrow eyes.

"Great." I grab a porcelain mug and turn my back to him. "Where's Gram and Constance?"

"Around here somewhere." He chuckles. "Probably polishing Gram's Oscars or something."

I don't laugh. He isn't funny. He's awkward and obvious and gives off this intrusive, invasive vibe that I can't fully explain.

Heading back to the kitchen, I don't find Gram's usual Saturday morning breakfast spread, no scent of bacon or steel cut oats, no buffet of fresh sliced strawberries and pineapples. She must've given her chef the day off.

"All right, well, I have to get to work," I say, striding toward the sliding door. "Good seeing you, Myles."

He stands. "You came all the way here for a cup of coffee?"

Pausing, I nod. "Gram has the good stuff."

His thin lips meld together and he exhales through his nose. "I see."

Reaching for the door handle, I give it a solid tug and embrace the mild morning air that hits my face.

Freedom.

Freedom from Myles Bridger.

I can't get back to the guesthouse fast enough. The way he stares. The way he stalls. The way his energy just lingers and clings and makes me feel like I need another shower.

By the time I get back to my place a minute later, I chide myself for overreacting. We had one date. One. And he was weird and tried to kiss me and he wasn't my type. He called me every day for two weeks afterwards and finally stopped when he got the hint.

He's just a nerdy, awkward guy. And he's nice. I don't give him enough credit for being nice. He's just ... not for me.

I should cut him some slack. I shouldn't fault him for having an innocent crush. The worst thing the guy ever did was try to kiss me after eating four pieces of garlic bread during a god-awful date at a horrendous hole-in-the-wall Italian place in South Gate.

Grabbing my apron and slipping into my work shoes, I find my keys and head out to my car, my mind returning to Isaiah's letter.

I promise myself I'll stop thinking about it. I promise myself I won't read into it anymore.

But promises are fragile.

And sometimes they break.

22

ISAIAH

THE DAY we get back from the Syrian border, I find a letter from Maritza lying on my bed. Dropping my bag, I take a seat and tear into the envelope.

DEAR ISAIAH,

Please accept my sincerest apologies for the care package. I hope my kindness didn't offend you. But seriously, get over yourself. We're friends and I'm allowed to do nice things for you.

I hope you're staying safe over there and I look forward to your next letter when you get back from your super-secret Army mission.

When are you coming home? Panoramic Sunrise is playing another show in five months in the Pacific Palisades. It's outdoor/open air. Should be fun ...

Oh. And I took your advice and slept with someone because you're right ... I am feeling a little tense lately. Anyway, it was awful. He was just some guy who was hitting on me at this bar I went to with Melrose. He had whiskey dick the whole time and I didn't even come. The next day he tried to kiss me with morning breath before he left. Who does that?! FYI – last time I take your advice, Corporal.

Yours,

Maritza the Waitress

P.S. I hate you ... because I blame you for the whiskey dick sex.

HER LETTER RESTS between my fingers and I read her words one more time—specifically the part about her fucking some random guy.

My blood heats, my body clenches. The thought of Maritza naked, some guy with his hands all over her body ... it doesn't sit right with me.

Yeah, I told her she needed to get laid. I pushed her in that direction.

But I didn't know it was going to feel like this—like a punch to the gut, and now I don't even fucking know how to process this or what to make of it.

I convinced myself she meant nothing, that she was just some smart-mouthed girl I hung out with for a week ... but now I don't know.

I don't fucking know.

All I know is there's this unsettled weight in my chest that wasn't there five minutes ago.

"Corporal, you ready?" Lieutenant Harbinger stands in the doorway. "Time to roll out again."

"We just got back."

"Yeah," he says. "And now we have to leave again. Another airstrike headed this way. Let's move it."

23

MARITZA

I LIED.

I broke one of my own hard rules.

But only by omission, which I don't think really justifies it fairly, but that's how I'm justifying it anyway.

When I told Isaiah I'd slept with some guy ... it wasn't just some random guy.

It was Myles.

And I'm not proud. In fact, I'm disgusted with myself. Melrose invited him to get drinks with us for some insane reason—I think she felt sorry for him or something. We were both plastered. It happened so fast and it happened without any forethought or thinking and as soon as it was over, I knew it was a mistake and I was appalled at my behavior.

Just thinking about that night, weeks later, makes me nauseous.

It was awkward, unsexy, and all around terrible, but it's

done. It occurred. I own it. And it's never going to happen again.

"Someone requested you." I finish pouring four ice waters and glance over at Rachael. "Some guy. Table eleven."

My heart pounds, my face blanketed in warmth before turning numb. I don't want to get my hopes up so I don't allow myself to think what I want to think, to assume what I want to assume.

Peeking out from the galley, I check out my newest table, only to have my stomach drop to the floor in the worst way possible.

Myles.

Fucking Myles is sitting at table eleven, thumbing through his phone and trying to nonchalantly scan the room in search of me.

"You know him?" Rachael asks.

Exhaling, I shake my head. "Unfortunately."

"Why do you say that? He looks cute ... like in a nerdy, endearing kind of way." Rachael takes him in from afar. "I like his glasses."

"It's a story for another time." I load the waters on a tray and head out, and when I'm finished, I hold my head high and make my way to table eleven. "Myles. Good morning."

He places his phone face down on the table and smiles wide when he sees me. "Maritza."

"Can I get you something to drink?" I ask, trying to keep this formal and impersonal. The night after we slept together, which has been weeks ago now, he called me.

And then he called me the next day.

And the next day.

His calls tapered off over the course of a couple of

weeks until they stopped completely and I found relief in the fact that he seemed to be getting the hint all over again.

"Been trying to get a hold of you for weeks," he says, voice low as he smiles through his bruised ego.

Wincing, I release a slow breath. "I'm so sorry."

Looking at him with his pitiful expression and his puppy dog eyes and falling smile, I feel like a giant piece of shit. I should've been an adult and told him right away that I wasn't feeling ... this ... instead I ignored him because I didn't want to hurt him—which only hurt him anyway. Faulty logic. Completely my fault.

"I shouldn't have brushed you off," I say, placing my hand over my heart. And I mean it. I feel awful. I knew he liked me, I slept with him which probably got his hopes up, and I ghosted him. "But I think we should just be friends."

He removes his disheartened gaze from mine, staring across the booth at the empty spot. His fingers tap on the table and he shifts in his seat.

"Myles, I'm so sorry," I say again. This isn't one of my finer moments, but I'm willing to accept full responsibility that I screwed this up and hurt him. At the time, the drinks were flowing and we were laughing and all I kept thinking about was how badly I needed a quick release and how sex is just sex ... but in my drunken stupor, I didn't stop to think that Myles and I weren't on the same page with that.

He folds his menu and shoves it across his table, exhaling hard. "Right. Heard you the first time."

"Maybe we can talk about this another time?" I ask, glancing at the man at the next table who's been trying to flag me down for the last minute. "When I'm not working?"

Myles' mouth presses flat.

"Sounds pretty pointless." Sliding out of his seat, he

squares his body with mine, his expensive cologne invading my personal space. "Guess I'll see you around."

He leaves.

I feel like shit.

Brushing my proverbial shoulders off, I check on the table behind him, refilling a man's coffee before returning to the galley.

"What was up with that?" Rachael asks, pouring an orange juice. "Why'd he leave?"

Drawing in a deep breath, I check the clock. "He's had a thing for me for a while. We slept together a few weeks ago and then I ghosted."

Her red lips form a crooked smirk. "You're so bad."

"I'm not bad. I'm cruel."

"Nah. You're not cruel, you're just being too hard on yourself. Men do that crap all the time. We do it once and we beat ourselves up about it for days," she says. "Let it go, sweets. He'll move on. They always do. And let's not dismiss the fact that you ignored him and he had the nerve to show up at your work to get your attention. Something's not right about him so don't go kicking yourself, all right? You didn't handle the situation perfectly, but neither did he. See? You're even."

Sighing, I say, "I love you, Rach."

"Love you too, Ritz." Rach gives me a side hug before grabbing the OJ and heading out to table seven.

The rest of the morning is a blur, which turns out to be a good thing. We're hit with our usual eight o'clock rush followed by a sightseeing tour bus full of retirees who traveled all the way from Reno to get their hands on our famous cinnamon pancakes.

By mid-afternoon, I'm back home with aching feet and a yawn that won't stop. I'm halfway to becoming an actual vegetable on the sofa when Melrose texts me and asks me to walk Murphy.

Peeling my faux zebra-skin blanket off my legs, I climb up and call for the world's most pampered pug before grabbing his leash by the door. The click-clack of his paws on the tile and the jingle of his collar follows and a second later he's attempting to jump into my arms. I hook him up and head out, passing by the mailbox once I'm outside the driveway gate.

Stopping, I reach my hand inside and retrieve a small stack of junk, bills, and Melrose's newest issue of Vogue.

Murphy relieves himself on a nearby palm tree.

Life goes on.

24

ISAIAH

I ALMOST DIED TODAY. Granted, that risk is always a given when I'm out here in the land of air strikes, land minds, and suicide bombers, but this was different. Fourteen of my men were injured today. On my watch, no less.

But one of us, Private Nathaniel Jansson, paid the ultimate price.

War doesn't care how old you are, how brave you are. War doesn't care how hard you work or how much you love your country. War doesn't care that you've got a woman back home waiting for you or that you're months away from becoming a father for the first time.

It could have been any of us, but today it was Jansson.

While he was young and green, he was going to be one of the best. I knew it. I saw it in him. He may have been new but he had a fire in his eyes and a dedication like none I've ever seen before, and now he's leaving behind a child that will only ever hear how brave and heroic their father was through secondhand stories.

My ears are still ringing and there's no time to sit around and process what just happened. We hadn't been back from our mission to the Syrian border but half a day when we found our base under siege. The flash of lights that preceded the deafening explosions and the sounds of men crying out in the dark will haunt my nightmares the rest of my life, but the strangest thing happened.

In the midst of all the chaos, when I wasn't focused on sheer fucking survival, I found myself thinking about *her*.

Maritza.

Coming this close to death does something to a man, it forces him to reevaluate his priorities and the things in life that he truly wants, forces him to question if the kind of life he's living has any sort of meaning at all or if he's just drifting through life like a fool believing his own lies—that he's happy alone, that he's never going to want anyone else for longer than a drunken night in a hotel room.

But I'm done lying to myself.

I want meaning.

I want her.

I want to get to know her, really know her. And I want to make her smile. I want to feel her strawberry lips on mine and brush her hair from her face. I want to do dorky touristy things together, things I'd never be caught dead doing with anyone else. I want to show her more constellations. I want to take her to another Panoramic Sunrise concert because god damn it, she deserves a do-over.

I want her to wait for me, to push my limits and do annoyingly sweet things and tell me she misses me.

And I don't want her sleeping with anyone else.

Shoving what's left of my things into an Army-issued

duffel bag, I find a crumpled scrap of paper—an old report of some kind, the edges burnt, and I grab a pen from my desk drawer. Scribbling a note, I fold the paper into fourths and tuck it in my pocket.

First chance I get, I'll send it.

"Corp, we gotta go."

I glance up to find Lt. Peters in my doorway, looking white as a ghost. The familiar, sickening sound of bombers breaking the sound barrier rumbles above us, vibrating through every breath, every thought.

I'm not a religious man much to my mother's dismay, but I find a handful of seconds to make a promise to God. Let me make it home alive, and I promise I'll tell her how I feel. I'll be the man she deserves, the man I'm supposed to be. I'll change. For good.

And I'll tell her *everything*.

25

MARITZA

MELROSE CUPS her dog's wrinkly face in her hands and rubs her nose against his. "You seem down lately."

"Me? Or the dog?" I ask.

She rolls her eyes before pulling her dog into her arms. "You. Murphy's always happy. He's living the good life."

"I'm not ... not happy," I say, reaching for my bottled water on the coffee table. I unscrew the cap and lift it to my mouth before adding, "I guess I've just been thinking about Isaiah lately."

"Still?" Melrose sits up straight in our leather arm chair. "You haven't seen him in, what ... several months? And you knew him all of a week?"

"I know, I know." I take a swig. "And it was nine days. I know, okay? Don't think I don't have this conversation with myself on a regular basis. I just guess I'm trying to make sense of how two people could hit it off so well and how we were writing these cute little letters back and forth and then he just ... stopped."

"You need a new hobby or something that doesn't involve obsessing over pointless stupid shit like Corporal Douche Bag."

"It's not like I've been moping around the last few months. I've been living my life, doing the exact same things I'd be doing had I never met him," I say. And it's true. I catch movies. I grab drinks with friends. I lunch with my favorite people. I read books and visit family. By no means am I sitting around waiting for the mailman or some serendipitous knock at my door. But it doesn't make this whole thing bother me any less. "I just want to know that he's okay, Mel. At this point, it doesn't matter why he stopped writing. I just want to know if he's safe. That's the only thing I care about."

Melrose begins to respond but my phone steals the show, vibrating across the coffee table.

"Ugh," I say, glancing at the screen and declining. "It's that blocked number again."

The few times I've answered, it's always been nothing—like someone's on the other end, muting their line.

"You're *still* getting those?" she asks, forehead wrinkled.

"Yup. At least every other day." They started a couple of months ago, and at the time I didn't think much of them. Most of the time they happen when I'm at work or in class and my phone is on silent. But now I get them almost every day, sometimes two or three times.

"For the love of God, will you change your phone number? It's the only way to make these stop." She cradles Murphy in her arms and kisses the top of his head.

Pulling in a haggard breath, I stare at the black glass in my hand. I've been putting it off for months ... maybe because a part of me wanted to make sure Isaiah had a way of contacting me should he need to or want to or whatever.

But that argument seems a bit moot at this point.

"I'll do it first thing tomorrow," I say. Rising, I head back to my room and grab my notebook—the one I'd been keeping all the letters I've written him the last several weeks, ones I vowed not to send until I'd heard from him again.

There are so many things I wish I could tell him—stupid things, really. Like I wish I could tell him I finally decided what I want to do with my life, that I finally picked a major and I'm starting classes this August. He'd be happy for me. At least, I think he would.

I guess I don't really know anymore.

At the end of the day, Melrose is right.

He's just some stranger I knew for nine days, and after all these months and all these letters, he's still just some stranger.

26

MARITZA

HE WOULD'VE COME home today.

At least, six months ago today was when he left, and he'd claimed his deployment was six months unless he decided to extend it.

I changed my number last week, which sort of signified the fact that I decided to let him go, to let go of the briefness of what was and all the questions that will never have answers. But still, he slips into my mind without permission on a regular basis. Melrose says I should learn to meditate, to mentally place my thoughts of Isaiah on a cloud and blow them away with a gentle exhalation.

I think she's full of shit.

I tried that ... a dozen times ... and not once did it work. If anything, those thoughts only came back with a vengeance, lingering longer and overstaying their welcome ten-fold.

It's like a sickness, an incurable disease.

Rach says I need closure. Mel says I need to see a shrink, which is a little dramatic in my opinion but she is her mother's daughter and her mother is of the opinion that shrinks are the answer to all of life's problems. That and Xanax.

All I know is I just want to move on with my life and be okay with not knowing why he stopped talking to me or why I continue to give a damn.

"You okay?" Rach ties her apron around her waist after clocking in Tuesday morning. "You look a little lost in thought."

I force a smile. "Yeah. I'm fine."

"Do I need to remind you that I'm a mother of three and my lie-dar is so strong it can pick up a lie from up to eighty yards away? You're lying, Ritz. Don't lie to me."

Tying my hair into a low ponytail, I turn to face her. "I stayed up all night checking all the public military casualty records I could find."

"Sweet Jesus. This is worse than I realized." Rach pinches her nose and places her palm on my shoulder. "Find what you were looking for?"

I bite my lip and shake my head. "I'm not proud, okay?"

"Is he alive?"

I shrug. "From what I can tell. Without being next-of-kin, there are certain records I couldn't access."

"You're going down a dark and winding path, my friend. Turn back now."

"I know, I know." I clamp my hand across my forehead. "It's just, I'm stuck between being scared sick that he's hurt or something happened to him and being furious at him for ghosting me like he did."

"Sweets, you have to let him go," she says, using the kind of tender tone she uses when her youngest kid falls off his bike and scrapes his knees, "because for whatever reason, the jackass let you go a long time ago."

I drag in a full breath of pancake-and-grease scented air, taking in the stainless-steel kitchen symphony going on in the background as patrons are being seated en masse.

"All right, fine," I say. "I'm letting him go—for real this time."

27

MARITZA

"LOVE, what are you doing this upcoming weekend?" Gram asks over tea the following Saturday afternoon. She saw me coming back from my jog and flagged me down, asking if I had a moment to chat, which always means she's up to something.

I'd spent all morning running around the Brentwood Pancake and Coffee like a crazy person then like an even crazier person, decided to go for a jog to clear my head when I got home from work.

"I haven't thought that far ahead. Why?" I ask, still trying to catch my breath as she pours me a steaming cup of her signature *Fortnum and Mason* Earl Grey and slides it my way. I slide the chair out beside her and have a seat, my sweaty tank top sticking to my skin and the hot tea looking particularly unappetizing.

"The reason I ask is because Constance is throwing her grandson—you know, Myles—a party at The Ivy. I guess he got some hotshot Hollywood producer to option this screenplay he wrote in film school and it's kind of a big deal. You should come. Oh, Lovey, he'd be tickled if you showed up to celebrate with us."

Gram's eyes light and her sweet face is aglow, and it isn't her Chanel makeup or the flattering light spilling in through the multitude of windows plastering the backside of her hacienda.

"You know he adores you," she says, pink lips pulled into a Cheshire grin. "Every time he comes around, he's always asking about you. In fact, just yesterday I ran into him and he was asking what you were up to. Even asked if you were seeing anyone ..."

"Are you serious?" I place my tea cup against my saucer, nearly knocking it over. Why would he ask my grandmother those kinds of questions when I made it perfectly clear I'm not interested in him?

Gram nods. "Serious as a heart attack."

"You know I hate when you say that." I roll my eyes. It'd be a little less of a big deal if Gram hadn't had one of her own a couple years back. "Too soon."

"Where's your sense of humor, Lovey?" she asks, narrow shoulders lifting and falling as she releases a dainty chuckle. "Anyway, there's this party and you should come. I'll even take you down to Rodeo Drive, let you pick out a new dress for the occasion."

Reaching for my jade green porcelain cup, I take a sip while I contemplate my answer. I don't want to hurt her, but I really need her to back off with the whole Myles thing.

"He said you two had a date several weeks back," she continues, head cocked. "He said it was one of the greatest nights of his life. You must have really left quite the impression on him."

Yeah …

"I just think the world of him," she continues. "He's so kind and intelligent. Your grandfather would've loved him. I'm sure your father would think the world of him, you know, if you ever feel like introducing the two of them. You know, I could invite—"

"—Gram," I say, steadying my trembling hands as I cut her off. I've never spoken to her with anything but love and respect in all of my twenty-four years, but I'm going to have to give it to her straight in order to put an end to her incessant prodding. "Myles is weird and awkward and we have nothing in common."

"Oh, come on now." She chuckles, like she doesn't take me seriously. "There's nothing wrong with him. Maybe he's just awkward around you because he likes you so much? You have that effect on boys, I've seen it. You make them nervous."

"Myles is broccoli. I've tried broccoli before, and I don't like it. I don't have a taste for it," I say. "And I tried it again just to make sure. Still didn't like it. So please quit forcing broccoli down my throat. I'm never going to like it."

Placing my cup on the saucer with a hard chink, I rise from her breakfast table and force myself to meet her gaze, taking in her wide eyes and gaping mouth.

"I'm sorry," I say. "I really am. I'm sorry. I don't like him. I can't. And I never will. Please, *please* stop, Gram. Please."

Her lips press together and she straightens her shoulders, glancing away. "Well, all right then."

Exhaling, I say, "Thank you. And I'm not leaving because of this conversation. I'm leaving because I have laundry to do and I told Melrose I'd do her hair."

"She's going out again tonight?" Gram asks.

"Yup."

"Are you planning to join her?"

I shrug. "I haven't decided yet."

I've been going out with Melrose all summer, weekend after weekend, Saturday after Saturday, sometimes staying out too late and hating myself the next morning when I'm rolling into work at 6 AM and other times calling it a night before half our friends even show up at the club *du nuit*.

But it's getting old.

Or maybe I am.

It's just not as fun as it used to be. The other day I sort of joked around with Mel that I felt like staying in and binge-watching Game of Thrones sounded more exciting than getting into 1 OAK and she looked at me like I had two heads. But the truth is, I'm in this gray area where going out sucks and staying in sucks and I don't know what the hell I want to do half the time, but I'm kind of okay with that because classes start next week and my priorities are about to shift and it's all for the best anyway.

Plus, I feel like everything happens for a reason.

And for the first time in a long time and in some kind of way that I can't fully explain, I feel like something exciting is just around the corner.

28

MARITZA

"YOU HAVE something stuck in your teeth." His name is Blake and he's a six-foot two former linebacker and current pharmacy student at USC.

My hand covers my mouth as my eyes widen. "Really? Where?"

"Right ... here." He flashes his perfect teeth and points between the two front ones.

"Oh, jeez. I'm always getting food stuck there, in the tiniest, most microscopic little gap. That's what I get for losing my retainer my freshman year of high school and thinking my teeth were going to stay perfectly in place for all eternity." I drag my tongue along my teeth before smiling. "Did I get it?"

"Yeah," he says. "But now I miss the little guy. He was kind of cute."

Laughing, I roll my eyes. "That's what I get for saying yes to the freshly ground pepper on my salad."

"Those pepper mills, man. They're irresistible." His hand rests on the white linen table cloth as his eyes catch mine over a flickering candle. We're dining al fresco on the rooftop of some Laguna Beach diamond-in-the-rough, the ocean waves crashing in the distance.

And speaking of diamond-in-the-rough, I'm pretty sure I'm sitting across from one right now—only this one was hiding on Tinder of all places. Tinder!

I only stumbled across him a couple of weeks ago because Melrose swore *by* Tinder and Rachael swore *off* Tinder and I agreed to settle their argument by selecting one lucky gentleman and giving it a go myself—for fun, of course. And science.

Looks like Melrose is winning the debate thus far.

"Whenever you're ready." Our server places the leather check wallet between us, skewing more toward Blake's side of the table and as soon as she leaves, we both reach for it at the same time.

He gets there first.

"I got it," he says, digging into his back pocket and retrieving a shiny American Express card.

"You sure?" I ask. I don't want to be that girl who makes an awkward thing out of paying for a check but this is only the third time we've hung out, he knows we're simply having fun, and this was by no means a stepping stone to boyfriend and girlfriend territory.

"Stop." He waves me off. A moment later, our server returns to grab his card. "So ... what are you doing after this?"

Resting my elbow on the table and my head in my hand, I sigh. "Homework. You?"

"Really? On a Friday night?"

I bite my lip. "Don't judge. I picked up a shift tomorrow so I have to go to bed early tonight anyway. It works out."

"All right, so what about tomorrow night? What are you doing then?"

I smirk. "What is this? What are you doing here?"

"Trying to ask you on a date."

"Like a *date* date? Or just hanging out?"

"What's the difference?" he asks, head cocked.

"Expectations," I say. "And wardrobe selection."

His blue eyes drift from my face to my collarbone and back. "Did you dress for a date tonight?"

"Not really ..." I look down at my ripped jeans and silk tank top, reaching for my Kendra Scott rose quartz earrings. "Was I supposed to? Was this a date? I thought we were just getting to know each other? Having fun?"

"What's the difference between that and dating?" he asks.

"Expectations. I told you that," I say with a teasing chuckle. "Get on my level, Blake. I'm losing you here."

Our server returns with his receipt, which he wastes no time signing. I gather my bag and he follows me to the exit, placing his hand on the small of my back as he walks me to the parking lot.

We stop at my car and he stands in such a way that I wonder if I should offer him some water because his feet are firmly planted, practically rooting into the ground beneath his leather boat shoes.

"I want to see you again, Maritza," he says.

Ordinarily when an intelligent, charming, well-studied man with impossibly good looks and a killer sense of humor looks at a girl like she's the prettiest thing he's ever seen and tells her he wants to see her again, she should feel something. A missed heartbeat, a flush in her cheeks, a tingle in her belly.

But I've got nothing, and it's not for lack of trying.

I want to feel something, anything.

But it's not something I can control—either a girl feels something or she doesn't. But maybe with time? Just because the fireworks aren't instantaneous doesn't mean they'll never be there at all.

"Casablanca is playing at the Vista Theatre tomorrow night," he says. "It's one of my favorites. Have you seen it?"

I nod. "Yeah. I have."

"You like it?" he asks.

"Love it."

"Good," he says. "So you'll see it with me tomorrow night. Pick you up at eight."

It hits me that earlier this year, I'd taken Isaiah to that same theatre to see that very same movie, and then it hits me even harder when I remember that Rick and Ilsa don't end up together in the end.

I've been doing so well lately, not thinking about the stranger I'd spent a week of Saturdays with once upon a time, but tonight it comes as one giant tidal wave, like everything I'd kept pent up all these months crashes over me at once.

I miss Isaiah.

I miss him for reasons I can't put into words, reasons I feel deep in my bones and in the pit of my stomach and in the ache in my chest I'd grown numb to.

But just as soon as the wave comes, it's gone, and I'm left with nothing but a handsome soon-to-be pharmacist with football player muscles who wants to take me to Casablanca tomorrow night.

I take this as a sign, and also as my closure.

29

MARITZA

"OH, HEY THERE." Melrose stands in my bedroom door as I'm feverishly typing out a term paper at my desk in the corner. "Was beginning to wonder if you still lived here. Feels like I haven't seen you in weeks."

"I know." I shut my laptop lid and face her. "I've been so busy with work and school."

"And Blake," she says, fighting a smirk as she takes a seat on my bed. "So what's up with him now? You guys official?"

Shaking my head, I say, "We're still just hanging out."

"But you're hanging out a lot."

Maybe a few times a week for the past few weeks. I'd hardly call that "a lot." And most of the time we're studying together or catching matinees.

I shrug. "So?"

"Clearly he likes you. And you like him too or you wouldn't spend so much time with him," she says, like she's the authority on the intricacies of Tinder dating in the modern age.

"He's fun," I say. "And he makes me laugh. And he's nice. And we have the same taste in music and movies. And for once, I've found a guy who believes me when I say I just want to have fun and not worry about labels. So yeah, I'm going to hang out with him."

Mel rolls her eyes. "You friend-zoned him. Nice."

"No. I fun-zoned him. There's a difference."

"Potato, po-tah-to." Murphy trots into my room and Mel scoops him up. "What do you think, Murph? Does she need to piss or get off the pot?" She places his smooshy face against her ear. "Yep. He's in agreement with me."

"Dork." I roll my eyes and turn back to my computer, about to lift the lid when a text comes through from Blake telling me he's outside the gate. Earlier today he texted, asking me to grab dinner with him. Said he needed some brain food for the all-nighter he was planning to pull studying for tomorrow's Pharmacogenetics test.

"Where you going?" Mel asks as I stand and scan the room for my bag.

"Dinner with a friend," I say, like it's no big thing. And it isn't. It's nothing—still. He even kissed me two weeks ago after we saw Casablanca. His lips were soft and his tongue was pure peppermint and his hands were in my hair and yet I felt ... nada.

Not a single, sleepy butterfly emerging from its cocoon.

"What are you doing, Ritz?" Mel asks.

My brows narrow. "Going out for dinner. I told you."

"No," she says, expression fading. "I mean, what are you doing with this guy? You don't even seem that excited to hang out with him."

I rest a hand on my hip. "I don't get where you're going with this."

"Are you waiting for yourself to like him? Because I can tell you, he doesn't make you light up half as much as Corporal Douche Bag did."

"Wow. Okay. You just went there ..."

"I just ... I don't want you to settle for someone who doesn't make you feel incredible," she says. "And I also don't want you to hold off on letting yourself feel incredible all because you're waiting for some jackass from your past to come waltzing through the door."

"Trust me. I haven't placed my happiness on hold for anyone and even if Isaiah came waltzing through my door like nothing happened, I'd have no problem telling him to fuck off," I say. "That train left the station a long time ago."

"Mm hm." Melrose gives me a side eye, which leads me to believe she doesn't buy it. But I don't care if she believes me or not. I know how I feel, and it's not my job to sell her on that.

If Corporal Isaiah Torres walks back into my life tomorrow like nothing happened, I'll waste no time telling him exactly what I think of him.

And it won't be pretty.

30

MARITZA

"UM, RITZ?" Rachael stands in the doorway of the galley as I mix three kid-sized chocolate milks—extra Hershey's syrup, her face white and looking like she's just seen a ghost. "You have a new table."

"Okay. Give me two secs." I give the final cup of milk an extra squeeze of chocolate.

Rach stands there, staring, watching, which is odd because she's always moving and we're mid-morning rush and all the other staff are go, go, going all around us.

"You okay?" I ask, loading the cups onto a plastic serving tray.

"Ritz ..."

I glance up at her only to find her staring out toward table ten where a dark-haired man sits with his back toward us. He turns for a second, but only slightly and only enough for me to recognize that chiseled jaw I'd remember anywhere.

The ground wobbles beneath my feet, I swear, and I suck in a deep breath before Rach grabs my wrist. My vision fades for a single, terrifying second. I've never had this kind of physical reaction to anything in my life.

"Don't do anything stupid," she says. "I know you want to let him have it—and he deserves it—but I don't want you to get fired. I need you here. I can't work here without you."

She offers a smile that lets me know she's half joking, half serious.

"I won't make a scene," I say, though I'm not sure if I'm trying to reassure her—or myself.

Clearing my throat and trying hard to deny the thrum and whoosh of my heartbeat in my ears, I deliver my chocolate milks with a smile before making my way to table ten.

Sliding my notepad from my apron and clicking the tip of my pen, I cock my head. "Good morning."

Isaiah places his menu flat on his table, drawing in a deep breath before checking his watch. "Just a coffee and eggs today, please."

My pen presses into my notepad with a slight tremble.

"Seriously?" I ask.

He glances up at me, his expression cold and distant. "I'm in a bit of a rush."

Lingering and at a total loss for words at the fact that he's treating me like a complete stranger, I clear my throat and let my notepad fall to my sides. My lips part as I try to say something, but the perfect words fail to find their way out of my jumbled brain.

A million thoughts spin around and there are a million things I probably should say to him right now, but I promised Rach I wouldn't do anything stupid and at the end of the day, I'm not willing to sacrifice my job over this jackass.

God help him if I ever meet him outside these four walls though ...

"No pancake today?" I ask, forcing a smile. If he wants to pretend we're a couple of strangers, then two can play that game.

He shakes his head. "Coffee and two eggs over easy."

"Really? Sure you don't want two pancakes?" I offer an incredulous chuckle, wondering, for a split second, why I feel the insane need to try to jog his memory. He didn't forget me. He couldn't have.

Isaiah points to the sign above the register. "Heard you guys are sticklers on that one-pancake rule. Figured I'd stick to something simple today."

The oceans and continents that once separated us have nothing on the distant gaze in his eyes when he looks at me.

Pressing my lips together and trying to stave off the stinging threat of tears, I take his menu. "I'll put that in for you right away."

Isaiah turns away from me, staring out the window to the sidewalk. His hair is a bit longer than it was before, which makes me think he's been home from his deployment for a while. And he's dressed in navy suit with a white button down, a far departure from the fitted ripped jeans and v-neck t-shirts I only ever knew him to wear before.

"You okay?" Rachael asks when she bumps into me back at the kitchen window.

I hang his order on the line and turn to face her, squeezing my eyes tight until the burn subsides. "He looked right through me, Rach. Like he didn't recognize me. Why would he come all the way here and pretend like we're strangers? What's he doing?"

Her nose wrinkles and her gaze skirts over my shoulder

and lands on him. "That's ... really weird. Did you say anything to him?"

Shaking my head, I say, "What am I supposed to say? 'Hey ... do you remember me? We slept together earlier this year...'"

"You'll think of the right thing to say. You're just in shock right now." She smooths her hand along my arm and offers a sympathetic head tilt before heading out to the floor.

Grabbing a full coffee carafe from a burner, I return to Isaiah's table and flip over his empty coffee cup.

"Room for two creams, half sugar?" I ask, hating that I remember the way he takes his coffee.

His brows narrow as he gazes up at me. "Lucky guess."

Lucky guess?

"Yeah, sometimes I think I'm psychic or something," I say, not so much as attempting to hide the biting snark in my tone.

"Thanks." He pulls his coffee closer and reaches for the sugar holder by the window.

"You look good," I say. And I mean it. As much as I want to rip his hair out and smack him across his pretty boy face and tell him what an asshole he is, a part of me is glad he made it home safe and unscathed. "I like the suit. It's a nice touch."

And my mother always said, you can never go wrong when you take the high road.

His dark brows meet as he turns my direction, studying me. "Thank you."

"Your eggs should be out soon." I leave and check on my three other tables before his order comes up, and when I return with his breakfast, he's on his phone. He doesn't acknowledge me or thank me with a quick wave of his hand when I place his plate in front of him. He simply reaches for a fork.

My stomach hardens, unsettling.

So much for the closure.

If anything, I'm more confused than I was before.

I spend the next fifteen minutes fully immersed in work, even pre-bussing some of Rachael's tables so I have every reason not to stand around fixating on why he's here and why he's pretending not to know me.

When he finally flags me down and asks for his check, a blanket of anxious heat warms my body and I will myself to find the right thing to say before he walks out of here.

"Thank you," he says a minute later, when I hand him the leather check wallet. His total was thirteen dollars and fifty-eight cents and I watch as he slips a ten and a five-dollar bill inside and tells me to "keep the change."

The dollar forty-two is a far cry from the hundred-dollar tip he once left.

"Why did you come here today?" I ask, hand on one hip and head cocked.

"I beg your pardon?"

"Why did you come here today?" I state my question clear as fucking day, enunciating every last syllable.

Isaiah frowns. "Is this some kind of trick question?"

"Why did you request me?" I ask.

"I ... didn't."

Pulling in a hard breath, I massage my temples before splaying my hand across my beating heart. "This doesn't make sense."

"Are you mad about the tip?" he asks. "I usually try to tip more, but you made me wait fifteen minutes for my check and now I'm going to be late for a client meeting."

"Oh, so now we're going to pretend this is about the tip

and not about the way you're treating me?" I ask. My mouth falls and I can sense the burn of cherry heat in my ears.

"The way *I'm* treating *you*?" He scoffs, sliding out of his booth and standing. "Ma'am, I think you're confused."

Ma'am.

He's back to calling me ma'am.

"Did you hit your head or something?" I ask. "Is that what happened? I'm not being facetious, it's a legitimate question. Do you have amnesia?"

Isaiah chuckles, like I'm being cute, and then he shakes his head. "Are we done here? Because I've got someone waiting for me back at the office."

At the office?

He's been back long enough to get a job in an office that requires a suit ...

He's not fresh off the military boat. Not at all. And at this point, I'm starting to wonder if he was ever really in the army. It could've all been a ruse, maybe something he tells girls so he can get laid and have an excuse never to see them again. Or maybe he was some method actor studying for a role?

Then again, the letters came from an APO ... so that couldn't be it.

Gram always says, "It takes all kinds," but I never knew what she meant until now, when I'm standing in front of one of the worst 'kinds' I've ever had the displeasure of knowing.

"If you'll excuse me," he says, squeezing past me, his meaty hands on my shoulders. Straightening his jacket, he gives me one last look—like I'm the crazy one here—and then he turns to leave.

Gathering his dirty dishes, I take them back to the

kitchen, scolding myself for all those wasted days and sleepless nights I spent worrying about that selfish prick.

When I said I wanted closure, I didn't know it was going to feel like this, and I didn't know it was possible to mean less than nothing to someone who meant more than something to me.

31

MARITZA

THE CLOCK on my nightstand reads 2:41 AM.

I've been tossing and turning since ten o'clock, when I took a Benadryl and a melatonin and thought I could force myself into a coma-like sleep.

All I wanted was to shut my mind off for two seconds, to stop the spinning and the madness and the questions that've been playing on a loop in my head since Isaiah walked into my café yesterday morning and pretended like he'd never seen me in his life.

Sitting up and finally accepting the fact that I'm not going to get a single minute of respite tonight, I click on my lamp and reach into the drawer of my bedside table, grabbing a pen and the notebook of letters I'd written Isaiah for a brief period of time when he was supposedly out on some mission—before the radio silence.

Flipping to an empty page in the middle, I write a letter that'll never be sent, but at least if I get it all on paper and out of my head, I might be able to catch some sleep before the sun comes up.

DEAR ISAIAH,

Eight months ago, you were just a soldier about to be deployed and I was just a waitress, sneaking you a free pancake and hoping you wouldn't notice that my gaze was lingering a little too long.

But you did notice.

We spent one life-changing week together before you left, and we said goodbye on day eight, exchanging addresses at the last minute.

I saved every letter you wrote me, your words quickly becoming my religion.

But you went radio silent on me months ago, and then you had the audacity to walk into my diner yesterday and act like you'd never seen me in your life.

To think ... I almost loved you and your beautifully complicated soul.

Almost.

Whatever your reason is—I hope it's a good one.

Maritza the Waitress

PS – I hate you, and this time ... I mean it.

PULLING IN A LONG, cool breath and letting it go, I close the notebook and tuck it away in the drawer before clicking my lamp off. Lying down and pulling the covers up, I stare at a dark ceiling before closing my eyes.

My mind is barely lighter than it was before, but my thoughts seem to have quieted a bit.

In the still, small minutes before I finally drift off, I

remind myself that LA is full of people who use people, people who do unscrupulous things and who have no qualms about hurting others.

Isaiah Torres was never anything special—he was just another run-of-the-mill LA asshole.

32

MARITZA

"MORNING, HOLLIE." I tie my apron around my waist and glance at the clock to confirm that I am, in fact, on time for work. Normally I can go a whole shift without seeing her because she's usually hiding in the back, door closed and only emerging when there's an issue.

But today it's like she was waiting.

"I need to see you in my office." My manager says a sentence I've never heard her say in all of my time here. She doesn't smile.

"Everything okay?" I ask, following her to the back.

Hollie says nothing and I find myself holding my breath without even thinking about it. Every silent second is torture.

"Close the door, please, Maritza," she says once we're there. "Have a seat."

Oh, god. I'm being fired.

Grabbing a sticky note off her computer monitor, she exhales. "I got a call from a customer last night."

I glance down at my lap, realizing I've been digging my nails into my palms this entire time.

"He had a very unsatisfactory experience here yesterday," she continues. "And he said you were his server."

"Hollie, I'm so sorry and I can explain." My gaze flicks into hers.

Her brows lift. "No need. He didn't want to get into specifics."

Leaning back against the chair, I peer to the side. None of this makes sense.

"Anyway, I wanted to tell you that each and every customer who walks through our door needs to have a five-star experience," she says. "And as a server, you're one of the many faces of this restaurant. It's your job to represent Brentwood Pancake and Coffee in a way that's going to keep them coming back."

"I know. And normally I do that, but this—"

"Rachael does a fine job," she says. "So does Harry. And Pam. And Chloe."

I bite my tongue. The comparisons aren't necessary and besides, I'm the one who trained all of them.

"If anything like this so much as happens again, Maritza, I'm going to have no choice but to let you go," she says, thin lips forming a hard line. "Anyway, I don't normally do this, but he was rather persistent and I wasn't in a place to disappoint him since he'd just had a God-awful experience with us, but here."

Hollie hands me the yellow sticky note where a phone number is scribbled in blue pen alongside the name "Torres."

It's an LA area code, but the last four digits of the number are unfamiliar—he must have changed his number.

"He'd like you to call him when you get a chance," she says, head tilting as she exhales. "While you have him on the phone, I'd highly recommend a profuse apology."

I nod, not sure what he's hoping to accomplish from this phone call—or if I'll even call him for that matter.

"Now, get back out there," she says, rising from her desk and adjusting her blouse. "Let's make today a better day than yesterday."

Piece of cake.

Any day would be better than yesterday.

33

MARITZA

"JUST CALL HIM," Melrose says, watching me pace my room. "For the love of God, just get it over with. See what he wants. Do it for yourself because you know and I know that if you don't do this, you're going to spend the rest of your life wondering what he wanted. Aren't you curious?"

"Of course I'm curious. I just can't decide if this is worth it—giving him another ounce of my time or energy."

Melrose pulls her legs onto my bed before bringing her knees against her chest. "Do you want me to do it? I can pretend to be you. I can talk the way you talk ... I took an impressions class last year."

I stop pacing for a second and give her a crazy-eyed glance. "Pass."

She shrugs. "Well, the offer still stands if you change your mind."

"I'm not afraid to talk to him. It's not that I'm physically incapable of calling him. I just don't want him to know that what he did got to me, you know? I don't want to give him that satisfaction."

"So call him and be a mega bitch," she says. "I know you're usually the nicest, sweetest person who ever did live, but maybe show him your super-secret evil crazy lady side. The one that comes out a few days a month ... only worse than that."

Taking a seat on the foot of my bed, I drag my thumb along my screen and pull up the keypad. The sticky note in my left hand is crumpled from shoving it into my apron after leaving Hollie's office earlier today, but the numbers are still legible.

"Screw it. I'm calling—but only because I just want to get this over with," I say, tapping out the numbers and hitting the green button.

Sucking in a lungful of vanilla candle-scented bedroom air, I chew my bottom lip and count the rings.

One ...

Two ...

Three ...

Four ...

"He's not answering," I say, a flash of panic washing over me. I didn't even consider the fact that he might not answer, and I hate playing phone tag.

"Hello," Isaiah answers a half-ring later, proving me wrong.

"Hey, it's Maritza," I say. "You wanted me to call you?"

"Maritza the waitress from Brentwood?" he asks.

I exhale, gaze locked with my cousin. "Yep. That's me."

The line is quiet for a split second, though for some reason that second feels like forever.

"So ... what do you have to say for yourself?" I ask

because I haven't got all night. "What was that about earlier?"

"Can you meet me somewhere?" he asks. "I need to speak to you. In person."

My jaw hangs. "I don't know. I've got a lot going on these days."

"It's important," he says. "And it won't take long."

"Is there a reason you can't tell me right now? Over the phone?" I chuff.

"Yeah," Isaiah says. "This is just something I'd rather tell you face to face."

34

MARITZA

"I WOULD'VE ORDERED you a coffee, but I wasn't sure what you drink." Isaiah stands when I arrive at the Coffee Bean and Tea Leaf on San Vincente the following morning. He's dressed in a gray suit sans jacket and his hand grazes against his skinny black tie when he sits.

"I don't remember you being this ... formal." My discerning gaze scans the length of him before returning to his familiar amber eyes.

Everything about him is *off* ... from the way he dresses to the way he carries himself and even the way he looks at me, but we established that two days ago.

Taking a seat and opting not to buy a drink because I don't plan to stay long, I fold my arms across my chest and give him my full attention.

"So?" I ask. "What is this thing you just had to tell me in person, Isaiah? And I can call you that, right? Since we're done playing this we've-never-met-before-in-our-lives bullshit game of yours?"

He offers a pained smile before licking his full lips and straightening his shoulders. "That's the thing ... I'm not Isaiah."

"Ha." I shake my head, rising and slinging my bag over my shoulder. "Right, right."

He's mental.

He's completely mental.

And now he's wasted my time.

"Maritza, please. Sit down. I'm not finished." He reaches into his back pocket, retrieving a brown leather wallet and flipping it open to his driver's license.

My eyes go to his photo. "Okay. What am I looking at?"

His thumb slides next to the name.

Ian Torres.

"Isaiah's my twin brother," he says, folding his wallet and returning it to his pocket. "My *identical* twin brother."

Swallowing the hard ball in my throat, I rub my lips together, studying his face. I suppose when you've only known someone a little over a week and you don't see them for the better part of a year and you don't know they have an identical twin ... it'd be easy to make assumptions when someone bearing their likeness walks into your life.

But out of all the crazy explanations my mind's been crafting up these last few days, this one seems to be the most plausible.

And it makes sense—the way he carries himself, the way he's dressed.

Nothing about the man sitting in front of me is familiar besides his golden stare and chiseled features.

"He never told me he had a brother," I manage to say.

Ian smirks, rapping his knuckles against the table top.

"Yeah, well, we don't exactly speak to each other these days. He likes to pretend I'm dead."

I can't stop staring as I let this sink in.

"After I went back to work the other day, I got to thinking about the way you were talking to me, like I was familiar to you, and then it dawned on me," he says. "You thought I was my brother."

"I'm sorry. I truly am."

He waves his hand. "Look, I've been cleaning up after his messes my whole life. This is nothing new. I just wanted to sit you down and tell you this in person. I just started a job in Brentwood at Cottage Financial Group so on the off-chance we bump into each other around town, I figured I should clear this up."

"Thank you, Ian. I appreciate you taking the time to do this."

Ian shrugs. "My brother, uh ... he's got some demons. Let me just put it that way."

"Demons?"

"He's not a good person, Maritza. I'm sorry you got mixed up with him."

"I didn't get mixed up with him. We spent a week together before he left for his deployment and we exchanged some letters and then I never heard from him again," I say. It sounds so simple when I summarize it.

Ian chuckles. "Yep. Sounds like him."

"What, is this his M.O. or something? Does he do this sort of thing a lot?" I ask.

His jaw juts forward as he contemplates an answer. "Let's just say he's a creature of habit."

Great.

"Isaiah tends to write people off once he gets what he needs from them," he says. "And then he moves on. I've seen him hurt people and destroy lives and not think twice about it. It's like he doesn't have a conscience."

My gaze narrows. "That sounds nothing like the guy I met."

"I know, right? He's good at what he does. He's good at seeming normal and likable and being the good time guy everyone thinks is cool, but he's anything but," Ian says.

We linger in silence, me soaking up this new reality and Ian reaching his hand across the table to cup mine. It's a sweet gesture if not a little awkward, seeing how we literally just met two days ago.

"Did he come home?" I ask. "From Afghanistan?"

Ian exhales through his nose, studying me. "He did."

My eyes burn, but I blink them away, hating that there's an ache in my chest more intense than the one that was there before.

"Look, I can see that he hurt you," Ian says, his palm still cupping the top of my hand. "But believe me when I say this, Maritza, you're better off without him in your life."

35

MARITZA

"SO YEAH, we were lying on his couch last night watching Interstellar and his phone kept going off. I saw him silence it. A half hour later he got another text and then he started acting weird and said I should probably leave because he had a test to study for all of a sudden ..." I tell Rachael about my night with Blake as we stand outside the back entrance to the café, waiting for Hollie to unlock the door. "So I called him on it. I refused to leave until he told me why he was acting so weird and then he confessed."

"Confessed *what*?" she asks.

"That he has a girlfriend," I say. "And he's had one the whole time."

"But you two weren't dating, right? And you haven't slept together."

"Right," I say. "But I don't want to be someone's side piece and I feel like we were headed in that direction."

Hollie opens the door and we shuffle in, one of the chefs staying a few steps behind us with his nose buried in his phone.

"I just feel like he left out a crucial piece of information," I say. "So we're done hanging out. I can't trust a guy who has a girlfriend and tries to meet girls on Tinder at the same time."

"That eliminates ninety-five percent of men in LA." Rachael clocks in and shoves a pen in her apron.

We check in at the hostess stand with Maddie and get our table assignments, but halfway through the morning rush, a new patron is seated at one of my tables.

"Ian. Hi," I say, flipping my notepad to a clean page.

"Morning." He glances up at me with a honey-brown gaze that crinkles at the sides. "Think I'll try one of those pancakes today. The guys at work won't shut up about them."

It's been a little over a week since I met with him at the coffee shop and he dropped an armful of bombshells in my lap. And I have to say, as wild of a ride as that was, I finally have some semblance of closure.

Everything makes sense now and it boils down to this ugly truth: Isaiah is a womanizer who lied and used me.

Nothing else really matters.

"Good choice," I say, jotting it down. "And coffee with room for cream and sugar?"

"I forgot. You're psychic," he says with a wink and a smirk.

Everything about Ian is sweet and disarming today, and while I don't know him, we almost have this common bond, this shared secret.

Leaving to grab a coffee carafe from the back, I return to

fill up his mug, leaving a couple inches at the top. "Going to work today?"

Ian adjusts his tie. "How'd you guess?"

"Promise I won't make you late this time."

His mouth curls at one side as he makes his coffee.

"I'll be back in a bit, all right?" I ask, resting my hand on his shoulder for a brief second.

"Oh, hey," he says when I turn to leave. I stop, spinning to face him once more. "Do you maybe ... want to grab a drink sometime?"

His question comes out of nowhere and my lips part but nothing comes out until I manage to muster a quick, "Can I ... can I think about it?"

"Of course." Ian's confidence doesn't appear to be shaken in the slightest and he reaches for his coffee mug with a steady hand.

Returning to the back, I bump into Rachael hanging a ticket on the line.

"Ian just asked if I wanted to get drinks sometime," I tell her, leaning close.

"What? No, he didn't."

I nod, biting my lip.

"What'd you tell him?" she asks.

"That I'd think about it," I say.

Rach rolls her eyes. "Which means you're going to say no."

"I need a break from men," I say. "And even if I didn't, I don't need to go out with the identical twin of the guy whose face I'd really love to punch right now. It's confusing. And I don't need that in my life."

"Amen, sister." Rachael laughs before heading back out to the floor.

Peering out toward my tables, I observe Ian for a minute or so, watching him scroll through his phone before tapping out a text and then turning his attention toward the sidewalk outside, people watching.

He's so sweet and from what I can tell, genuine.

Then again, apparently I'm a horrible judge of character.

I can't pick the good ones from the bad ones to save my life.

As soon as Ian's order is up, I run it out to him, making sure to grab a warm bottle of maple syrup on my way.

"You're not going to regret this," I tell him.

"These things are like crack, I hear," he says. "Is it true you only get one?"

"Yeah," I say.

He spreads a pat of cinnamon butter across the 'cake. "Sounds like a genius marketing ploy."

"Right?"

"Anyway," he says. "I'm going out with some friends this Friday. Dos Rios. If you and your friends want to meet up for drinks, cool. If not, no big deal. Just thought I'd ask."

"Never been to Dos Rios. Is it any good?"

"It's incredible," he says. "Best margaritas in the city. You like margaritas?"

"Margaritas are my jam."

Ian chuckles. "Then you should go. If not for me, then for the margaritas. They'll change your life."

"Now that sounds like a marketing ploy." I give him a playful wink. "I'll be back in a bit."

He slices into his Brentwood pancake and I head off to check on another table, wiping the dopey grin off my face before I get there. I can't remember the last time I smiled like that, over something so silly, but Ian's so easy to talk to. He puts me at ease without even trying. He's disarming in a way that Isaiah never was.

I suppose one margarita never hurt anyone ...

36

MARITZA

MELROSE IS on her third hibiscus margarita by the time Ian and his friends show up to Dos Rios Friday night.

"Hey." Ian takes the chair next to mine at the high-top table we saved. A few of his friends, all of them suit-and-tie business types, fill in around us. His golden gaze lights when it finds mine in the dark bar. "Glad you could make it."

"Thanks for the invite," I say, the taste of flowers and tequila on my tongue.

"It's crazy how much you look like him," Melrose leans over me, pointing her finger in Ian's face.

"Right," I place my hand around her arm and guide her back to her spot, "since they're identical twins. Ian, this is Melrose, my cousin."

"You two must get mixed up all the time," she says, her elbow in front of me as her chin rests on her hand.

Ian nods. "It happens more than I like."

He looks to me.

"But it isn't always a bad thing," he adds.

Melrose's jaw falls and she nudges me, making an awkward deal out of nothing. "Can I ask you something, Ian?"

"Anything," he says as another one of his friends approaches the table and starts handing out bottles of Dos Equis like it's going out of style—two per person. These guys don't mess around, though I imagine working in finance has got to be stressful. It's so unpredictable, so volatile at times. Too many highs and lows for the average person to handle. "What do you want to know?"

"So what's the deal with your brother?" Mel asks. "Why is he such a fucking dickwad?"

I hide my eyes in my hand. Here we go. Once the filter comes off, it's impossible to put it back on.

"Can we *not* make tonight about him?" I ask.

Ian takes a sip of his beer as his gaze passes between the two of us. "I don't know why he is the way he is. I just know that the only thing we have in common is the way we look. Other than that, we're night and day in every way possible."

"Who just freaking ghosts the nicest, smartest, prettiest girl in the world?" Melrose asks, barely trying to hide the slur in her voice.

Ian looks to me, his lips curled at one side. "A fool. That's who."

My cheeks warm as I turn my attention to my margarita, twisting the stem of the glass between my fingers.

"My brother hates commitment. He's a closed book. He holds grudges longer than any bastard I know. He has a nephew he won't acknowledge. And see, the thing about my brother is that if he's not in control at all times, you'll lose him. He'll turn his back on you and not think twice," Ian says, taking a generous swig. "My family singlehandedly blames him for what happened to my father a decade ago. He's got demons."

"What happened to your father?" Melrose asks.

I elbow her in the ribs. "Mel, enough. It's none of our business."

Ian picks at the label on his bottle for a moment. "He died in an accident when we were seventeen."

My hand lifts to his. "Oh, god. I'm so sorry to hear that."

He offers an equally as apologetic smile and holds my gaze before his expression softens. "What do you say you finish that drink so I can buy you another one?"

"You really don't have to—"

His mouth pulls up at the sides and for a split second, I see Isaiah in him more than I ever have before, in the mischievous, sexy smirk that once made me fall harder than I ever anticipated.

But the man sitting in front of me is the furthest thing from the man who once wrapped his arms around me and pointed out constellations on a perfect spring evening, and it isn't fair to compare the two of them after learning what I've learned, after experiencing what I've experienced, after feeling the way I've felt.

I don't know Ian quite yet.

And as it turns out, I never really knew Isaiah.

The only thing I do know is that I'll never allow a man to make me feel half as disposable as Isaiah made me feel.

Never again.

37

ISAIAH

NERVOUS IS NOT a sensation I'm familiar with.

Scared is a feeling I've ever truly known once before, when my life literally flashed before my eyes and settled in a cloud of smoke so dark I couldn't see the screaming comrade in front of me.

But none of that compares to the way I feel right now, standing outside Maritza's café, watching her stride across the checkered floor in her little black shorts and little green apron, smiling at everyone she passes, not a care in the world.

There's something light and buoyant about her, and for a moment, like a woman who moved on from the meaningless fling she had eight months ago and found someone new to love her and treat her the way she deserves.

I wouldn't fault her for it, but sometimes life happens and impossible things get in the way of the things we want most and there isn't a damn thing we can do about it.

I've been home three weeks now.

I've stopped by the café seven times, each time only to find that it was her day off or I'd already missed her.

But today the stars aligned because here I am and there she is and there's a letter in my pocket with her name on it—a letter that survived Syrian air strikes and Army hospitals and rehabilitation centers.

Drawing in a deep breath, I head in. The bell jingles with the door and the hostess glances up from her stand with a practiced smile.

"How many in your party, sir?" she asks, pretending this isn't the eighth time she's seen me in three weeks.

"I won't be eating today. Just here to see someone."

The hostess gives me a stale smile and directs me to have a seat at the breakfast bar.

Thanking her with a nod, I make a beeline for the restroom first. I need to gather myself, splash a little water on my face—anything to keep myself from sounding like a bumbling idiot when I see her.

Vulnerability is a horrible look on me, but then again, so are these burn scars covering the left side of my torso and curling up the back of my arms.

If she'll hear me out ...

If she can see past the burns and the limp in my gait and the distant look I get in my eyes when I'm having a flashback ... then maybe we can pick up where we left off.

The men's room is empty and the scent of lemon cleaner and bleach invades my lungs. Hunched over one of the sinks, I twist the right handle and cup a handful of cool water, lifting it to my face.

A second later, I dry off with a paper towel, give myself a once over, and take five long, deep breaths.

This is about as good as it's going to get and I'm about as prepared as I'll ever be.

Yanking the door open, I step out into the hallway, only to run head first into Maritza herself. She startles, taking a step back until she's up against a wall between a USA Today newspaper rack and an antique gumball machine.

"Maritza," I say, stepping toward her.

"What are you doing here?" Her face is pinched and this isn't exactly the warm, joyous reunion I'd hoped for.

"I came to see you." Reaching for her hand, I stop when she waves my assistance away.

"Seriously, Isaiah? You think you can just ... disappear from my life for months and months without any kind of explanation and then walk back in here and act like you did nothing wrong?" Her hands lift to the sides of her forehead as she rants. "Do you have any idea how worried sick I was for you? How many nights I spent checking casualty reports and death records because I was certain the only reason you'd stop talking to me was because something bad happened—"

I smirk, cutting her off. "—Maritza."

"—No. Let me finish," she says. "I've waited a long time to be able to say these things to you, and you're going to stand here and let me say them. Do you understand?"

My arms fold. She's so fucking adorable when she's angry. "Sure."

"I don't know how you can just stand there being all flippant after what you did to me," she says. "But you know what? I'm done being angry. I'm just annoyed. And I'm not even annoyed at you. I'm annoyed at myself for being dumb enough to think that the time we spent together meant anything. Looking back, it was all so silly, wasn't it? The stupid wax museum. The observatory. The farmer's market.

I assigned all this meaning to everything because I guess, somewhere deep inside, I wanted it to mean something because underneath it all, I was starting to fall for you."

"Maritza ..." I lift a hand, hoping she'll let me get a word in.

"I'm not done yet."

"All right." I anchor my feet to the ground, arms still crossed as I give her my attention. Maybe in a moment, she'll give me a chance to explain why I couldn't get a hold of her, maybe she'll give me a chance to tell her that I thought of her every minute of every hour of every day while I was fighting for my life, lying comatose in a hospital for weeks and waking up with a nurse telling me the doctors were trying to figure out a way to save my leg.

"You know, I'm glad this happened," she says, dragging her hands through her hair as her lips pull into an incredulous grin. "Because if anything, I learned that there are kinder, better, nicer people out there than you and you're not the person I thought you were. You saved me from ... you. So thank you. Thank you so much, Isaiah."

She turns to leave, but I hook my hand around her elbow, reeling her back to me.

"I can explain," I say. "I can explain everything."

"Yeah, well, I accepted a long time ago that I was never going to have your explanation and now that you're offering it to me, I don't want it." Her words slice through the tight space between us. "Whatever reason it was that you stopped talking to me ... it's inconsequential now. I've moved on."

"I get that you're angry," I say. "But I think you've made some assumptions ..."

"Assumptions?" Her dark eyes widen and her brows arch. "You're right, Isaiah. I did. I assumed you were a good person. I assumed we were on the same page with the no lies and bullshit rule. And I assumed we had something special—or at the very least a friendship."

"No," I say, lifting my hand, but she continues to talk.

"You've been home a while, haven't you?" she asks.

"A few weeks, yes," I say.

"Tell me," she says, squaring her shoulders with mine. "Is it true you have a nephew you don't acknowledge?"

My eyes narrow. How the fuck would she know that?

"And is it true you've ruined peoples' lives, Isaiah?" she asks. "Is it true you ... is it true your family blames you for your father's death?"

Dragging my hand down my face, I look her dead in the eyes. "Yeah. It's true. All of it."

Maritza exhales, her glassy coffee-colored eyes settling in mine. "You should go. And please don't come back here again. You're not the person I thought you were, and I don't want to be with you. I don't want to pick up where we left off. Not now. Not ever."

With that, she pushes past me and disappears behind the swinging door to the ladies' room.

A blue-eyed blonde donning a matching uniform rounds the corner, stopping in her tracks when she sees me.

"Oh. Hi," she says, looking at me like I'm a bomb that needs to be defused. "Have you seen Maritza?"

I point to the ladies' room.

"Right," she says, offering a tepid smile. The waitress makes her way past me before stopping and turning back. "You should probably leave."

"I know."

"And you should probably never come back here again."

Dragging my hand along my mouth, I linger.

A second later, I remember the letter, and I dig into my pocket to retrieve it.

"Give this to her," I say, handing it off to the blonde.

I don't wait for her to respond or refuse it.

I get the hell out of there.

I don't want to upset Maritza any more than I already have.

It hurts like hell to see how much pain I caused her, and not just because I care about her but because she wouldn't be so hurt if she hadn't cared so much about me.

Our feelings? They were mutual at one point.

But evidently not anymore.

Not now. Now ever.

38

MARITZA

"HEY. YOU OKAY IN HERE?" Rachael pushes past the restroom door and stands next to me in front of the mirror.

"Yeah. I'm fine." I force a smile. The swell of tears in my eyes subsided about a minute ago, the second I removed myself from his presence.

I didn't know seeing him again was going to get to me like that. When I first saw him, for a half of a second, I thought it was Ian, but then I saw the faded t-shirt and the shorter hair and the weighted look in his eyes, and I knew.

"Is he still out there?" I ask.

Rachael rubs circles into my back like the devout mother-figure that she is and sighs. "Nope. I told him to get lost. And I told him never to come back here again."

I chuckle at the idea of five-foot-two Rachael giving strapping Isaiah the what for.

"But before he left, he asked me to give you this." Rach

digs into her apron and retrieves a folded, faded piece of paper and hands it over.

"I don't want it," I say, taking a step back.

"Ritz..."

"No, seriously. I'm done." I shake my head, staring at a water-stained tile on the ceiling. "I don't know why he thinks a letter is going to change anything. It's not going to change the fact that he let me go first, Rach. He let me go first."

"I'll hold onto it for you." She offers a tepid smile. "In case you change your mind."

"We should probably head out there before we get fired," I say. "How's my mascara?"

"You pass the raccoon eyes test."

I glance at my face in the mirror. My rosy cheeks and glassy eyes are a dead giveaway that I temporarily lost my cool, but a couple of deep breaths later, I'm somewhat more presentable.

Stepping out into the hallway where Isaiah stood just minutes ago, I round the corner and watch out the window as he climbs into his vintage Porsche outside the café.

A second later, he's gone.

Gone from my life just as quickly as he came into it.

39

ISAIAH

"HEY, MA. BROUGHT YOU SOME LUNCH," I call out as I walk through her door. The doctors put her on this new medication while I was gone and she's been less sleepy lately, spending most of her time in the living room and taking the occasional five or ten-minute walk around the apartment complex when she's feeling up to it. "Got you the clams casino from Bertocelli's."

It's a step in the right direction, that's for damn sure.

"Isaiah," Mom says. "We have company!"

Placing the brown paper bag on her kitchen counter, I drop my keys beside it and turn to face her, only to find my brother, Ian, relaxing on her sofa.

"Corporal." Ian rises, coming at me with his right hand extended, and I glance at my mother to find her all smiles, as if she expects that we've suddenly made up after all these years. I shake his hand with terse hesitation, but he pulls me into a hug. "Been a long time. You're looking good. Glad you made it home safe."

Bullshit.

All of it.

Ian's the phoniest fucking bastard I've ever known, and I know him better than anyone.

"Come on. Have a seat. We should catch up," Ian says, waving me toward the living room. "Was just telling Mom about this girl I've been talking to."

Mom turns to me, her dark eyes lit. "She sounds perfect, Isaiah. Ian, tell your brother what you just told me."

Ian wears a shit-eating grin to go with his shit-brown belt and his shit-brown shoes and takes a seat in the center of the sofa beside our mother, taking her hands in his.

"Well, she's sweet and funny and kind," he says. "And she's got the prettiest eyes I've ever seen."

"What did you say her name was again?" Ma asks.

"Maritza," Ian says, directing his gaze to me as he answers. "Maritza Claiborne."

I'm going to fucking *murder* him.

And now it makes sense ... all those things she knew at the restaurant, she learned from him, and I'm two-hundred percent sure he painted me in the worst possible light because that's what Ian does.

It's what he's always done.

We were never close.

We were never brothers.

We were always competitors—at least in his eyes.

Everything I ever had, everything I ever worked my ass off for, Ian wanted.

Everything.

My fists clench at my sides and my jaw tightens. Ian is rambling on and on about how wonderful she is and my mother is lapping it up like a kitten to milk, telling him how she can't wait to meet her and how she's so happy he's finally met someone special.

"I'm going to introduce her to Benson soon," he says, referring to his son—the son that was almost mine until my girlfriend—*ex*-girlfriend—dropped the ultimate bombshell on me at the last minute.

"You know my birthday is in a couple of weeks," Ma says, clapping her hands together. "Calista wants to throw a barbecue at some park by her house. You should bring her then!"

"That's the plan, Ma," Ian says, the smug bastard's gaze careening into mine.

"Excuse me, boys. I'll be right back." Ma pushes herself up from her chair and makes her way to the bathroom down the hall.

"I'm going to fucking *kill* you," I say under my breath.

Ian stands, adjusting his tie. He looks like a goddamn buffoon. Or a kid playing dress up in his father's clothes. He's nothing more than a snake oil salesman trying to project an image of success, but I see through it.

I've always seen through everything he's done over the years, like it's some skill I've honed and practiced and fine-tuned.

"Okay, so if you killed me ... how many would that be? What's your running total?" he asks.

"Fuck you."

"What does it feel like to kill people you don't even know? I've always wanted to know," he says. "Do you ever feel bad about it? Do you ever feel like, hey, maybe I shouldn't fight this war I have no business fighting and maybe I shouldn't kill people if I don't have the decency to fucking look them in the eyes when I do it."

"Go to hell." My shoulders rise and fall with each hard breath and I clench my fist to keep from strangling the jackass. "You're lucky Mom's in the next room."

I step closer to him, until our faces are mere inches apart.

"What exactly are you doing?" I ask. "With Maritza? What's your plan here?"

"I like her."

"Bullshit." I shake my head, hands hooked on my hips.

"I'm being the better man. Being the man you could never be," he says. "She had no idea what a piece of shit you were until I told her."

"The fuck did you tell her?" I spit my words at him.

"Nothing that isn't true." Ian tosses his hands in the air and wears a sneer that every part of me is seconds from ripping off his face.

Pulling in a hard breath, I try to calm myself down before I do something stupid.

But it doesn't work.

And within an instant, I've got his shirt collar and tie bunched in my right fist and his back is slammed against the living room wall. His face is turning red and he's struggling to say something, his eyes wide and fearful.

I've done some things in my life that I'm not proud of, but I'm a fucking saint compared to Ian ...

"Stop seeing her," I say, letting him go and watching him slink down the wall like the pathetic slug he is.

"Or what?" he asks.

"Boys, what's going on?" Ma's voice disrupts this shit show and Ian adjusts his tie. "Please tell me you two aren't fighting. You haven't seen each other in so long and then I walk out for a few minutes and—"

"It's fine, Ma," Ian says, offering a reassuring, fake-as-hell smile. "We're good now, but I should get going. I'm taking Maritza out to dinner tonight."

His eyes settle on mine, a silent "fuck you," and then he's gone.

If he so much as thinks about hurting her, he's a dead man.

40

MARITZA

PRESSING 'SAVE' on my Word file, I close out of my research paper and email it to my professor. Heading out to the kitchen, I grab a drink of water and check the time. I'm supposed to get dinner with Ian tonight, who's surprisingly becoming a good friend.

He's an amazing listener, extremely sympathetic for being a guy, and gives the best advice.

And he's normal.

Just a nice, normal guy.

No gimmicks, no shtick, just a what-you-see-is-what-you-get kind of person.

Grabbing a bottled water from the fridge, I unscrew the cap and lift it to my lips, only to spill it down my shirt the second someone knocks on my door. It wouldn't be Mel or Gram because they both have the code to the lock, and I'm not expecting company and even if I were, I never have people ring the buzzer at the gate because I don't want to bother Gram so I usually have them text me when they're here.

Dabbing the wet splotches of my shirt with a dish towel, I get as much as I can before tiptoeing across the guesthouse toward the front entrance. Peering through the peephole, I squint until the face comes into focus.

Myles.

Exhaling, I debate pretending not to be home but quickly decide I'm a grown ass woman who doesn't need to hide from anyone ... and also my car is parked out front.

"Myles, hey," I say when I get the door. "Come on in."

"Hey." There's a sadness in his eyes that wasn't there before, like a wistful longing when he looks at me.

"What's up?" I slide my hands down my back pockets and linger in the doorway next to him.

"Was just visiting with my grandmother," he says. "Thought I'd stop over and say hi. Haven't seen you in a while ..."

"Yeah. I'm sorry. I've been swamped lately with school and work and everything," I say. "How've you been?"

"Good," he says. "Was actually going to see if you wanted to go to the Art Con Awards with me next month. As my date." He flashes a nervous grin that disappears in seconds. "You know, as friends."

"Myles ..." I drag in a heavy breath, tilting my head. "I don't think that's a good idea. I'm so sorry."

He wrings his hands before shoving his thick glasses up his nose. "I tried calling you a while back. You change your number or something?"

"I did. Some psycho kept calling me from a blocked number," I say.

His gaze immediately falls to the floor and his lips press flat. "I see."

Oh my God.

It was probably Myles.

The buzzing of my phone in my pocket sends a quick startle to my heart, and I waste no time redirecting my attention.

It's Ian.

"I'm sorry," I say, pointing to my phone. "I have to take this. Good seeing you though. Congrats on the script option."

I get the door, giving him no time to protest or linger, and he leaves without making things more awkward than they already were. Next time I talk to Gram, I'll have to tell her my suspicions. Maybe then she'll finally stop wishing and hoping and praying there's a chance.

"Ian, what's up?" I answer.

"Hey, I'm so sorry," he says, the sound of traffic fills the background. He must be driving. "I'm going to have to cancel dinner. My mom had a fall this afternoon and she's in the hospital. I'm on my way to see her right now."

"Oh my God. Is she okay?"

He hesitates. "I don't know. Doctors are trying to figure out why she fell. She said she blacked out, but that's all we really know right now."

Ian's voice breaks a little and the seriousness in his tone breaks my heart. Just last week he was going on and on about how amazing his mother is and all the things she did for him and his siblings before she got sick.

"I want to be there for you," I say. "Which hospital is she at?"

"Maritza, you don't have to do that."

"Ian, we're friends. That's what friends do. Let me be there for you. If there's anything your family needs, I'll be the gopher. If anyone needs a babysitter or someone to entertain the kids or something, I can be that person."

He hesitates at first and for a moment I wonder if I've overstepped some boundary I never knew was there, like when I sent Isaiah the giant care package.

"You're incredible," he says. "That would be amazing. Thank you. She's at Good Samaritan on Wilshire."

"Perfect. I'll be there as soon as I can."

41

ISAIAH

CALISTA CHECKS her phone before shoving it in her pocket. "Ian's on his way."

Reaching for Mom's hand, I shrug. "So? I'm not leaving."

She lifts her hands. "Wasn't saying you should. Just thought you'd want to know. He's in the building. Just texted me for Mom's room number, so he'll be here any second."

Mom is sound asleep in her hospital bed at Good Samaritan, monitors beeping as the scent of bleached bedding and antibacterial soap fills the air around us. In the corner, my other sisters, Layla and Raya, talk amongst themselves. My older brother, Marco, is down the hall chatting up one of the nurses, though he claimed he was just going to get an update.

Guess the gang's all here.

"When are you two going to bury the hatchet?" Calista asks. "Hasn't it been long enough?"

I shoot her a look.

Forever would never be long enough.

"Hey," Calista says a minute later, peering across the room where the man of the fucking hour stands in the doorway, looking like he's about to shed a tear or something.

I don't buy it.

If he truly cared about our mother, he would've taken care of her when I was gone instead of running around knocking up other people's girlfriends.

"Hey, Cal." Ian strides across the room, ignoring me as he heads toward Calista and gives her a side hug. "How's she doing?"

"She's stable," Calista says. "Just resting right now. They're waiting on some labs. Thinking maybe her meds interacted or something, but we won't know for sure until we get the results."

Ian greets the other girls next, heading across the room and leaning against the wall, arms crossed and making small talk.

It's funny how years ago we were all on the same page about Ian and his penchant for lying and cheating and scamming and generally only looking out for his own interests, but I go away for years on end and suddenly it's like he's taken my place and everyone loves him again. And it's not that I'm jealous—this isn't a fucking competition—I just hate that some of us seem to have forgotten what a vile human being he is.

Ian won't stop checking his phone and after a minute, I watch as he types out a quick message and shoves it back into his pocket before returning to his conversation.

"She's going to be okay, Isaiah," Calista says, voice low.

"I know."

"You've been here since 6 AM," she says, "and you haven't left her side once. Go. Get something to eat. Grab a coffee. Stretch your legs. Just do ... something."

"I'm good."

Calista marches around Mom's hospital bed, arms folded. "I'm serious. Go for a walk. It's better than sitting here stewing, which is exactly what you're doing."

"I'm not stewing." My nose wrinkles.

She rolls her eyes before grabbing the sleeve of my t-shirt and yanking me into a standing position.

Exhaling, I straighten my shirt, smooth out the wrinkles, and squeeze between my obnoxious older sister and the wall beside Ma's bed. Ian, Raya, and Layla watch as I leave, and I walk with purpose, like I have somewhere to go, when I don't know what the hell I'm going to do.

I'm not hungry.

I don't want a coffee.

I don't want to go walking around a germ-y hospital.

It's cold as hell outside.

Passing the nurses' station, I spot my older brother flirting with a copper-haired, freckle-faced girl-next-door type in lavender scrubs, and he's so far gone he doesn't notice me.

Rounding the next corner, I stop mid-trek when I nearly bump into a familiar face.

"Oh. Hi." Maritza brushes a strand of dark hair from her eyes, tucking it behind her left ear. "I'm just ... I came here to support Ian."

"Obviously."

Her expression softens and she's a little less bent out of shape than she was yesterday morning at the café, and I take this opportunity to share a few things on the off-chance she might be more receptive this time around.

"You know, I came home a few weeks ago," I said. "Tried to call you, but your number was disconnected. Tried stopping by the café, but you were never there. I couldn't remember your address because I'd kept it in this book in my tent and we lost it in one of the airstrikes, and to be honest, ever since the coma, parts of my memory are a little foggy sometimes. Couldn't even remember how to get to your place when I came back."

Her dark eyes point toward the ground and she pulls in a breath of purified hospital air.

"But the one thing I didn't forget was you, Maritza," I say. "I never stopped thinking about you for two seconds. I don't know what he told you, but I can—"

"Maritza." Ian's voice over my shoulder brings my commentary to a screeching halt. "Everything okay over here? Just came to find you. Wasn't sure if you got lost."

Her gaze lifts, traveling between us, and she nods. "Yeah. It's fine."

"No, everything is not fine." My voice is a harsh growl and my jaw tightens. "Go back to Mom's room. Go back to pretending like you're some stand-up guy."

"Isaiah." Maritza's voice is somewhat scolding, like she thinks I'm being hard on him, but if she only knew ...

"You can't date him, Maritza," I say. "Date *anyone* else. Just not him."

"You can't tell her who to fucking date," Ian says, trying to step between us. I place my hand on his chest and shove him out of the way, keeping my eyes trained on her.

"What makes you think we're together?" Her arms fold across her chest and her gaze narrows.

Chuffing, I say, "Because that's what he said ..."

"Ian, is that true?" Maritza peers over my shoulder to where my brother stands. "Did you say we were seeing each other?"

I answer for him. "Yeah. He was telling our mom all about you, how he was going to introduce you to the family soon and all this other shit."

"I never once said we were *dating*," Ian says, the embarrassment in his tone obvious, but that's what he gets for lying.

"But you sure as hell made it sound that way." I talk to my brother but I'm looking at her. "See, Maritza? He's a liar, a master manipulator. You can't date him."

"*I'm not*." Her pretty face is red and twisted and she glares at both of us with the same disdain. "I'm not dating Ian. We're just friends."

"Good. You deserve better than that jackass," I say.

"What, like you're any better?" Ian chuckles.

Turning to face him, I rush him against the wall and gather his shirt in my hands, giving him a good, hard shove until that stupid fucking smile of his disappears.

"Whoa, whoa, whoa." A hand on my back gathers a fistful of my shirt and yanks me away.

Calista.

"The hell are you two doing out here? Having a pissing match? In the middle of a hospital? Are you both *insane*?" Our sister splays her hand on Ian's chest, keeping him from making any sudden moves as he stands there seething.

He's lucky I didn't bash his fucking head in.

"I'm sorry, it was a bad idea coming here. I'm going to go." Maritza turns to leave before anyone has a chance to stop her.

"Is that the girl you like, Isaiah?" Calista asks. "The concert girl? How does she know Ian?"

Maritza turns for a split second, as if she heard my sister, but then she's gone.

As much as I hate the fact that I didn't get to say my piece and explain everything the way I wanted to, at least she got to see firsthand what a Svengali my brother is. If I can keep her from so much as thinking about dating him ... I've secured a small victory.

But the war is far from over and I'm hardly done fighting.

I won't stop fighting until I win her back.

42

MARITZA

"THANKS FOR MEETING ME TODAY," I say when Ian arrives at the Coffee Bean on San Vincente. I feel like it's only fitting that we have this conversation here, where we first "officially" met. "How's your mother? Is she okay?"

He takes a seat. "Yeah. She's going home today. They think there was some kind of mix-up with her meds, so they're getting that straightened out and she should be good to go."

My hand covers my chest. "So glad to hear that."

"And before you say anything," Ian says, "let me just apologize for yesterday. For Isaiah. You shouldn't have been put in the middle of that, and I hate that he made you feel uncomfortable."

"You don't need to apologize for your brother," I say, noting the way he wasted no time placing all of the blame on Isaiah.

"Sorry." His full lips twist into a smile. "Old habit."

"But I wanted to talk to you about what he said ... about you telling your mom about me and wanting to introduce me to your family ..."

He sits up straight, eyes locked on mine.

"I thought I made it clear that I didn't want to date you," I say. "And you said you only saw me as a friend."

Dragging his hang along his smooth jaw, he flashes a disarming smirk. "Yeah, I guess ... I guess my feelings changed, Maritza. And I got a little ahead of myself."

"Why'd you give him the impression we were dating?"

He shrugs. "I don't know why he interpreted it that way."

I'm beginning to see through him, little by little, piece by piece. There are all these little nuances in the way he talks, the word choices he uses. It's crazy that I didn't see these things before, but I can't stop seeing them now.

"Anyway, I wanted to meet up today because I was thinking," I begin, "and after what happened yesterday, I don't think it's a good idea that we continue our friendship."

Ian's expression falls, his gaze shaded in disbelief. "You can't *break up* with a friend, Maritza. Who does that?"

"It's not a break-up. I just don't want to cause any more rifts between you and your brother, and I don't want to give you the wrong impression about my intentions," I say. "For now, I think it'd be in everyone's best interest if we all just went our own ways."

His chiseled jaw unclenches and he clears his throat before scanning the room. He doesn't have to say anything for me to see his ego in real time.

We linger a bit, neither of us saying anything. I've already said my part, but apparently I've left Ian speechless.

My phone vibrates in my bag and I reach down to silence it, catching Rachael's name flashing across the screen. I told her I was coming here today to have this talk with Ian, so she's probably just checking to see how it went. I'll call her back when I leave.

"You okay?" I ask, brows lifted. "You're so quiet over there."

"You're still in love with Isaiah, aren't you? That's what this is about. He came home, you saw him, and you—"

I laugh. "Don't be ridiculous. This has nothing to do with him. And I was never in love with him."

Ian rolls his eyes before checking his watch. "All right. Well, you're not that fucking special anyway."

"Ian." I half-chuckle because I can't tell if he's joking.

He rises, straightening his red silk tie. "You're just a waitress with nice tits."

"*Excuse* me?"

"You heard me." His honey eyes scan the length of me and his full mouth twists at one side, as if he's suddenly judging me.

"Evidently, Isaiah was right about you," I say.

Ian scoffs. "Believe what you want to believe, Maritza. At the end of the day, I know the truth about the kind of person he is, and honestly, you two deserve each other."

His chair screeches across the tile floor, and just like that he's pushing past a handful of teenage girls with iced coffees in their manicured hands.

Way to make an exit, jackass.

Good riddance ...

My phone buzzes one more time and I glance down to see Rachael's calling again. Sliding my thumb across the screen, I lift it to my ear and answer.

"Rach, what's up? He just left," I say. "And let me tell you, he *reallllly* doesn't like being rejected. Holy shit. You should've seen hi—"

"—Cooper has a fever of a hundred and four and he's saying his ear hurts," she cuts me off. "I'm so sorry. I hate to ask you this, but I can't get a hold of my mom or the sitter. Would you mind staying with the other two while I run him to urgent care?"

Rising and gathering my things, I say, "No, of course not. I'm on my way."

"Thanks, sweets. I swear this is his third ear infection in three months." Rachael sighs, and my heart goes out to her. I have no idea what single motherhood is like and I imagine it's the hardest thing in the world, but she always handles it like a trooper.

"Don't stress, okay? I'm leaving now."

43

ISAIAH

"WHAT'S IN THERE?" A wide-eyed, blonde-haired, lanky-armed spawn of Rachael peers into the small cardboard box I brought over.

"Stuff," I say.

"What are you going to do with that stuff?" she asks.

"Things."

"What kind of things?" she asks.

"Caitlyn," Rachael says, striding into the room in a sweatshirt and leggings and guiding her daughter away. "I'm sorry. She asks a million questions and she doesn't know when to stop."

"It's fine." I'm seated on a worn-down sofa covered in flowers in the cozy living room of Maritza's co-worker's bungalow.

It's surreal being here and I have no idea if I'm going to make the world's biggest fool of myself or walk away with the ultimate victory, but I have to try.

I owe it to myself. And to her. To Us.

"Thanks again for doing this for me," I tell her, slicking my hands together.

"Of course." She waves her hand. "She's going to kill me for lying to her, but I think—I hope—everything's going to work out for you guys."

Earlier this morning, I stopped into the restaurant hoping to catch Rachael. All I wanted to know was if she gave Maritza the letter because I couldn't comprehend why she'd still be so distant and upset with me if she knew the truth.

But when Rachael told me Maritza refused to read it, she unexpectedly softened the blow by offering to help in any way she could.

"She's a stubborn old mule sometimes," Rachael says. "Usually she's this happy-go-lucky girl flitting around with a smile on her face but once she digs her heels into the ground, there's rarely any moving them."

"You think she's going to be pissed when she shows up?" I ask with a slight chuckle, imagining how fucking cute she looks when she's angry, her pretty face all pinched and her delicate hands resting on her hips.

"I mean, I don't think she's going to be running into your arms in slow motion, if that's what you're wondering." Rachael rolls her eyes. "But all we need is for her to come on and hear you out. Cooper's prepared to lock the door if I say the magic word and Calla's going to hide her car keys if it comes to that."

Shaking my head, I smirk. I know she's just trying to lighten the mood and take the edge off a bit, but all I keep thinking about is the way she looked at me the other morning at the restaurant and the way that everything I said at the hospital seemed to go in one ear and out the other, like she wasn't even listening.

If she doesn't want to hear me out, if she's so convinced I quit talking to her on purpose, then I can't change that.

But it won't stop me from trying.

"Mom, she's here!" Rachael's son shouts from the front window.

"Okay, okay. I heard you. Now take your sisters and go back to your room for a bit," she says, brushing her fingers through his wavy blond hair. "And only come out if you hear me shout the magic word."

Cooper nods and takes his sisters by their little hands, leading them down a hallway. It's only now, in the stifling quiet, that I realize my heart's beating like a kick drum in my chest and my palms are sweating up a storm.

I've never been so fucking nervous in my life, but I swallow it down. I stuff it down where I can't see it or feel it or hear it anymore, because I have to get her back. I have to prove to her that I care about her more than I've ever cared about anyone in my life, and I can't do that if I'm a bumbling mess bracing myself for the worst.

The doorbell chimes and Rachael strides across the room. Maritza's shadow moves on the other side of the opaque glass door.

"Don't hate me," Rachael says when she answers.

"Where's Coop?" Maritza asks, stepping in. "And why would I hate you? You had an emergency."

Her eyes scan the empty house until they land on me and her smile fades like it was never there at all.

"What is this ...?" she asks, pointing to me. "Why is he here?"

"You two need to talk," Rachael says, placing her hand

on the small of Maritza's back and all but shoving her toward me. "I think you should hear him out, Ritz."

She stands before me, eyes searching mine and feet frozen. Her lips part, as if she's about to say something, but then she stops.

Rachael glances at the two of us before drawing in a deep breath. "All right. I'll be out back with the kids if you need me for any reason, babe."

As soon as we're alone, Maritza folds her arms across her chest, eyes narrowing, and I pat the seat beside me on the sofa.

"I'm fine standing, but thank you," she says.

I roll my eyes, patting the seat a little harder. She still won't budge.

"Fine," I say. "Suit yourself."

"So?" she asks, eyes traveling to the cardboard box beside me. "What did you need to say so badly that you had to involve my best friend and force her to lie to me?"

I lift a palm. "Nobody forced anybody to do anything. This was all her idea, actually. Having you come here."

She lifts her brows, fighting a smirk. "Fair enough. I can believe that."

Placing the box in my lap, I reach in and retrieve the first item: a photo from earlier this year from Madame Tussaud's, where she's standing next to Miley Cyrus' wax likeness, her tongue sticking out of the side of her mouth.

"Why did you print this?" she asks, examining the singed edges.

"I took it with me over there."

"You had this printed before you left?" she asks.

"CVS one-hour photo."

"Why's it burnt?"

"It was on my right side, resting in an interior pocket,

when the first explosion happened," I say. "Fire and shrapnel mostly hit my left side. I'm convinced you were my lucky charm that day."

Her mouth turns up at one side, though every other part of her is still trying to pretend she's still angry with me; her intense stare, her rigid posture and crossed arms.

"I kept it with me from hospital to hospital while I recovered." I drink her in, studying the way her features soften, like she doesn't want to hate me anymore. "Made all the nurses hang it up in my room each time they moved me."

Maritza steps closer, finally taking a seat next to me. Drawing in a long breath, she rests her eyes in mine.

"I had no idea you were hurt." Her voice is softer now.

Lips pressed flat, I reach for the top button of my shirt and begin to unfasten it, then the next and the next. When I'm finished, I pull the left side down my arm and show her the burned, scarred mess of skin that trails all along my left side and stops at the base of my shoulder.

"Does it hurt?" she asks.

I nod. "It hurt like hell at first. They had me in a coma for a couple of weeks after it first happened. When I woke up, I was in so much pain I'd pray every night for God to just let me die, but I think it was the drugs talking. Doctors said had the burns traveled to the other half of my torso, I wouldn't be here today."

I don't even touch on the fact that I almost lost a leg from the hip down. That'll be a story for another day.

Her chest rises and falls slowly and she studies the marks that cover my flesh.

"I wanted to talk to you. I wanted to write you letters," I say. "I lost your address. I didn't have your number memorized. There was no way for me to reach you, Maritza, and the idea of you thinking I'd written you off fucking killed me."

Maritza's eyes flick to the floor, focusing on the hardwood beneath our feet. "There were so many times I had this feeling ... this gut feeling that something happened to you and that that was why I hadn't heard from you. I believed that for so long. And then when I met your brother, he said you weren't hurt and that you'd been home for a while."

"Of course he did. That's what he does—he lies."

She shakes her head. "I'm so sorry. If you had any idea what a rollercoaster these last six months have been for me ... all the nights I stayed up worrying about you, wondering where you went and what happened ..."

I slip my shirt back over my arm before taking her hands between mine. "I can only imagine. And I hate that I put you through that."

"When I got back, Ma had left the guest room exactly the way it was when I'd left," I tell her, "and I found these sitting on the nightstand."

Reaching into the box, I retrieve a couple of small items.

"The receipt from our sushi lunch where I accidentally Back-to-the-Future'd your future children," I say. She chuckles, taking the thin slip of paper from my hands. "And the ticket stub from the tar pits, where I kissed you in front of a woolly mammoth."

"Why'd you hold on to these?" she asks.

Shrugging, I say, "I don't know. Believe me, I'm not a sentimental guy. I don't hold onto anything. But I guess I wasn't quite ready to throw them away."

"That's kind of ... romantic," she says, head tilted as her lips lift in one corner.

"I don't know about romantic," I say, reaching for the bouquet of blue hydrangeas I'd picked up on the way here.

"Blue hydrangeas?" she asks, bringing the flowers under her nose. "I can't believe you remembered."

I smirk. "There's this little flower shop over by Ma's place. And every time I passed it these last few weeks, I saw hydrangeas in the window. They were usually white or pink or purple, but today they were blue. And this girl I know once told me to always stop for blue hydrangeas."

Maritza's perfect teeth drag along her lower lip and her eyes are lit, glassy almost, but the smile forming on her face tells me this is a good thing.

"I never stopped thinking about you, Maritza," I say. "Not once. And I didn't realize what that meant until it was too late to tell you."

"I'm sorry I wouldn't listen to you," she says, exhaling. "Your brother was just so convincing ... and I'd been trying for months to make sense of everything and then he came along and filled in the missing blanks and I was so sure I had it all figured out, I was so sure you were this horrible person who went around hurting people and not thinking twice."

Skimming my palm along my jaw, I blow a hard breath between my lips. "Yeah, well. I'm not perfect, Maritza. I've done some things I'm not proud of. I've taken the low road way more than I probably should have, but there's something about finding the girl of your dreams and then watching your life flash before your eyes that does something to a man."

"The girl of your dreams?" She laughs.

"It's cliché, I know." And it's not really a phrase that's ever been in my vocabulary until I met her. "I don't know how else to describe you other than you're everything I never knew I wanted, everything I never knew was possible to have."

Reaching into the box, I retrieve the burnt letter Rachael had given back to me after Maritza refused to read it.

"Here," I say.

Our eyes catch and she hesitates before taking the folded paper from my hands and gazing over the faded, smudged ink.

Dear Maritza,

I almost died today.

And I don't say that because I want your sympathy or I want you to worry about me. I say it because in those deafening seconds when I thought it was the end for me, I found myself thinking about one person and one person only.

You.

Something happens to a man when he's on the brink of death, and truth be told, it's as cliché as it is profound. You look back on your life, namely your regrets, and you realize you only had one shot—and either you made the most of it or you didn't.

It's that simple.

I haven't even touched thirty and sure I've served my country, but what else have I done? Pissed away the best years of my life on women and beer? Walking around with a chip on my shoulder because my life didn't go the way I thought it would?

Like I said, I almost died today. And in a way, I did die because I'm not the man I once was.

For the first time in my life, I've realized what I truly want and that's meaning. I want a girl to miss and a girl that misses me. I want the corny letters and care packages. I want to come home and wrap my arms around you, swinging you around in a gymnasium around all the other guys reuniting with their family. I want to get to know you. I want to make you smile and do ridiculous things together. I want to push your limits and I want you to push mine. I want to get in fights with you and I want to have crazy makeup sex when they're over.

There are so many more constellations I want to show you, Maritza.

Just months ago, I lost myself in your smile and I found myself in your kiss. You were the one. I was just too afraid to say it. If only I'd told you sooner, maybe you'd be mine right now.

I guess what I'm trying to say is ... wait for me.

Yours,

Isaiah

P.S. I could never hate you.

When she's finished, she folds the letter and presses it against her chest, staring at me with through glassy, squinted eyes.

"You knew me all of nine days ..." her voice is broken, tapering into nothing.

"I spent more time with you in those nine days than I've spent with any other woman in my adult life," I say. "Well, aside from Cassie."

"Who's Cassie?"

"We dated all through high school," I explain, rubbing my hands together. I don't talk about her and I can't remember the last time I said her name out loud, but I promised myself that if Maritza gave me another chance, I'd tell her anything she ever wanted to know, bullshit-free. No filter. "Summer after senior year, she showed up with this positive pregnancy stick in her hand. We were both scared shitless. Within a couple of weeks, I'd gone down to the nearest Army recruiter and enlisted myself."

"Oh my God. That's a little extreme."

I shrug. "It was either that or working minimum wage jobs to support us, hoping someday maybe we could go to college if the stars aligned. Plus, I was just a kid. An eighteen-year-old kid who didn't know anything about anything. I was terrified and I just wanted to do right by her."

"That's really sweet."

"Yeah, well. I came back from basic training, wanting to surprise her. Ending up getting a bit of a surprise myself," I say, rubbing my lips together as I pause. I can still picture this clear as day. "Walked in on Cassie and Ian in bed together. Damn near murdered him that day and had Cassie not been there, shrieking and pregnant, I just might have. But I let him go. And Cassie confessed that they'd had a thing for quite some time—the better part of our senior year, actually. And not only that, but she said the baby was his and that she'd lied about how far along she was so I wouldn't know."

"Jesus." She cups her hand over her mouth. "So you were betrayed not only by the girl you loved but your twin brother."

I shrug. "I expected that sort of thing from Ian. He was always chasing after everything I had, wanting everything I wanted. He was so jealous of me it drove him to do stupid shit all the time. It was like his life mission was to see how many times he could get me in trouble with our parents. He once pretended to be me and showed up at my work acting crazy and yelling at customers just to get me fired, and it almost fucking worked."

"Is he mental? Who does that?"

Rolling my eyes, I continue, "You know, he'd done so much shit to me over the years, and all I wanted to do was get him really good. So when we were seventeen, I stole my dad's car and parked it in some gas station parking lot a couple of miles from our house. When I got home, I dumped the car keys in Ian's room and waited for Dad to get up for work. Well, my little plan worked at first. Dad blamed Ian for the missing car and I told Dad I saw a dented-up Buick like his parked at the Conoco down the street. Anyway, long story short, I guess Dad had been late for work a few times when Mom had been sick and he was on his last write-up. His boss said if he was late again, he was fired, no questions asked."

"My god. What happened?"

I pause. I've never told this story, not to anyone, not out loud. Maritza's hand lifts to my back and she scoots closer.

"I told him the truth," I said. "And he left. We don't know if he was walking down to the Conoco to get his car or if he'd just had enough ... caring for his sick wife and trying to support his six kids ... but he never came home after that. The next day, we got a call. Someone found his body in a ditch off the highway a few miles from our house. He'd been mugged, assaulted, left for dead. He died for a Timex watch and the twenty-dollar bill in his wallet."

My hands form a bridge over my nose and I take a few moments to compose myself.

"Isaiah ..." Maritza nudges her cheek against my shoulder. "I'm so sorry."

"My whole family blamed me for a long time. Now they don't talk much about it," I say. "Ma doesn't know exactly what happened of course—she doesn't know about the car keys thing and me trying to get back at Ian. But everyone else does. Ian made damn sure they all knew."

"So when your brother said you had demons and that you ruin lives ... is that what he was talking about?"

"I imagine so, yeah."

Her hand lifts to cup the side of my face and for a moment we just sit and breathe, her warmth mixing with mine.

"I hope someday you'll be able to let that go," she says. "I hope you'll be able to stop blaming yourself."

"Yeah," I say. "Maybe someday."

Sitting up, she rests her palm on my face and her eyes lock on mine. "Thank you for sharing that with me."

A moment later, her pillow soft lips graze mine and she breathes me in, but before we kiss, I have to say one more thing.

"I'm not a perfect man," I say, my voice low and soft. "And I've made a lot of mistakes in my life. But letting you go? Letting you walk away without a fight? That might be the biggest one of all. And I can't do that, Maritza. I can't let you go."

Pulling her into my lap, I hold her stare and reach for her face, guiding her mouth closer, until I taste her familiar strawberry lips and peppermint tongue.

"Then don't," she says a moment later, coming up for air. "Don't let me go."

44

MARITZA

IT'S crazy how much life can change in an instant.

One minute I'm serving pancakes, the next minute I'm spending a week with an Army corporal who makes my stomach somersault every time I look at him.

One minute I'm writing him letters, the next minute I'm writing him off.

But now we're here—in the present moment.

And all those minutes have added up, turning into days and nights and weeks and months and now that same broody Army corporal is standing in my grandmother's trophy room listening to her wax poetic about her Hollywood golden years.

"And that's how I knew Richard Burton was going to go back to Elizabeth," Gram says with a melancholic sigh, twisting her pearls around her fingers. "They were just meant to be. But it's all right. Everything worked out. Had I not met my husband, I wouldn't have had my two boys or my two beautiful granddaughters."

Isaiah turns toward me and I give him a wink.

"Everything always has a way of working out, doesn't it?" he asks.

"Always." Gram smiles. So far she seems to be quite taken with him, at least judging by the fact that she's been leading him from room to room ever since breakfast this morning, showing off her awards and movie props and costumes. Isaiah seemed to take a particular interest in the white bikini from the Davida's Desire poster, even going so far as to jokingly ask if she ever loaned out any of her costumes.

I smacked his arm when she wasn't looking.

Sicko.

"We should probably get going, Gram," I tell her when she attempts to lead us to the room where she keeps her framed posters and the actual baby grand piano she danced on in 1968's Sunset Sonata.

"So soon, Lovey?" She pouts, turning to face me. "But you two just got here. And I wanted to show him my posters."

I check the time on my phone. "We're catching Splendor in the Grass at the Vista. Starts in an hour."

Gram's eyes shift between the two of us and she wears a knowing smirk. "Well, all right. Some other time, then, Isaiah?"

"Of course, Mrs. Claiborne," he says.

She bats her hand. "Please. Gloria's fine. And I do hope I'll be seeing more of you around here. It's good to see the sparkle back in my granddaughter's eyes. It'd been gone for so long."

I saunter up to Isaiah, sliding my hand into his and grinning at him the way I haven't been able to stop doing since yesterday, when we had our heart to heart.

"Pretty sure it's here to stay this time, Gram," I say.

She hooks a hand on her narrow hip before pointing at Isaiah. "But if she ever loses it again—"

"She won't," he says, giving her his full attention. "I'm not going anywhere. I can promise you that."

"Have fun at the movies, you two ..." Gram sashays down the hall in her fur-lined, white satin robe, disappearing into her master bedroom and closing the door.

"You want to hear something completely insane?" I ask him when she's gone.

"What? You think you love me?" he asks.

My jaw falls. Of all the things that could come out of that gorgeous mouth of his, I wasn't expecting that.

"I was going to say that this week is my parents' twenty-fifth anniversary and that my mom had to choose between my father and my uncle but ..." I draw in a deep breath, "yeah, I *do* think I love you."

His lips curl into a slow smile, the very same one he wore this morning in my bed as he peeled the sheets from my naked body and climbed over top of me for the third time in under twenty-four hours.

With his hands cupping my waist, he pulls me in and crushes my lips with his. My body surrenders and I'm having second thoughts about going to that movie because suddenly I'm thinking spending the afternoon in bed with this guy sounds like a lot more fun.

"You just going to leave me hanging, Corp?" I ask, my mouth brushing against his as he kisses me again. "I just told you I think I love you."

"I heard you," he says, stopping to stare into my eyes. "I

just wanted to let it soak in first before I said it back. I want to remember how this feels for the rest of my life."

Isaiah's fingers lace up the back of my neck, his palm cupping my jaw, and he brings his mouth onto mine once more.

"I love you, Maritza," he whispers. "And I've known it was going to come to this since the day I left LA with your picture in my pocket. It just took losing you completely for me to finally accept it that my feelings were real and they weren't going anywhere."

45

ISAIAH

"SO THIS IS HER? This is the girl who put the smile back on your face?" Ma rises from her chair as I bring Maritza inside.

The doctor's switched up her prescriptions a bit since her hospitalization last week and ever since then, she's become a completely different person, almost a better version of her previous self—the woman she was before she got sick. Granted, she still has a few moments where she'll be tired or achy, but we've improved leaps and bounds from where we were before.

Originally, I didn't want to bring Maritza around Mom until Mom was feeling up for visitors ... just didn't know it'd be so soon.

"Mom, this is Maritza." I give my girl's hand a reassuring squeeze that she probably doesn't need. She didn't seem the slightest bit nervous on our drive over here. In fact, she was pretty excited. "Maritza, this is my mother, Alba."

Maritza releases my hand and meets my mother more than halfway across the small living room. "It's so nice to finally meet you."

"Likewise," Ma says, eyes twinkling as she smiles. "I hear you'll be joining us at Calista's barbecue in a couple of weeks?"

Maritza nods. "Can't wait. Isaiah says it's your birthday?"

Ma's brows rise and she swats her hand. "It's a family barbecue that just so happens to be on my birthday. Honestly, I couldn't even tell you how old I'll be. I quit counting a long time ago. And Isaiah, can you believe Ian said he can't make it? Said he's traveling for work or something."

"I can believe it. And you'll be fifty-seven," I remind her.

"Shhh, shh, sh." Ma silences me, wagging her finger. "In my mind, I'm still thirty-five. Forever thirty-five."

"We're only as old as we feel, right?" Maritza asks.

"Right!" Ma cups her hands, laughing, and leads her to the sofa. "So have a seat. I want to hear how you two met."

"He hasn't told you?" she asks.

"No, he has." Ma rolls her eyes. "But I have a feeling his version is a bit condensed. I want to hear your side of the story—the unabridged version. Women have more of a penchant for the important details, don't you think?"

Maritza glances at me. "I'd have to agree."

"All right. I'm all ears." Ma leans in. "Tell me how my favorite son finally took my advice and found a nice, sweet girl to spend time with."

I exchange smirks with Maritza from across the room as she starts from the top, when it all began with a stolen pancake and ends with a stolen heart.

When the story's over, I kiss the top of Ma's head. "Sorry to have to bail, but I've got something special planned for Maritza tonight."

"You do?" Maritza asks. "You didn't mention anything earlier ..."

"It's a surprise," I say, taking her hand. "Bye, Ma."

"Be good, you two." Mom waves from her chair, and I take Maritza to my car.

"Okay, so where are you taking me?" She asks a minute later, fastening her seatbelt.

Starting the engine, I glance across the console at a wild-eyed girl with contagious excitement. I still struggle to believe she's finally mine. And while I never would've believed she was my type, she's somehow exactly what I need.

"I have it on good authority that there's this little band you love having a jam session at the lead singer's house in Malibu ... and I also have it on good authority that we've been invited to sit in and watch." And by invited, I mean ... I called my brother-in-law who put me in touch with Case Malbec so I could explain how important it was that I give Maritza the Panoramic Sunrise experience she deserves.

"Shut. Up." She reaches for my hand, squeezing it hard as she bounces in her seat. "You're joking. Tell me this is a joke. I don't believe you."

I laugh. She's so freaking cute when she's all worked up. "It's no joke. We're going to Case Malbec's place to watch the band write some new songs."

And then just like that, her eyes begin to well with tears and she covers her face with her hands.

"Are you ... are you crying?" I ask, yanking away one of her hands so I can see her face.

Thick tears slide down her cheeks and I can't tell if she's laughing or crying or both.

"Maritza, are you crying?" I ask again. "What's wrong?"

Dabbing her wet cheeks on the backs of her hands, she peers at me through glassy, chocolate-colored eyes. "These are happy tears."

Unfastening her seatbelt, she leans across the console, cups my face in her hands, and kisses me harder than she's ever kissed me before.

"I've never been this happy in my life," she says. "You make me so happy, Isaiah. You're *everything*."

There aren't enough words in the English language to convey to her just how mutual those feelings are, so instead I kiss her back, slow and lingering, savoring her soft lips and relishing in the fact that this woman, this beautiful, sweet, loving soul ... has a heart of gold that beats only for me.

She's mine.

And I'm hers. God, am I hers.

46

MARITZA

"I'M NOT REENLISTING AFTER THIS." Isaiah hooks his hands around my waist as we skinny dip in Gram's pool under a moonlit, midnight sky on an unusually warm spring night.

This marks the first time in for-ev-er that I've had Gram's place to myself for a full week. Melrose is shooting some Lifetime movie on location in Vancouver and Gram decided to tag along before she embarks on a fourteen-day Alaskan cruise with Constance.

"Really?" I ask, circling my weightless legs around his hips.

"Yeah. Really." He pulls me against him and I kiss his chlorine-flavored mouth. "I think it's time to start thinking about what comes next."

"Sounds like a good idea to me." I hug him, our wet, naked bodies gliding against one another as we bob in the water. "What do you think you'll do?"

"Maybe I'll go to school for astronomy or physics?"

"God, you'd be the sexiest freaking nerd I've ever seen in my life." I throw my head back. "Do it."

Isaiah chuckles. "I've got three years to figure it out, but I'm leaning that way. How are your classes going by the way? Finally made it through all those letters."

I smirk, thinking about how I'd handed him that old notebook from my nightstand where I'd written all those letters I never had the chance to send.

"That was fast," I say.

"I devoured them," he says. "And I'm so fucking proud of you, by the way."

"You are?"

"Yeah. When you thought I'd ghosted you, you dealt with it, you acknowledged how you felt, and then you forced yourself to move on with your life," he says. "Makes me proud as hell to know you respect yourself like that."

"Thanks, Corp." I kiss his wet lips again, my legs cinching tighter around him.

"You keep rubbing yourself against me like that and I'm going to have to take you right here, right now."

"Is that a threat? Or a promise?" My hips circle against his growing hardness and I wear a teasing smile that I bury in the solid bend of his neck. His corded steel arms wrap around me, holding me tight, and I swear I could live here in this moment for the rest of my life and be perfectly content.

Striding to a shallower corner of the pool and taking a seat on the steps, Isaiah's hands slide up my outer thighs before gripping my ass and pushing me down onto him.

I exhale as he fills me and I lower myself deeper before tossing my head back and holding onto the back of his neck. He takes a pointed nipple between his lips as I grind against him, rocking slow then fast then slow again.

We've got all night.

And all day tomorrow.

And the rest of the week.

Hell—the rest of our lives.

Neither of us are going anywhere.

Isaiah's rough palms skid along my slick body, the pool water lapping around us, ripples of water kissing our skin as we move.

Dragging my hands along his sculpted shoulders, I lower my lips to his neck, peppering kisses along his collarbone then working my way up to his jaw before finishing at his mouth. I could kiss Isaiah a million times and it still wouldn't be enough to show just how crazy I am for him.

"You're so fucking beautiful," he says, lips tracing mine as he drives himself into me, our bodies rocking in tandem. "You're the best thing that's ever happened to me, Maritza. And I'm going to spend the rest of my life proving that to you. I love you, Maritza the Waitress."

My lips curl. "I love you, too, Corporal Torres."

EPILOGUE

ISAIAH

THREE YEARS Later

DEAR ISAIAH,

It's so strange to think that this will be the last letter you ever get from me while overseas. In a way, it's bittersweet, like the closing chapter of an amazing book you've spent years devouring, but mostly it's just sweet because now we get to start our sequel.

No more goodbyes. No more sleepless nights. No more waiting. No more worrying.

I don't know about you, but I've spent a lot of time thinking about what's next for us. I've always kind of liked not knowing what was next, and I've always thought it'd be nice to wing it with you because I can't imagine any scenario being less than amazing as long as you're in it.

In your last letter you mentioned that you'd never wanted kids until you met me, and that one night you dreamt we had three kids and it got you excited. To be honest, it caught me off guard because I never knew if I wanted to have a family either. Being an only child with one cousin and parents who were never around all that much doesn't really instill much for family values, but since I've met you, I've been thinking ...

And I want a big, loud, crazy family and I want it with you.

So yes. Let's do it. Because I can't imagine doing it with anyone else.

See you soon ...

Yours forever,

Maritza

P.S. I love you.

I spot her from the other side of a high school gymnasium in Burbank, where my troop is making their official homecoming entrance. It's loud as hell in here, people crying tears of joy and shouting and running into each other's arms, but there's my girl, standing under a basketball hoop in a pretty floral sundress, scanning the room.

It only takes a moment until our eyes catch and the way her face lights sends a shock of joy to my chest. A second later, she runs to me, jumping into my arms and wrapping her long legs around me.

"We made it, baby," I say, holding her tighter than I've ever held her before. "I'm done. I'm all yours now."

She kisses my neck and breathes me in again and again. "I've waited so long for this day."

I think about everything we've been through. Our chance meeting. The fact that, against all odds, we somehow couldn't get enough of each other. I've never once believed in fate, but I've always believed in karma, and I like to believe I did something right to get an effervescent girl like her to fall head over heels in love with a damaged soul like me.

Maritza slides down, but she doesn't let me go and she won't stop looking at me. It's been six months since I've seen her last, but this is my fourth deployment since she's met me. It never gets any easier and there's always that unspoken chance that I might not make it home this time.

But I made it home in one piece.

The last few tours were some of the hardest of my life. Turns out things are different when you've got someone waiting for you back home, but my stint in the Army is officially over and I'm never going back.

Maritza is my home now. She's the place I run to when life gets hard. She's my refuge and my solace from the storm. When I'm with her, all my worries and cares and demons tend to fade into the background, sometimes melting away entirely.

"Ian's probation got denied," she tells me, biting a smirk.

"Good." The bastard got caught last year embezzling money from the brokerage firm he was working for in Brentwood. Wouldn't surprise me if he was another Bernie Madoff in the making, but now we'll never know because he's serving time at some white-collar facility on the east coast and once he's out, he'll never be allowed to work in finance again.

"Your sister called and told me this morning. Wanted to personally deliver the news. Kind of sad though. Almost feel bad for him."

"I don't," I chuff. "I feel bad for all the people who trusted him with their money."

"True ... anyway, let's focus on the important stuff. Like

the fact that you're home for good and the fact that I cannot wait to show you my new office space in Riverside and introduce you to my newly hired assistant." She does a little jump. "It's so weird being someone's boss but I kind of love it."

I kiss her forehead. During my latest deployment, she opened a small PR and web development firm out of some cheap office space in Riverside. From what she's told me, everything's going well, but I've yet to see it in person. "I knew you'd find your element. Never doubted you for a sec."

I make my rounds, saying goodbye to all the familiar faces, and then we head out to the parking lot where Maritza parked my vintage Porsche.

"I knew you'd want to drive her first thing when you got back," she says, handing me the keys, which I gladly accept before stealing a kiss from that sweet mouth of hers. As soon as we get to the car, Maritza flings her arms around me once more. She does this whenever I get back, hugs me and kisses me and touches me a hundred thousand times, like she has to make sure I'm real, that I'm here to stay. "So what next? What do you want to do now?"

Resting my hand beneath her chin, I peer into her gorgeous dark eyes and smile. "First I'm going to marry you. Finally. And then I'm going to buy you a house. And we're going to fill it with lots of babies. After that, I think I'm going to spend the rest of my life growing old with you. A lifetime of Saturdays. How's that sound?"

Maritza chuckles. "I meant, like ... are you hungry? Do you want to grab dinner? Do you want to stop at your mom's? But I like your answer. It sounds pretty perfect to me."

I kiss her, threading my hand through hers and pinning her back against my car.

Our future starts right here, right now, in this high school parking lot, just a former waitress, a former Army corporal, and a lifetime of memories ahead of them.

THE END

DREAM CAST

DREAM CAST

Isaiah – Milo Ventimiglia
Maritza – Olivia Culpo
Melrose – Jennifer Lawrence
Rachael – Rachel McAdams
Gram – Susan Sarandon
Murphy – Murphy Renshaw
Myles – Matthew Gray Gubler

ACKNOWLEDGMENTS

This book would not have been possible if it weren't for the help of the following amazing individuals. In no particular order ...

Lou, the cover is absolutely incredible! One of my favorites yet! Thank you, thank you, thank you.

Sandy, thank you for being so patient, sweet, and kind over the past several months. I'm so thrilled to finally put your work on my cover! Your talent is second to none.

Ashley, thank you for beta'ing as always. I couldn't do this without you, and I love your brutal honesty to the moon and back.

K, C, and M—hoes for life!

Wendy, thank you for being so flexible! You're a dream to work with, as always.

Neda, Rachel, and Liz, thank you for ALL the behind-the-scenes stuff you do. Your service is invaluable and you are a joy to work with!

Last, but not least, thank you to all the readers and book bloggers, whether you're a longtime loyalist or reading me for the first time. It's because of you that I get to live my dream, and I'm forever grateful for that.

CLICK HERE FOR BOOKS BY WINTER RENSHAW

The Never SeriesThe Arrogant Series

Never Kiss a Stranger(free!)Arrogant Bastard (free!)
Never Is a PromiseArrogant Master
Never Say NeverArrogant Playboy
Bitter Rivals Claim Your FREE Copy!

Rixton FallsAmato Brothers

RoyalHeartless
BachelorReckless
FilthyPriceless
Priceless (an Amato Brothers crossover)

The Montgomery Brothers DuetStandalones

Dark ParadiseVegas Baby
Dark PromisesCold Hearted
The Perfect Illusion

ABOUT THE AUTHOR

Wall Street Journal and #1 Amazon bestselling author Winter Renshaw is a bona fide daydream believer. She lives somewhere in the middle of the USA and can rarely be seen without her trusty Mead notebook and ultra-portable laptop. When she's not writing, she's living the American Dream with her husband, three kids, the laziest puggle this side of the Mississippi, and a busy pug pup that officially owes her three pairs of shoes, one lamp cord, and an office chair (don't ask).

Winter also writes psychological suspense under the name Minka Kent. Her debut novel, THE MEMORY WATCHER, was optioned by NBC Universal in January 2018.

Winter is represented by Jill Marsal of Marsal Lyon Literary Agency.

Like Winter on Facebook.

Join the private mailing list.

Join Winter's Facebook reader group/discussion group/street team, CAMP WINTER.

MORE ABOUT THE AUTHOR

Vogue's 73 Things About Me

1. What's your favorite movie? Right now it's The Big Sick

2. Favorite movie in the past five years? Interstellar

3. Favorite Hitchcock film? The Birds

4. A book you plan on reading? The Last Mrs. Parrish

5. A book that you read in school that positively shaped you? The Crucible

6. Favorite TV show that's currently on? This Is Us

7. On a scale of one to ten how excited are you about life right now? A solid 9

8. iPhone or Android? iPhone 4-eva

9. Twitter or Instagram? Insta

10. Who should EVERYONE be following right now? F*ck Jerry

11. What's your favorite food? Soup (very general, I know)

12. Least favorite food? Mushrooms

13. What do you love on your pizza? Ham and pineapple or pepperoni and broccoli.

14. Favorite drink? Starbucks Chai (iced, 5 pumps, nonfat)

15. Favorite dessert? Tiramisu

16. Dark chocolate or milk chocolate? Milk

17. Coffee or tea? Green tea

18. What's the hardest part about being a mum? EVERYTHING

19. What's your favorite band? The Avett Brothers

20. Favorite solo artist? Sam Beam (Iron and Wine)

21. Favorite song? Coffee by Sylvan Esso

22. If you could sing a duet with anyone, who would it be? Sufjan Stevens

23. If you could master one instrument, what would it be? Piano. Took lessons as a kid then quit because I didn't want to do the recital. Dumbest move ever.

24. If you had a tattoo, where would it be? Maybe inner wrist?

25. To be or not to be? To be.

26. Dogs or cats? Doggos

27. Bird-watching or whale-watching? Whales

28. Best gift you've ever received? My babies. <3

29. Best gift you've ever given? My babies. <3

30. Last gift you gave a friend? I gave Marin Montgomery a Kindle!

31. What's your favorite board game? Sorry!

32. What's your favorite country to visit? I've only ever been to Mexico.

33. What's the last country you visited? Mexico. Lol.

34. What country do you wish to visit? England

35. What's your favorite color? Cerulean blue

36. Least favorite color? Orange. I dislike everything orange (oranges, orange pop, orange juice, etc).

37. Diamonds or pearls? Diamonds

38. Heels or flats? Wedges

39. Pilates or yoga? Pilates

40. Jogging or swimming? Um, neither?

41. Best way to de-stress? Sleep for a million years. Or read.

42. If you had one superpower, what would it be? Time travel.

43. What's the weirdest word in the English language? Dongle.

44. What's your favorite flower? Hydrangeas

45. When was the last time you cried? Watching The Zookeeper's Wife. I had to turn it off halfway through. It was brutal.

46. Do you like your handwriting? Hate it.

47. Do you bake? Sometimes.

48. What is your least favorite thing about yourself? I get stuck in my own head sometimes and work myself up.

49. What is your most favorite thing about yourself? My ambitiousness.

50. Who do you miss most? My grandpa.

51. What are you listening to right now? The sound of my elliptical in the next room because I forgot to turn it off. Whoops.

52. Favorite smell? Coffee or leather.

53. Who was the last person you talked to on the phone? The chiropractor's office—spaced off my last appointment. Oops.

54. Who was the last person you sent a text to? The hubs.

55. A sport you wish you could play? Tennis. I like it but I kind of suck.

56. Hair color? Blonde

57. Eye color? Dark blue

58. Scary film or happy endings? Both!

59. Favorite season? Spring

60. Three people alive or dead that you would like to have dinner with? Oprah, Jason Momoa, and Nick Kroll

61. Hugs or kisses? Depends on the person ;-)

62. Rolling Stones or the Beatles? Stones

63. Where were you born? Iowa

64. What is the farthest you have been from home? Mexico lol

65. Sweet or savory? Savory

66. Lipstick or lip gloss? Lipstick

67. What book have you read again and again? YOU by Caroline Kepnes

68. Favorite bedtime story? The Man With the Golden Arm

69. What would be the title of your autobiography? Don't Quit Your Daydream

70. Favorite sound? My kids' giggling and playing together. Close second – my dogs snoring.

71. Favorite animal? Elephants

72. Who is your girl crush? Melanie Ervin

73. Last photograph you took? A "before" picture. I just started 80 Day Obsession. Going to crush it!

Made in the USA
Lexington, KY
05 June 2018